# Weary Men

»»»»»»»»» «««««««««

# Arne Garborg

# Weary Men

TRANSLATED FROM THE NORWEGIAN

BY SVERRE LYNGSTAD

WITH AN AFTERWORD BY PER BUVIK

NORTHWESTERN UNIVERSITY PRESS
EVANSTON, ILLINOIS

»»»»»»»»» «««««««««

Northwestern University Press
Evanston, Illinois 60208-4210

Originally published in Norwegian in 1891 under the title *Trætte Mænd*.
English translation copyright © 1999 by Northwestern University Press.
All rights reserved.

Printed in the United States of America

ISBN 0-8101-1600-6

**Library of Congress Cataloging-in-Publication Data**

Garborg, Arne, 1851–1924
    [Trætte mænd. English]
    Weary men / Arne Garborg ; translated from the Norwegian by Sverre
Lyngstad ; with an afterword by Per Buvik.
        p.   cm.
    ISBN 0-8101-1600-6  (paper)
    I. Lyngstad, Sverre.   II. Title.
PT8848.G2T713 1999
839.8'336—dc21                                         98–45904
                                                           CIP

# »»» CONTENTS «««

6/5/1885, midnight

"Friends are a poor breed. They're good for nothing but dining with, and for hanging their heads at our gravesides. They like the latter the best. 'At last, we're rid of *him*,' they sigh, and may, in their joy, manage to get up a collection of 200 kroner for the widow."

This (roughly) was what I told Jonathan, the attorney, this afternoon over the burgundy (that fellow has connections—genuine burgundy!), and as usual he started moralizing.

"A proud person arranges his life in such a way that he doesn't need friends," he said.

"Well, I've certainly needed them," I said, "and could use some even today, but—it's like with the police: when you need them—. I often wonder what happens to them."

George Jonathan stroked his whiskers and said, with a playful allusion to my thinning crown, "You may just as well ask what happens to the hairs on your head, my friend. They simply get lost. One by one. You don't notice it—until you discover some day that you have to wear a hairpiece . . . in other words, form a whist club."

Ah, yes, they do get lost. Or, one might say, you "outgrow them," shake them off as you continue growing. Dear Lord, I do miss them now and then, but if I could have them back I wouldn't be able to make use of them. If I meet one of them now, I can think of nothing else to say but "Should we go to Ingebret's and have an absinthe?" So we sit at Ingebret's for an hour or so, talking about wind and weather and the latest scandal, while each of us feels there is a sort of void fixed between us. When, after a while, this feeling has given us both a cold, we get up and say with a certain relief, "Goodbye, old fellow; God be with you."

Friendship is the subtlest kind of selfishness, much more subtle than love, for example; one wants, after all, to devour the other only spiritually. Nevertheless, the end result is that each consumes the other, whereupon both chuck the other onto the bone heap. I can look back on many a skeleton that I have picked clean and thrown away at different stages of my life's journey; and I myself lie chewed up on several bone heaps, I can imagine.

Real friends we have only in our teens, before we get hold of our first girl. Oh, all right: till we get hold of our second girl; for the first one is so fascinating that you must have someone with whom to talk about her, and about your own remarkable talent as a Don Juan. As soon as you're past twenty, you start spreading out, acquiring edges and angularities, and then begin those frictions between friends that lead to a break or separation. A friend to whom you can pour out your lovesickness certainly doesn't exist for a fellow of thirty-eight. Instead of keeping quiet and nodding and understanding, they say, "Ha-ha! Pshaw, one of those girlie stories. You aren't going to eat your heart out over something like that, are you?" Or they cut in and relate their own latest lascivious adventure—a tale from an altogether different quarter. Or they dismiss the matter with a couple of inane words and continue, "From one thing to another, what is your opinion of the Sverdrup cabinet?"

Ah.

Hssh . . . steps on the stairs.

Nonsense. A good glass and then to bed.

Sunday forenoon

George Jonathan is an intelligent friend and a stylish fellow, which I like. But intimacy—? Oh dear! His cold English manner doesn't invite that; and he's not interested in individual cases. To him every love story turns into a social issue: "When women become more intelligent . . . ," "when they get to understand that they have just one life to live and, in that life, only one youth. . . ." But how can that help me! As it happens, she was *not* very intelligent; so here I am, going around sighing. Nothing is as crashingly indifferent to me as the question of what women will do and think in the next century.

I mourn myself, her, the whole world. This little ridiculous affair, which really wasn't an affair, has derailed my existence.

"Resignation" was humbug. Up till your thirtieth year you can rest content with the thought that people will be happy at some future time, but when you are approaching forty a voice inside you begins to talk louder and louder, "What about you, you, you yourself, aren't you supposed to live too?"

I'm one note, a single, thin tune that demands, *demands,* to be harmonized. My inward musical ear is tortured to the point of madness by continually hearing this thin, lone, unison tune, borne upon the desert air of my existence. She was my harmonization—not wholly, I'm afraid, it was not pure enough—and now the lonely tune sounds even more lonely and sad and godforsaken through my wasted existence.

Evening

If it had been real love, all right! But that's the ludicrous, impossible aspect of my unhappiness: I wasn't even in love.

Not à la Romeo. Not à la Werther. This is the horror of being past thirty: your love is no longer blind.

I was hopelessly infatuated, but my eyes were open. I saw all her shortcomings, everything that was wrong, with painful clarity. If I could undo my latest cruel folly, being ever so sure that she loved me, would I? Would I dare to? I don't think so. Though—. But what if matters stood as they did then? No. I wouldn't be man enough, I know that. It is a painful, sick, divided love, a dissolution of my being; my senses and my soul are engaged and fascinated, but my consciousness is cold, clear, mocking—remorseful and exasperated at the very fascination that I cannot master.

Who can understand such things? Who among all these coarsely hewn, thickset, naive sailor types and Bohemians, George Jonathan included?

In the final analysis I don't understand it myself.

Sunday morning

My sins are
as the sand of the sea . . .

Another half a beer.

"He seeks his murderer." I could write a farce-tragedy with myself as the hero under that title.

### Murderer Sought.

Able and experienced murderer may find employment. Whopping reward on preliminary inquiry to would-be murderee. Useless to apply without the best references. For further information, contact the business office.

Rubbish, it won't do.

### Notice!

Famished art students, literary men, and so forth are notified that I still have 100 kroner on me (well hidden), beside a letter addressed to a friend indicating I have died by my own hand. . . .

Ick. Idiocy. Nonsense. Alcoholism. Another half a beer.

My sins are
as the sand of the sea,
manifold as the rays
of the sun.
God, set me free
from the curse of sin,
now and in the hour
of death.
You will not
see me lost,
who gave me breath!
Save me
through your abounding grace!

Weep. Pray. Our Lady, Holy Virgin, pure and blessed among women, who still understands, you *Schmerzensreiche, ach, neige dein Antlitz gnädig meiner Not. . . . Was mein armes Herz hier banget, was es zittert, was verlanget, weisst nur du, nur du allein. . . .*

I shall go to my father confessor. I shall confess to him that I've once again been the prodigal son, eating with the swine and drinking with the swillpots, and that in the end I—oh! not even Mathilde . . . God, strike that out, with a very thick stroke. Another glass of beer. . . .

It won't work. It simply won't work, you see. This presumed cure is worse than the disease. I'm simply turning into an idiot, going mad. . . .

Miserable and sick at heart, I sit there among bandits aching for her; in the vilest, most dissolute company of witty dogs and convivial swine my tongue thirsts to utter her name, to say something that will remind me of her, that will bring me close to her; say something that could betray me, betray my ridiculous, *ridiculous* love. But they are common and godless, talking about tarts and bluestockings and other things that don't concern me; and Blytt tells dirty jokes, and Bjølsvik is yelling about the devil and his swizzle stick. I drink and drink and swallow my agony, until I'm no longer able to. I jump up and leave: Mathilde, Mathilde. . . . Even the most humble woman would understand my anguish better than these vile men. But of course she is not home, the goose—not home on this of all evenings. I'll flip out! Can't possibly head for smug, boring Homansby now. I have to see someone, talk, jabber, display my bleeding heart, even if it were to . . . ugh.

I'll do as I am in the habit of doing: pretend to be a writer. Confide in paper—at least it's clean. And someday, maybe, *this* could become a novel! Who knows. At all events: gather, arrange, all these notes and impressions I've jotted down during the last year; write about her, all, all about her; dive in and drown among those strange, lovely, foolish little memories. And meanwhile she'll sit here, behind me, looking over my shoulder, gazing in surprise at all those strange things with her deep, dark eyes. Oh, I notice her, all right, she's here, especially in the evening; I often hear her breath around me then. This thing will be my way of getting in touch, of corresponding with her. But good Lord, I'm mad! Why not just as well be mad, then!

Lock the door carefully! It will be my work and my company every evening; then the bandits can be where they damn well please.

And so I'm saved!—for the time being.

Oh, these old notebooks with their half-indecipherable penciled entries, and all these odd loose papers, envelopes, reverses of letters, large folio leaves and small, fine letter-size sheets on which I've jotted down the impressions of the day, experiences, whims, and moods in solitary hours! Nearly every slip of paper and every note have their own specific recollection: this one was taken down in this or that dive, where I sat alone waiting for the right moment or was annoyed that I had nothing to wait for that evening; that one was written on a stone up in the Frogner Woods or on a tree stump out by Ekeberg, where I was trying to forget; that one again hails from a lonely midnight hour here at home, in my apartment, as I let the preceding day pass in review over my last glass and my last cigarette. Vague sentimental twilight moods rise from these multifarious scribblings, enveloping me like a soft, warm fog.

》》》 《《《

# Part One

## Weary Men

### I

This complete calm, even coldness, when I'm with her, when she's really there! It's odd. Am I *that* old? For she's lovely. Well, it's probably just that, at close range, I see her all too clearly "as she is"; there's no idealizing distance anymore, no falsifying atmospheric layer such as makes faraway hills so romantic.

What an excellent idea it was that I, a weary, elderly gentleman, should arrange such a spiritual marriage, an ideal relationship without a trace of the ordinary or common, something that every cockerel can bring off with every chick: sex! The relationship has a charm that's quite unique. You feel free; she has no "claim"—this annoying, tiresome claim that the mistress has on her lover; you come and go when you please, you are who you please. There can be no question of "betrayal" or suspicion, nor consequently of scenes or any of the trouble that always goes with having a mistress. Freedom is, after all, the highest good.

And yet, at the same time a touch of piquancy, something a bit uncertain and "promising."

The mere fact of having exchanged one's old, used-up boon companions for a young, sensible woman is a huge benefit. A woman brings an extra stimulus, something special, "feminine," that has a uniquely animating effect on a man, at once exciting and tranquilizing; it calls forth a certain agreeable sentimentality while keeping all his more prideful instincts awake.

She appears cool, almost strict; short of being prudish, she has a tinge of remoteness, of the untouchable, in her manner: she's presumably not of a very sexual nature. There are none of those sticky, cloying ways most little girls have—those who constantly go around waiting for that something wonderful to happen and, before you know it, hang themselves around your neck. This one is on the thin side, pale and almost angular, and her lips have a tiny, easily evoked trace of mockery that makes her look quite disdainful. (She laughs too much, that's bad. . . . Oh well, you'll never find perfection.) She's on the whole extremely self-assured and seems to have a very definite sense of her own worth. She can't be won simply by holding out one's hand, and that is very much to her advantage. Having tired of soft, round little girls and obvious coquetry, I feel strongly attracted by her rather English, governess-like manner, for which I really have the utmost dislike. And therefore, thank goodness, there can't be any question of actually falling in love with her (later note: ha-ha!).

But her large, dark eyes with their slightly tuberculous expression form a curious, piquant contrast to the rest of her person, suggesting that a volcano might be hidden under the snow and that her "self-assurance" vis-à-vis men could have other reasons. Altogether, there's something about those eyes that makes one feel unsure. She's probably what she seems to be, but it's not absolutely impossible that she could be one of the more clever coquettes.

She's not a young chick at any rate, the good lady; for that she has a much too unaffected way of talking about certain things, besides a not inconsiderable knowledge. It's incredible how different she is from the little impertinent brat that trotted about with my goofy friend Aas at one time; she has gone through something or other in the meantime. But when she tries to make me believe that she has never had a love affair, she strikes me as disagreeably matronly: they all say that. I'm convinced that if you married a widow with seven children and asked her on your wedding night if she had ever had such an experience, she would spontaneously exclaim, "No, I swear! How could you imagine anything of the sort?!"

Well, however that may be, to me the matter is quite clear. I have made no move, nor do I intend to. It's a friendship on a straightforward foundation. As I get to know her better, I can give some more thought to the matter. If one finds it worthwhile, one can go further, of course; conversely, the whole thing will dissolve of itself. For the moment I'm happy to have found something that occupies me to some extent; after all, to "live" means to be occupied.

## II

"And you have really been able to take this life? Year in, year out—not a single affair you got really caught up in?"

"Yes, I *have* been able to take it."

"Unbelievable."

"But true."

Pause. Then she laughs and says: "When I was small, I naturally believed that my life would be an interesting novel. With princes and counts and all sorts of things. . . . And all it has come to is this miserable nonsense which doesn't have a trace of reality in it. Not a pennyworth of sense or interest. And it will go on just the same. (Me: "Hmm—?") Oh yes, it won't change, just get worse and worse, obviously, the older I get. And so I try to imagine that this so-called life here and now is merely the first part of the novel, and in the first part, you know, what happens is often rather muddled: you can't make any sense of it, one thing seems more stupid than another. You begin to understand it only when you get to the other parts; and in the end, when you're through with all the parts, the whole thing adds up. This way I figure we shall live several lives, travel from one planet to another (you've read Flammarion, haven't you?); and so my life would turn out to be an interesting novel after all, don't you see!"

"I would like to say that, as far as I am concerned, the first part of the novel will doubtless be more than sufficient."

"But I *believe* in Flammarion! I *want to* believe in him!"

"Go ahead. Believe, if it makes you happy."

"Bah, how boring you are. You really don't believe in Flammarion?

Oh, please, say that you believe. Say that you believe, you too."

"I'm damned if I will!"

"Oh dear, how difficult you are."

"But that shouldn't prevent you from believing."

"Sure it does; because, you see, I don't believe in him very much either." (Laughter.)

*(At the statue of Wergeland.)* SHE. Isn't it really the greatest thing on earth: being a poet?

ME. Oh well. What did that one accomplish, for example? Who reads him? A couple of literary scholars. What did he accomplish? He brought Jews to this country, that's about the only thing. The rest of his ideas were deluged and drowned out by romanticism and religious bigotry; it wasn't Henrik Wergeland but Hans Hauge who created the Norwegian nineteenth century. Alas no; it's not much use. You have to write with a dagger—and not use ink, but blood—if you want to make an impression on these wads of wool that people carry in their heads, instead of brains.

SHE *(crying out)*. Is it possible? Have you really been to Paris? Oh, tell me, tell me. . . . Oh, really, you've been to Paris, how lucky you are!

ME. Tell about Paris? Hmm. There are a great many streets, and some of them are very long. Some are also very wide, and tree-lined: they're called boulevards.

SHE. Yes, and then of course there's such a lot of splendid big stores with silk and gold and diamonds—real, genuine diamonds.

ME. Oh yes; many nice things. And then there is the large square with the obelisk and the tall stone figures, and many other large squares; and then there's the Seine.

SHE. Yes, the Seine! It must be magnificent.

ME. At least four times as wide as the Aker River, and at least eight times as dirty.

SHE *(disillusioned)*. Dirty?

ME. Horribly. Quite greenish-yellow. Oh yes, Paris is lovely. I intend to go there several times, especially to look at attractive ladies' costumes.

SHE *(uncertain)*. Really?

ME. Yes. You know, such a truly stylish dinner dress—well, it simply affects you like a musical composition: nothing but rhythm, harmony, graceful movement. Honestly, it touches my heart like a voluptuous, graceful, seductive chord, warm and soft and subtle and delicate and—damn it, I can't find words for it. But it's certainly beautiful. Well, an elegant men's outfit can also be worth looking at, of course; but men's clothes are, and will continue to be, essentially devoid of poetry. A woman's body, with its soft undulations and musical rondures, is also a far more rewarding subject for composition, of course, than the straight-lined, architectonic, sober male body.

*(Pause.)*

ME *(continuing)*. But it's awful to come back home again.

SHE *(slightly sullen)*. Yes, of course, here at home we have no idea how to dress.

ME. No—all due respect, incidentally! The women here certainly don't. Then it's better with us, in Bergen. Well, you probably don't know that I am from Bergen; after all, I speak like a native of Kristiania now. Good grief, there are honorable exceptions, to be sure, but in general you see nothing here except unskilled seamstresses' maltreatment of everything that's called rhythm and form. That's why, I believe, I can never fall properly in love in this country.

SHE. No, as long as you look just at the clothes—

ME. *Just* the clothes—oh, dear! Go to Paris, miss, and then try, when you come back, to say in that tone: "*just* the clothes"!

SHE. Well, I didn't quite mean—

ME. In general we're a bunch of abominable barbarians. Yankees, that's what we are. The only remaining trace of our old beautiful life—everything considered, the only fine or festive thing we ever had up here among the icebergs—is, you see, this bit of female beauty. And now that, too, will be undone—naturally! Covered up by homespun and heavy boots and reform dresses. As ugly as possible, hence practical and healthy, say the emancipated—and moral, say the lay preachers; for then the men won't be seduced to sinful thoughts, and so there will be no sinning at all. Ugh, the devil take this everlasting philistinism! Soon, of course, the women will cut off their hair too, all for utilitarian reasons—and because long, beautiful hair is so frightfully romantic. And someday women will be forbidden to wear gloves, since an attractive, white hand can also turn a man's head. In the end, all perfumes will be prohibited. Isn't it more virtuous and natural to smell with perspiration than to exude a fragrance of violets?

SHE *(laughs, a little embarrassed)*. Oh dear, I'd rather you—

ME. All right, beg pardon. Well. What was I about to tell you?

SHE. You said it was so horrible to come back home again.

ME. Yes, of course. Yes, one stares in horror at the silent, empty streets with their cultural-historical paving and all those naturalistic piles of horse manure—I beg pardon! And one's fellow citizens! Those long-shanked, bony figures dangling and slouching along in their threadbare trousers, with smudged collars and broad, crooked faces that have never expressed joy—phew! How slowly and sadly they crawl along, with their crooked knees and long, trudging strides! There's certainly no fun in store where they are headed, that you can tell by their looks. Then you go farther up Karl Johan Street and meet the lions; oh, ye gods! *(Shrug.)* Small town! Small town! Shabby-looking clothes and a day-old stubble—the beauty expecting these fellows is anything but demanding! Sometimes you get the impression they have barely taken the trouble to wash. And what the hell should they wash themselves for, in this town! Only now and then do you meet a correct gentleman in top hat and gloves, and with a pretension to style in his appearance; but . . . they're so few. With a coachman on the box looking like a lay preacher, I sat in my cab saying to myself, Next time you'll go ashore at Arendal or Larvik, so you won't come home to this beloved capital so completely unprepared.

SHE. I've heard others say it's supposed to be absolutely delightful to come home to Norway.

ME. To Norway, sure! That's something else. But our sorry capital? Oh well, all due respect, all due respect—.

### III

That she would go along with this joke! Who is she really? What does she think, what sort of opinions does she have? Is she in love? A pretty pass that would be!

But no; then she wouldn't have gone along, naturally. "Women always act illogically."

And yet—I do get that feeling every once in a while.

And since I am a decent fellow and not the least bit cruel, that would really give me pain (later note: ha-ha!); consequently I take to slandering myself—something I can do perfectly well without offending against the truth.

I'm old, I tell her. Old from birth, that is, an impossible blend of old and young. It's an inherited trait, no doubt; anyway, everything is supposed to be heredity these days. My father was a spent old man about town, a pensioned-off captain; in the end this wreck falls into the arms of his housekeeper, a small, buxom, thirty-year-old girl from Voss.

"Did he marry her?" she interrupts, interested.

"No, he had that much taste anyhow; meanwhile . . . the consequence of this fall was me. Old, tired, thin blood, see, mixed with young, thick peasant blood—nothing whole could come out of that, obviously. For example, I don't believe I've ever loved anyone, never completely—if at all, it would have to be when I was sixteen or seventeen and became enamored of the neighbor's maid. Always only half—half attracted, half cold, blinded by love in one eye and fully alert in the other; and therefore, obviously, I'll end up by becoming what I least of all want to be, namely, an old bachelor."

"Why don't you want to? You men have nothing to worry about; it's only we old maids who become laughingstocks."

"I'm not quite sure. It's probably my childhood memories from this so-called home, a peculiar, unpleasant lack of order in one's affairs—it must be from this that I've acquired a distaste for everything irregular and im—; well, I really find it in poor taste."

"But if your father loved that girl from Voss—"

"Good grief, I'm not reproaching him with anything; I'm only saying that such things are in poor taste. Because it really is."

Pause.

"And therefore," I added, "I didn't marry that maid either, you see. Thank God for that, such things won't do. One should marry according to one's station in life—birds of a feather, you know. . . . And then build a home for oneself that's sufficiently proof against invasion by the public. One should be *comme il faut* in those things. Everything else has a bad aftertaste."

Pause.

*

"One shouldn't make light of that which 'looks seemly.' Hang it, when all is said and done, one's first moral duty is to avoid offending one's fellow humans with dirty cuffs. I often wonder what's worth more: an elegant woman's foot or a serious philosophy of life!"

She laughs; I get excited.

"Yes, do what we will, we'll never go beyond *Erscheinungen*. Consequently, the beautiful *Erscheinung* is the highest thing that exists— for us, naturally; it is this that constitutes the 'realization of the idea' and the 'solution to life's riddle.' A beautiful woman, whose glance is like the night, whose breath is youth, whose gait is music—"

"And so on, and so forth!"

"Yes—we may rummage for truth in every nook and cranny of existence, but 'the meaning of life' is revealed in her."

"It sounds pretty—"

"Thanks, I know the continuation. But it is *not* just nonsense, you know!"

Why should she fall in love with me, an elderly gentleman past his prime?

It's written in every comedy: woman's innate penchant for saving and repairing. It is really very decent, touching; but it's stupid. It's bad economy to repair what is run-down; let it go to wrack and ruin, for God's sake! The sooner the better. When a woman falls in love with such trash, she betrays decadence; her duty to her kind is to choose the best, the young, the healthy, those most suited to be fathers to her children.

She's in a great rush to let me know that this—namely, this going around with me—is "the only thing she has," "the only enjoyable thing in her life."

But then comes the thought, If she were in love, she would never say such a thing!

Nonsense. You conceited old duffer. Let things take their course. There's certainly no danger in that quarter. Only, how stupid—she could become the subject of gossip. That is, the stupid part is that it would be entirely without foundation. (Later note: aha!)

It's just *too* ridiculous to go around and be "friends" in this way with a young, attractive girl; the male in me feels a bit ashamed. One could use the time to better advantage. (Aha!)

Just imagine: not even to make an attempt at bringing about a more intimate relation, which is the only possible and natural thing between man and woman! Not even to want to, in fact! It's ridiculous, it's indecent. She must simply despise me.

And in the meantime I'm regarded as a hell of a guy, and she perhaps soon as—something else.

It's no good. Either forward or back; this is idiocy. But one of the two I won't accept, I just *can't*, even if I were willing to get involved—she's not like that; she shows a friend's absolute trust, and it is disarming. So it must be the other: end it. Anyway, she's beginning to occupy me to a degree that borders on the unwholesome for a respectable bachelor and government official. It won't do, it's just absurd.

End of chapter!

*IV*

Pro tem. Bergen, 20 July

Obviously, the chapter did not end. I wanted to show consideration, not make a clean break; withdraw from the affair slowly and elegantly and inconspicuously. And it turned out accordingly. Whereupon I used "the vacation" as a pretext and made off.

So here I am, walking around, and I'm not in Bergen. After the lapse of several long years I saw the old haunts again without any particular emotion. Only with a certain indifferent surprise: was it really that small? And I suddenly realized that I had no idea what to do in a town where Miss Holmsen wasn't taking her evening walks.

In love?! For the 199th time? Oh no; no such luck, I almost said. Only a bit sentimental. My "love" is merely a certain sense of discomfort when she's gone. If she were here, I wouldn't give a damn about her—with reservations.

And so here I am, hovering about the above-mentioned old haunts and seeing nothing. Feeling nothing either. Only a certain uneasiness and desolation in my breast: will these three weeks ever come to an end? Considering that a day and night has 24 hours, 3 minutes, and 56.56 seconds (?), there's certainly not much hope. To pass the time I go walking and sailing; I also intend to take a trip to Hardanger. Almost everybody is in the country; and as for my family, I'm a black sheep, thank God. Anyway, I haven't got a family.

So it's not for "her" sake that I want to go back to Kristiania; I'm now definitely set on "getting weaned of" her—by God I am! But I still miss the city—the hangouts. I miss the Grand Café and Gravesen's, and in general those beginnings of European urban life that can be found (here there is absolutely nothing); I even miss George Jonathan and his burgundy—I would be quite happy to have his social revolutions thrown into the bargain.

I'm bored—that's the word. Bored, bored! I'll be bored in Kristiania too, but still, still. . . .

The ridiculous thing is that I catch myself being jealous every once in a while. By now she has obviously found someone else. She is at an age when young women usually want to get down to business. And besides, you know: this almost too sweet face with those almost too tumultuous curls and those almost too irresistible eyes—I can see him! Next time I meet her she'll be walking arm in arm with him and admiring his wisdom. What business is it of mine? And yet, it bothers me.

No, it certainly isn't just fun. There she goes and finds happiness, sailing into port with someone or other with whom she will live out her life in tranquillity, while I shall be left to drift in this glacial desert alone, cold and worn out, finally to die a lonely death in some ditch, as crows and other black birds sit around sharpening their beaks.

Strange. To sail and sail and all the time know for certain that you won't ever reach port, but only that you'll spring a leak some night and go to the bottom—to the bottom with the whole kit and caboodle.

But since we are bound to go to the bottom anyway, why for God's sake do we lie tormenting ourselves with this voyage in the first place?

Phew, it's warm today. The brain turns soft and lapses into banalities. Out and take a swim.

Could I really refrain from looking her up if she were sufficiently close to—

Fiddle-faddle. There is, worse luck, no possibility of falling into temptation.

(Still, I don't go to bed a single evening without again and again—for at least two hours—dreaming the ridiculous dream that, in her insane love, she has set out in search of me, has looked me up and now, suddenly, stands outside my window. . . .

May heaven bring you ease, you old gallant.)

This Miss Berner, whom I see every now and then, is more sensible than she appears. Her simple correctness and flawless ordinariness fooled me in this respect. After such a long period of native genius, we have swallowed the idea that a human being whose breeding does not fall short in one way or another cannot be much good.

I had her for my dinner companion this evening at the place of an acquaintance—a kindred spirit who, like me, does reviews for the newspapers and indulges the vice of writing poetry on the sly. And then and there, Miss Berner revealed a more than usual intelligence with regard to gastronomy. We spoke about food in truly European fashion for three quarters of an hour. Various ragouts, oysters in this or that form, lobster, a new English sauce, etc., etc., subjects that Miss Berner handled with excellent understanding. That's how she attracted my attention—after all, women have no understanding of food as a rule—and so I began to talk to her about love. Miss Berner passed the test with a grade of "Not unfit": she argued the case for marriage of convenience contra love matches in a truly talented manner, and at the same time so discreetly, without any show of feeling, without fishing for agreeable objections.

"After all, a marriage of convenience is far less risky," she said. "If you can't get along, well, that's too bad, but it really doesn't matter; you can just quietly agree to live like other acquaintances who dine together. It does happen, though, that they develop an affection for each other, and then the marriage becomes a pleasant surprise, whereas in the case of love matches I believe it's all too often an unpleasant one."

I replied that I, too, had all due respect for an intelligent marriage of convenience, but that I had still always considered it an advantage if considerations of convenience and inclination went together. "Call it my tribute to moral sentimentality. You seem almost ready to agree with our elders, who say that circumstances of social station, fortune, and education must in any case be in order, and that love is something that 'will come with time.'"

"Our elders are always right." Miss Berner smiled.

"Well, I suppose one can't always feel assured that love 'will come,' so you must mean to say that well-bred people can, in a pinch, manage without it."

"Yes. They very often have to anyway."

In the end I couldn't help asking her if perhaps she was quietly at work on a novel; she had made observations, I could tell, perhaps she also had experiences (she's twenty-eight), and her thoughts were orderly and consistent. She dismissed the insinuation with the most restrained contempt. "In any case, you are one of the few who might be entitled to write," I complimented her; "but I must admit that my respect for you is not diminished by your leaving the pen-pushing alone."

She smiled. Her smile is agreeable, intelligent, and gentle— *geräuschlos*, as a German would say.

*That* could be a wife for me—!


Pro tem. Hardanger

Still, a bit of romanticism is a good thing for a change. It's refreshing and restful. You become quiet, turned inward, religious. Your soul becomes clear like the fjord with its strange double depth, ostensibly sky blue and transparent and smiling but in reality dim, dark, black, with starfish and nixies and sunken bodies. Green leafy slopes and steep cliffs are reflected in absorbed, dreamy silence in this bewildering double depth. Now and then a boat cuts its way in slow motion through the calm, perilous expanse.

I can sit up here on the hillside for hours on end, looking and looking and forgetting to think; and the world rushes off into nothingness and turns into the beautiful empty appearance that I believe it really is. Slowly, like an insect, a boat glides along the fjord in the glowing sunshine, and in the boat sits a human animal with its head full of tiny worries that it takes seriously.

Silence. Silence. Buzzing bumblebees, purling brooks. Light flashing and glittering. The rhythm of slow strokes of the oars. The tranquillity of thousands of years. Isn't it curious that this is, ultimately, nothing but hydrogen and oxygen, carbon and nitrogen, $HO_2$ and $HO_3$?

Some beastly Mr. Smith or other came sailing yesterday in his own yacht, with wife and children and cattle and goats and sheep, and rented the entire hotel.

As for me, a mere paltry Norwegian who has, accordingly, been treated with studied nonchalance all along in this connection, both by the (Swedish) hotel proprietor and his Norwegian stock of slaves—the only one who's been really kind to me is a little half-depraved chambermaid from Bergen—well, I was simply deprived of my room and asked to do them the favor of sharing a room with another Norwegian, a miserable fellow from Kristiania with a university degree, I believe.

It's the dawning glory of tourism—"Norway's glory" in a new version—in this same "marvelously beautiful Hardanger."

The university fellow is an idiot. He says he can "tell from my dialect" that I am from Bergen. Well, every once in a while perhaps, when I get excited.

And I did get excited. "That's how it is!" I said. "Mr. Smith and Brother Lundström—they simply threw us out of our own house. Good old Norway is becoming a summer sanatorium for English coal merchants. Brother Lundström and Mr. Schultze-Müller build the hotels and take the profit; the 'Norwegian people' become waiters and the 'Norwegian woman' a whore for European tourists. A good Norwegian who sets out on foot to gratify his soul's joyous urge to visit the valleys of Norway will simply not be able to find a place to stay anymore, not unless he can speak English at any rate. Oh, the glory of Norway! Oh, what progress the country has made under the blessings of democracy! There's only a single being in the whole country that doesn't grasp where we are headed, and that being is called the Storting. The yeoman class is sliding at dizzying speed down the slippery slope of mortgaging their farms; the foreigner is buying up the nation's property piece by piece, everything that has some value—mines, ports, building lots, waterfalls: the Storting sits there watching, happy that 'money is coming in.' In another fifty years our minicomedy of a Norwegian state will be nothing more than a legend! And yet there are some half-educated individuals who go around declaiming about 'Norway's future'! Oh yes! Oh yes!"

"Well," the university man says, with the guardedness of a prospective government official, "the development of tourism does have its drawbacks, that's true. Pardon me, but I can tell by your dialect that you are from Bergen. . . ."

I'm leaving by the coastal steamer tomorrow.


Bergen

We got up a bit of a spree at the end all the same—nothing but boredom, by the way. Today hangovers all along the line, and I would feel ripe for the halter if the newspaper hadn't told me it was August already. A stab of joy shoots through my breast: then I can leave in a couple of days.

But . . . Yes, of course.

Of course. After all, I'm just about "weaned." No strolls anymore, none at all. I'll be absolute reason personified. But still . . . All right.

Just to be leaving!


*V*


Kr—ia, 20 (or rather 21) Aug.

Queer fellow, that George Jonathan.

Like this idea of his of building a collection of paintings!

Sure, if he had a flair for painting! But he boasts that he can't tell a Thaulow from a Werenskiold. "Constructional drawing is the only thing I care about, for that I know myself!" Jonathan says.

However, he is really building that collection. "It will provide background, a foil, position," he says. "A man who's known as the owner of fifty paintings is a curiosity in this country, something unique, a paragon, about the same as a paleface among the redskins. And if you wish to rise in the world, you must first of all astonish your fellow citizens. You have to provide yourself with a nimbus, you see. The money spent on this humbug will bring a nice rate of interest."

I reply that such a nimbus will rather scare the redskins. They will respect him but shun him. He will be viewed as someone who is artistic and literary and Bohemian, as someone unpractical. How the hell can a person who takes an interest in something so transcendental as art know anything about matters like poor relief and the sewer system!

He manages a shrug. "The patriotic aspect of the case will be palatable," he says.

"The patriotic aspect? Well, it's nice of course that someone slams down a few hundred-krone bills for artists every once in a while—"

"I'll tell you one thing," Jonathan replies seriously. "A time will come when Europe will flock to Kristiania to see the *Norwegians*, just as people now flock to Italy to see the Florentines. And that means money in the till for the merchants, you see; and it will dawn on them after a while."

I give a shrug.

He solemnly "unveiled" this evening—in the presence of Dr. Kvaale, the painter Blytt, and my own humble person—his most recently purchased picture, which I could almost believe he had bought on account of me. For I suppose he knows it was she who was my "previous" one. Anyway, it's not a portrait, it's an interior, and she is mere decor. Her father painted it, it's from the time before she got married. The artistic interest of the picture is the delicate treatment of light—or of shadow, if you will; but it was only her that I saw, my once so ardently loved Elinè. She stands in the background looking out of the window. It's wonderful how nicely she is set off against the dull, grayish-white—masonry-gray white—light outside. I recognized her in every line. That small distinctive head (with the plentiful reddish-blond hair in a chignon at the back) has just the right, graceful slant, and that tiny watchful, oblique, half-upward tilt. The pale-brown back of her neck with its string of corals gleams delicately forth through the penumbra; under her rich wavy hair a small, blushing ear peeks forth inquisitively with its rather gypsy-like gold trinkets. Over her fine, strong shoulders and her delicately but firmly modeled back, a reddish-brown damask robe, making the nether part seem a smidgen too low. My heart grew faint, but it quickly passed. She is a finished chapter, unfortunately.

When she went off and married that disgusting hunchback— what was it we called him? Oh yes, Peter Tordenskjold, the shamscape painter!—my infatuation seemed to be instantly wiped out. It was just too sickening. To picture her being besmirched by his kisses, ugh; more than enough.

What a dreadful idiot I was. She probably did it simply to annoy me. I believe I was the one she'd chosen for herself. And then to frighten her off with all kinds of accursed foolishness and lack of manners—ah! It was *her* I should have had. When I let happiness slip away from me then—well, I think it really sealed my fate.

As for my current "friend," I think I am well on my way to being cured. The wound is reopened only off and on—like the other day when I heard that a lady had come by and asked for me; it *could* have been her!—but, hang it, it's not the first time I swallow my love. Coming down here had a cooling and tranquillizing effect on me. She's nearby, after all. Now I just have to be brave and stick it out, and in a couple of months it will be over.

A painful thought, as it happens. It's as though I'm killing something in myself, something dear and valuable, a possibility of life; tearing up the roots of something beautiful and rich that was eager to grow and put forth leaves, grow and thrive and enfold me in a profusion of flowers, white, pink, full of fragrance—.

## VI

30 Sept.

Fall is my season, especially when there's rain and fog. Then I spend long afternoons taking walks outside and around the city; I enjoy the wanness of the fields and the turning leaves, sickly and flushing, yellowing and falling. And I wallow in mournful moods.

The birds are silent and fly away, everything seeks shelter and safety. A strange, whirring tune suggestive of fairy music drones from the small human dwellings scattered around on hills and knolls; it is the threshing machines working, working for the winter. People know what is in store; they are getting ready with everything—provisions, clothes, reading matter—as if before a long siege.

On such days it may happen that I perpetrate verses. What follows below was made by my humble self—which does not mean that I dare guarantee its originality.

> A banner, big and black,
> casts a shadow on the earth.
> Death rides his shabby mount,
> the bane of life and mirth.
> Death rides his shabby gray
> along a barren trail.

The sun hangs low and pale,
its life dying away.

Fading leaves are everywhere,
and shriveling buds on plants.
The woods sway darkly in the storm,
singing funeral chants.
Black and silent, the streams flow by,
'tween bushes yellowed by fall;
they can't anymore recall
the blue of the summer sky.

All human dwelling places
close quietly for the winter.
The farmer garners his last potato,
better sooner than later.
The leaves rustle down and down
like dying butterflies.
To his winter lair the bear hies,
he wants to be left alone.

We shed our summer things,
the snow may come any day.
An end to summer outings!
"We'll go to the café.
The paper, may I, please excuse!
What's doing in parliament?
Nothing? The same old predicament.
From Paris, what's the news?"

One might get scared and sad,
seeing life so decimated.
But think of all the myriad
seeds the summer created!

We can bear the black moods of fall,
as long as they are not forgot . . .
They're laughing in some secret spot,
"We've survived, one and all!"

## VII

I was beginning to feel better now, but the good Lord had found
out about it, and naturally he let the pale girl with the tousled hair
turn the corner of Kirke and Karl Johan Street the very same moment I was about to round that dangerous corner—in the opposite
direction. She obviously didn't see me, and even if she had seen
me? What am I to her? A funny windbag, a queer fellow. . . . Well,
no. Anyway, I did see her, though God knows how—I have a very
distinct feeling that I closed both my eyes quite firmly.

She was very pale. With such a peculiarly downcast expression
in her eyes—those large, sick, dangerous eyes, those swimming,
absent eyes that looked out into the world so wistfully without discovering a way or a destination, staring into a black abyss. Her
brown curls falling in the most hopeless confusion down those
snow-white, blue-veined temples. I felt a jolt through my whole
being, I haven't had a moment's peace since. It's all been opened up
again; it gnaws, tears, eats into me—as before. I looked up Bjølsvik,
coaxed him into going out with me and tried to drink and be merry;
but the old refrain that says, "If you want to be merry, you have to
drink," is a lie. The truth is that, if you are going to drink, you have
to be merry, and of course I was not. I collapsed time and again and
sat staring at the woman turning the corner yonder. . . . She's constantly turning the corner of Kirke and Karl Johan Street; I constantly see this glimpse of pale despair under an abundance of
brown curls, and of two large, sick eyes staring into some black
abyss. And each time, my breast is filled afresh with those vague,

miserable, lacerating pains that writhe and wind themselves around and into one another, like serpents in a snake pit.

(Here follow several attempts to make pen and pencil drawings of her. None of them is any good.)

I've been on something of a drinking spree for a week. Last night I had a bad time again. And now, here I sit, soft in the head and quite stupefied with liquor. My sins are . . .

What my department head will say? Who cares! More beer—.

I'll simply go to bed again. My sins are—ugh!

Evening the same day

Waking up after a bad spree, you find yourself in a special state: there is this picture of a very long, pliant sword settling itself quite slowly into your breast, vertically and securely, straight through the heart. I can see it; and in a way I can feel it, it does me good. It cools me, comforts me. A big, white, elegant hand with glittering diamond rings sits up by the hilt guiding it, securely and steadily, slowly and agreeably; but there's hardly any arm.

This picture alternates with another one: it's a sort of guillotine, formed like a large breadknife, and under this knife—a very broad knife, shiny, thin, whistlingly cold, and so sharp that it sinks through the flesh almost by itself—lies my throat; and a woman, a nice elderly, housewifely woman, is cutting this throat, slowly, thoughtfully, as you'd cut a slice of rye bread. I lie in a comfortable position—on my left side—and enjoy the situation. Ah!—lovely.

This evening I have mostly fantasies of hanging. At every moment I instinctively feel my throat with my hand, in the place where the cord would be; then I bring my hand upward, toward the ceiling, where the cord would be fastened, and for a moment I imagine that I'm dangling, giving out a gasping sound with my tongue hanging out. It calms and cools me. It must be lovely to soar like that, above it all, above all the serpents and lizards on earth; they can't get to me anymore now, I'm through, once and for all, with the vermin and the filth.

Everything might be all right if it weren't for my tremor, a strange, obscure tremor that I can't figure out—it must be inside, a sort of vibration of the internal muscles, odd and disagreeable. I become so unsure of myself, so dizzy, so weightless, without a center of gravity—a tiny little quivering tremor throughout my whole person. It's maddening. I know what it is, of course—alcoholism, damn it! But that doesn't help any. A faint sense of queasiness below my chest. No real headache, just a peculiar foggy feeling of emptiness around my head—there is a sort of gap between me and the world, a soughing remoteness; and the things around me aren't really things, they are stage sets, they are . . . As a matter of fact, the things that stand there are just so many tricks, while trying to pass themselves off as this, that or the other, sofa, cabinet, chairs, and so on; but they know very well they aren't. It troubles me a little. I can't bother watching this comedy.

But under, undermost, underneath, behind, in the background, in the subterranean layer of my being, sits this dangerous anxiety, heavy as lead, a kind of secret, locked-up madness that starts swelling up and, swelling, wants to let out a roar. It's my bad conscience, or a kind of dread, a feeling of terrible degradation, and a sort of strange, idiotic horror at something or other, God knows what. A desperately sick yearning to throw myself at the feet of someone or other, a woman, a priest, a god, and howl, weep, confess, be whipped, cursed, condemned, finally to be lifted up by a pair of trusty, loving arms like a sick child.

I have to be a bit careful, I might get the horrors. But it's good for my infatuation. It divides things up. The woes of love are swallowed up in the sea of another kind of anguish. Love becomes remote, sentimental, freed from desire; you feel so unworthy—you wouldn't touch her with your little finger even if permitted to. And you fool around with your suicidal mania and nurse your nerves and delusions and mumble aloud to yourself: what an old pig I am! Oh no, with God's help she's not going to fall prey to someone like that! And you feel noble and good and get tears in your eyes.

Fanny, listen! Why can't you come to me now, just ring the bell. I won't hurt you; we'll just have a sweet moment together.

I catch myself looking for the same roads where she and I went for walks. I religiously drink bad, ice-cold beer in those country restaurants where she and I have been together. On the quiet I probably hope to meet her, though that's precisely what I don't want at any price. And not having met her, I walk home again with my tail between my legs.

Death is the only thing that's certain, people say. Sure; but still, you know, it isn't to be trusted. It will come, all right, but it doesn't come at the right moment.

The good Lord, who pinned us onto life so that we should squirm for his greater glory, doesn't like to remove us from the pin until we have performed every squirming trick we possibly can. But by that time we've begun to feel almost comfortable on the point of our pin; for we can get used to anything, even to going on living.

Shoot oneself? It requires so much initiative. And one rarely hits the correct spot. And besides, it's in such execrable taste.

Maybe Dr. Kvaale could bring himself to give me a vial of morphine, just in case?

*(The latest scandal.)* A young, attractive wife has had a love affair with a sea captain. Consequently, everybody raises an outcry— with conviction! The men because they envy him, and the women because they envy her.

I, for one, envy him. Provided, that is, "she" were the one *I* am thinking of.

Right Honorable Gabriel Jeronimus Gram! Really, what sort of stupidities are these?

I almost fell over with amazement when this self-evident thing dawned on me—up in Bogstad Road someplace; I simply cannot understand where I have been.

You see, it is morality, that familiar jackass, which has been after me. The greatest possible happiness, the smallest possible unhappiness—willy-nilly these commonplaces (may they be damned!) interfere with emancipated people's reasoning.

Feeling good? I would rather feel bad (as long as it wasn't a stomach ache, that is). This soulless, slack satiety that people call feeling good may be all right for cabinet ministers and clergymen, but it certainly is not for human beings.

Feeling bad in one way or another—longing, loss, pain, and worry—that's just what life *is*. It makes you do your utmost, fills the time, keeps your psychic mechanism going, breeds feelings, stirrings of the will, thoughts, energy, while being satiated and content—well, that is simply the end of everything.

Just look at those few chancy hours when you live fully! When all the vital spirits are active, your entire being aglow and working, your soul all trembling! It has no resemblance to satiety, feeling good, and such; all real pleasure is at least half pain—after all, mastered pain is the definition of pleasure! Such hours can be achieved only by means of some stimulus or other: wine, love, gambling, enthusiasm. But the moralists say: Watch out! Above all, no intoxication! Tomorrow you'll have a hangover! I would prefer even an unadulterated hangover to their sated boredom—much more so when I get life's great moments into the bargain!

And yet here I am, avoiding and shunning this stimulus, which even now could impart some vibrancy to me, for fear of the suffering that will come, for fear of a little hopeless love! Gabriel, Gabriel, I don't recognize you anymore.

I want to see her again, I want to spend time with her—*in order to* fall "hopelessly in love," in short.


## VIII


Old man! You cannot love. Go home and lie down among the ashes like Job, and scrape yourself with a potsherd.

She interests me essentially as a problem. I like working on it, feel an urge to solve it. But this is obviously not the sort of interest a man should take in a woman.

Ay, ay—and then a bit of maudlin sentimentality when she's absent again. A kind of longing. In certain moods this longing can be painful. But there is no passion whatever.

Cupid, Cupid, I'll sacrifice a hecatomb to you if you make me blind. . . .


I feel content in a fashion. That irksome sense of loss is gone; I have peace of mind.

It's not healthy to keep your distance. Imagination and feeling mutually egg each other on, until you have changed the young girl in question into "woman," into a madonna in the clouds, Eve among the roses. Then bold dreams add fuel, until you walk around like Saint Anthony, who would have been capable of marrying a market woman if he'd met her.

Eleven o'clock in the evening. A pleasant feeling of being *comme il faut*. Everything in order. Supped in proper fashion with her; talked wittily and sensibly and effortlessly, with a flattering sense of being appreciated.

A man is not completely satisfied with himself until he feels he's admired by a woman.

I recognize in her many quaint and antediluvian things—many of my own former viewpoints and periods; thus, she is patriotic, among other things—naturally! Loves Norway and so forth. "And hopefully you do the same?"—"Oh yes; Norway isn't bad at all, heavens no, considering the circumstances."—"Phooey!"

Ah yes, we mortals are clever. We transform our necessities and limitations into virtues and are proud of them. Just as we change our instinct to perpetuate the species into "love," the brutal fact that we are creatures of habit, and physically and spiritually bound to a specific milieu, gets transfigured in our fantasy into the poetic illusion of "love of country."

Loving a piece of geography, what a ridiculous idea! "Loving" 226,560 square miles!

I truly believe that my being so cool about the above-mentioned square miles makes her suffer; at any rate she keeps coming back to the subject, and now and then she lets me have it.

I defend myself.

"Well, patriotism, you know, is in reality nothing but self-love raised to a higher power. We are so precious to ourselves that we value everything we come in contact with in any way whatever, be it nothing more than the places where we live, or even those places that just have some judicial or administrative connection with them. However, *enfin! That* doesn't mean patriotism isn't justified."

"Justified! What a disgusting, insipid word!"

"Dear me, what shall I do! Where should I take love of country from? I come from an old family of civil servants; I therefore belong to that homeless horde of nomads that are parasites on the great body of the people, move from place to place, from one position to another, just as the Lapps move from pasture to pasture in the mountains. No feeling for one's country can develop among such a breed. Patriotism belongs to the viewpoint of those who are settled. It is developed along with agriculture and architecture. To the tiller of the soil the plot of ground he has started using really means something, and before long also the entire territory that goes with it; but for the nomads the old saying is absolutely valid: *Ubi bene, ibi patria*—your fatherland is where you make the most money."

"So, without further ado, you could go and make a Swede of yourself, if you got nicely paid—"

"Hmm, a well-paid job in the Swedish foreign ministry, for example—why not?"

"Should it ever come to war, you'll be the first one I'll shoot!" She smiles, her eyes blazing, charmingly pretty.

I lift my hat and bow.


She's a democrat, naturally. She speaks with intense rage about "the little thieves who get hanged, while the big ones go free," as if *that* could be of any avail.

I walk around like a professional damper and fireman; she irritates me every moment with her exaggerations and her injustice, based on the most naive ignorance.

"Well, of course the little thieves get hanged," I say, "just as we kill vermin. On the other hand, we cannot help developing a certain respect for those who steal on a grand scale, as we do for everything of a certain magnitude. They are masters of their craft, artists, and people have respect for art, for mastery, and ought to have respect for it, even when the art in question is nothing but the art of stealing. We feel revulsion at a miserable petty larcenist and pickpocket, who turns himself into a louse for a bit of change and lets himself be caught and punished to boot. But we take an interest in Ole Høiland and Gjest Bårdsen and tip our hats to Rothschild and Vanderbilt."

She gets angry and protests with excessive energy, failing to understand that mixture of weary seriousness and gallows humor that unintentionally becomes the tone of someone who has experienced resignation. She takes everything with solemn seriousness, as a cow does a green door or a college student "the republic."

We came today across a poor woman sitting, pale and blue, on a staircase with a frozen baby in her arms. Fanny nervously tore open her purse, gave the woman something and hurried on; when she began to talk again after a short while, her voice was nearly choking with tears. I felt at the moment somewhat embarrassed; my thought on seeing the woman had naturally been, Aha, a gyp artist! She has bought or stolen a poor child, which she uses for bait—where the hell is the police? And the naive girl goes off and bursts into tears, then hands the female her last penny.

It's more noble, of course.

She put my feeling to flight at once.

"And there inside," she said, "sits rich Mrs. Hartmann, who spends so much money on makeup and powder and perfume alone that such an unfortunate creature could support herself and raise her child on it, and . . . they should be *hanged!*"

The last word was hissed forth; it was the hiss of the lower classes, full of hate, devoid of understanding. Such things make a terribly half-educated impression.

I overcame my annoyance and said, "The bad part is that they are both right and wrong, Mrs. Hartmann as well as the beggar woman. It's quite possible that both ought to be hanged, in principle; at any rate, that would be best for them. But in practice, you know, we'll have to accept that they both go free. I, too, have suffered a lot from compassion with those who are hungry; but as time goes on it dawns on you that they're not the ones who are worst off."

"Who, then, are the worst off?" she asked bitterly.

"Those who are the best off," I replied. "You see, they have the fewest illusions."

"Pooh," I believe I heard. I went on.

"Every human being can endure a certain amount of suffering; if this quantity is exceeded, the person concerned throws himself into the Aker River. It doesn't cost anything; admission is free down there. Accordingly, as long as a person doesn't throw himself into the Aker River, one can assume that his sufferings have not exceeded the limit of the endurable. (A skeptical 'Hmm?' was heard.) Oh yes, that inference is pretty certain. But as a matter of fact, relatively few of the hungry ones throw themselves into the Aker River. From that I conclude that there are worse sufferings than hunger, more unbearable, more hopeless. It is simply false to weigh the sufferings of these pariahs on our scale. They don't feel the way we would feel under similar circumstances. The human being is an elastic creature: it can get used to anything."

"Only not to starving."

"Oh yes; that, too, to a certain degree."

"Have you tried it?"

"No, of course not."

"How can you be so sure, then?"

"I base it on my Aker River statistics."

"Maybe the starving don't throw themselves into the Aker River very often, but that's probably because they die so quickly anyway. I have read in some paper that three or four times as many per thousand of the poor people die as of the well-to-do."

ME (*with a shrug*). We'll die in any case, you know. Nothing much is gained by living.

"But then it would be better to kill them in a hurry, it seems to me."

"Hmm!" A shrug.

Pause.

## IX

If only I could understand—.

Marrying me is clearly not on her mind, that I conclude both from her various utterances and from her behavior. If she had something like that in mind, she would obviously be far more reserved, that's part and parcel of the most simple, innate feminine tact. Besides, a woman of twenty-four knows that a man of culture won't marry someone who gives cause for any sort of doubt by her behavior, toward him or others.

Just to "banish boredom," is it?

To say to hell with her reputation, her future, all that is important and sacred to a woman, just to banish "boredom" during a few afternoons? Can anybody pretend to believe something like that?

Or might there still be love at the back of it?

That would be nice, wouldn't it! To disturb a woman's peace of mind without any reason or purpose whatsoever, to make her unhappy for life perhaps without being willing or able to give her any kind of compensation, not as much as a remembrance to live on—really great!

Ha-ha, you old pious fraud, you simpleton—are you there again, eh? The idea of her becoming "unhappy"! She's happy now, then, is she? Is it better to be bored to death than to die from grief? "Moral" is almost always synonymous with cowardly. I "don't want to make her unhappy" means: I know that she'll be unhappy in any case, but simply refuse any responsibility or trouble on my own account. The girl will be ruined, so let her rather be ruined by boredom—then I'll be out of it!

It is called "to have a clear conscience."

Anyway, there's no danger. She's not sexy—many strikingly beautiful women are that way. That's why it happens relatively often that they stay unmarried. And that's also why people say that it is the plain Janes who are loved the most. They have the most sex, you see. The beautiful and cold ones seldom fall in love, and accordingly seldom inspire love in return; if they marry it's out of curiosity as a rule, or for the sake of social position, and so on. When Miss Holmsen gets tired of being a virgin one of these days, she'll take some rich guy who can keep her supplied with horses and diamonds.

All in all, a woman does not love as we do. Her love means that her children simply must have a father; it's not very important whether it turns out to be one or the other. If she can't have the best one, she cries and takes the next best.

And if she doesn't get married at all, it doesn't matter very much either. These old maids do pretty well for themselves, by gosh. In fact, "women's emancipation" aims at producing even more old maids. For women there's only one social question: being provided for. If they manage to provide for themselves, they don't give a damn about either husband or marriage; it's so lovely to be independent of these disgusting, conceited men.

Women always have to use these big, broad, general words, which are so crude and so devoid of nuance. A thing is either one or the other: "lovely" or "beastly." Toward a person they feel one way or the other: "love" or "disgust." With regard to general questions and circumstances, they are either "madly enthusiastic" or they hate them—underscored. One or the other: black or white. A more subtle characterization doesn't interest them.

"Sure; but how can you expect anything else, when we haven't had an education!" Fanny says.

Strange. I actually used to be almost fond of Mathilde; she seemed so naïve and childlike and deliciously frivolous. Now I sit there feeling indisposed and thinking about Fanny.

This evening I finally had to close my eyes and imagine it was *her* I was holding in my arms.

It's always only what we *don't* have that seems desirable, isn't it?

We should marry young, otherwise we'll never get around to it.

On the one hand, our own scruples increase in number; on the other hand, we experience too much—through married friends.

Great God, look at all those distressed married men! They put on a happy face as long as possible, saying, "Get married, my friend, it's the only thing." But if you catch them alone over their third glass (if they dare permit themselves a third glass), there's no telling what may happen.

They begin talking about "woman." In general terms, in the form of common theories. They have heard other married men say—; this or that well-known women's physician is of the opinion that—; I have read Dr. N. N.'s famous physiology of women, and there it says—. And when men start talking in general terms about "woman" one must prick up one's ears, because there's always an ulterior motive behind it.

I'm familiar with two main categories of matrimonial lamentations.

Some say, Woman is cold. She takes little or no interest in "that sort of thing," but does it merely out of a sense of duty and obedience. And they lower their voices to a whisper and say, "You have no idea how common that is; more than one married man has told me in confidence that he . . ."

Incidentally, I've never believed any of that. As a rule, it probably means no more than that the woman in question married without love, which does happen now and then.

Well, it can be bad enough all the same. But it seems to be even worse for those husbands whose wives are in love—at any rate if I am to believe Dr. Kvaale.

I meet that man off and on at Jonathan's. But he seems a bit surly, I can't rightly get him to open up. This evening, however, we happened to sit together for a while over a toddy, and I prodded him so long that he actually came out a little.

An odd fellow. A peasant student, shy, withdrawn, with a broad, irregular face and small, queer eyes. He's really bright, has thought and gone through a lot—and "lived" a good deal, it seems; indeed, an interesting man. He risked the experiment of marrying his youthful sweetheart, but so tardily that both she and he were rather faded.

"By the way, most husbands say that women are cold," I said, egging him on.

He gave a little shrug, then barked in his somewhat piercing voice, "Those are men who have no talent for awakening woman, my good man. Once she's awakened, there won't be any reason to complain about coldness, as a rule."

"So—? I would be very much surprised."

"After all, woman is the sexual being *par excellence*," he snarled. "It's quite natural. Monandry is a trick of the devil."

I argued with him until I had a fairly clear idea of his situation, and in the end I felt quite uneasy. Miss Berner, with her marriage of convenience, is right despite everything.

All kinds of awful stories of marriage come to mind. Today I saw Lunde, the agent, on the street, and it made me recall what he had once told me.

"Aha, what a damn farce: we spend our youth trying to find a woman, and in our manhood years we have a hard time getting rid of her again. For the latter is a damn sight more difficult than the former."

"But, uh—isn't the law actually quite liberal?"

"The law? Ha, it sure is stupid enough. But you can always get around that; no, it's the wife, naturally."

"Oh well, you could make her bored with you, couldn't you?"

He laughed. "Bored—she certainly was; but to get divorced—haw-haw-haw! So then, you see, I had to try scandal. Oh yes; and openly, you know, so she would find out about it."

"Well?"

He laughed again, with an internal, wheezing laughter that sounded disagreeably nervous. "She forgave me!" he said.

"Yes, but in the long run—"

"Oh no, time after time. Bawled a little, sure, and brought off a couple of fits; but since propriety was saved, you see, she presented me with her pardon on a platter—haw-haw-haw-haw! And one does have some manners, after all; it would simply not do to insult the lady."

"Hmm."

"One time I went so far that she enacted the last scene of that comedy, you know—Nora, of course. She ran away, you see. Thank God, I thought, and went to my club; and there I celebrated my deliverance as it behooved, I can tell you. But when I came home—oh, haw-haw-haw—who is sitting in the drawing room but my wife? In full traveling gear and red-eyed and awful-looking, with her despair spread all over the chairs—haw-haw-haw-haw!"

"Well, but then you could simply—"

"She brought off yet another fit, naturally, extra special, first class, A-1 with a star. I bore it like a man, needless to say, and thought: It's the last time! Finally she saw the method wasn't working anymore and that somehow there was danger afoot, and so she threw her arms around my neck—haw-haw-haw—and forgave me. Oho, sure; she was not without a sense of humor."

I no longer remember everything the fellow had perpetrated to guard against his wife's forgiveness, but I do remember his melancholy final remarks.

"Aha, yes. At one time I was really a good soul, you know; good-humored, a nice fellow. But in the course of those six years I had become—uh, a gorilla. A gorilla, sure. Well, what the hell can you do? Why, once you have inflicted a woman on yourself there's only one medicine for that sickness: a tremendously long patience, you bet. Or, if you don't carry that kind of merchandise, try a good, strong hemp rope! Yeah. Ay-ay-ay! We haven't been put on this earth to enjoy ourselves, that's for sure! But I for my part, you see, was obstinate and thought, I'll be damned if I can't get you in hand, my cutie! And so, that was my way of getting the better of her."

The worst of it is that the fellow loves his wife even today.

A strange thought is pursuing me. This fellow Lunde, the agent, is an exact replica of Fanny's father (she tells me about her parents when I ask her to tell me about herself; rather mysterious). Suppose I got married to Fanny (who would after a while, as likely as not, be just like her mother); then I too would in all probability become such a wretched fellow—a Mr. Holmsen, an Agent Lunde. I can see myself in that role, trudging from dive to dive, heavy with beer and sweaty with cognac, and philosophizing about "woman."

But what the hell, I don't want to get married to her; what sort of nonsense is this? After all, that is precisely what I *don't* want to do: get married to Miss Holmsen!

## X

One of the funniest things that can happen is for two former boon companions and hell-raisers to meet again after a lapse of many years, and one of them has been faithful to his past while the other has become a clergyman. I met this evening my former "co-carouser" and "fellow boozehound" Frits, alias the Lieutenant, as the very reverend Pastor Løchen.

We had whooped it up many a night together, the two of us—

"helling around" through the night, to use our expression of that time. God only knows if he still remembers it. He was a fine, handsome man, dashing and smart-looking, with a pale-yellow martial mustache (hence his pet name, the Lieutenant), diligent with his glass and merry with the girls, the best fellow boozer you could ask for. He sang well and was a good raconteur, bubbling over with jokes and piquant stories; he also made up jokes and stories himself. Besides, he was an able student actor; I believe the key question of his life was whether to become a writer or an actor.

In the end there was rather too much celebration; he broke off, became an earnest person and went in for theology. And we drifted apart and began to speak our separate languages, until neither of us understood the other any longer. Soon we only greeted each other across the street; his circle of acquaintance became more and more white-tie. He himself too. His face grew longer and longer and paler and paler; at last the mustache was gone, too, and the *cand. theol.* was complete.

This evening I met him again after the lapse of a year. He was barely recognizable. A clergyman from top to toe. His face, with all its long clerical lines and broad clerical features, almost completely new; he also had another mouth, a wide, mildly grave, devout clergyman's mouth. Only up around his eyes a few traces were left of the fellow carouser of yore.

It was almost like meeting a man who had died and come alive again. He doubtless had a similar feeling about me; at any rate he said a couple of times, not without sadness, "It's amazing how you have changed, Gram." I replied, with an irony he hardly sensed, "You aren't quite the same either, Reverend."

"And how are you doing, my dear friend?" He made a rather well-meant attempt to be a fellow human.

"I'm doing all right, thank you. I'm bored eight days a week and have fun otherwise."

"Hmm, bored." He smiled, becoming a clergyman again. "Well, yes, I'm quite familiar with it—from former times."

"Only from former times?"

"Yes. To tell the truth, I believe the expression 'to be bored' doesn't exist in the vocabulary of a Christian."

The old quibbler and blabbermouth was about to awaken inside me, but then I discovered the hostess nearby; she had a rather worried look in her eyes, and so I checked myself. I said something extremely polite to the effect that perhaps it was with the Christians as with those of us "who have undergone the great resignation in another way: we know that boredom is part and parcel of it and so we accept it, like a cross, without any particular grumbling—in the end as something that has to be that way, as normal, something that is no longer noticed."

But he said no. It was not resignation. On the contrary. It was hope, faith, spirit—zest for life. "Every single hour, every minute, is occupied—and occupied with something that's really worthwhile."

"Ah, if one could be sure of that," I said, changing the subject. We parted in the "hope" of meeting again. Alas, much good that would do!

He is no doubt happier than I am. But I cannot in any way bring myself to envy him. In the last analysis it is *not* happiness we seek; it's something else, something higher. . . .

## XI

"You seem to be a little tired this evening, miss?"

"Me? Oh—oh, no. Nothing much."

"How are you doing these days in general? Taking it easy, I suppose? One day at a time?"

She answers quickly, as if deprecatingly, "Let's not talk about it."

Pause.

*Why* doesn't she want to talk about it? If I only knew what she's like inside, what she thinks about during the day, what she's busy with; what longings, dreams, memories, or worries are bothering her. For I gather from all she says that she's anything but happy. But to get her to explain herself, to make herself totally transparent to me—no, she constantly eludes me. Can't she figure me out?

I'm annoyed that two sensible people should walk side by side and be utter strangers to one another.

I wonder how she feels, this young woman who walks beside me, leaning on my arm. Sometimes I have an impression that she leans more heavily than is strictly necessary, looking for a pretext to press my arm onto her breast. A pleasant warmth runs through me, and I say to myself, Perhaps just a tiny kiss now and the ice would be broken. . . .

But to kiss a girl is like signing a check: Can, will, should I accept all the consequences? And the kiss doesn't come off, and the ice remains.

"Well, here we are, I'm home."

"Yes. All things come to an end."

"And you, poor man, who has such a long walk home."

She snatches my hand and squeezes it softly and warmly. "Thanks for a nice evening."

"Thank you, miss. When shall we meet again?"

"When you wish. I take this walk every day."

"So long, then. Good night."

"So long."

I drag myself home. I have no reason to hurry.

No, no, not write. I have too much to think about.

It has become my routine now: a glass and a cigarette, and then sitting in the rocking chair daydreaming—for hours on end.

Who is she? What does she want? What does she mean? How

shall I handle this business anyway? It has to end sometime. Well, it's interesting too, of course. As a study, at least. She's different. . . .

Should I stake something on this card? Should I take a risk? Perhaps I'm mistaken about her; she seems a bit odd to me. But still, once the ice was broken perhaps—getting to know her through and through—? Perhaps she may yet be—not just partly but in every essential—the one and only I could get along with, being a bit odd myself.

I sit for hours debating these same questions over and over again, without end and without a beginning. The result is invariably negative, but the game is no less tempting. And I go to bed at two, to wake up tomorrow with every nerve quivering.

No, not write . . .

Sunday evening

This fellow Kvaale is a damn pessimist.

"They're so naïve, these Bohemians," he barked this evening at Jonathan's. "They think that marriage can 'be founded on love'; did you ever hear the likes? What is love? After all, it's nothing but want, thirst, or whatever you'd call it; and blast it, once you've had a chance to drink you aren't thirsty anymore."

"Well," I said, "if the wine is good, you get thirstier the longer you go on drinking."

"Yes, but if you drink a drop too many, you get a hangover. That's physiology."

"But it passes, and you drink again."

"That's habitual drinking, and that's the crux of the matter, you see: marriage is not founded on love but on habit. You don't care for each other in the least, but stick together anyway, because of habit, which I assure you is often quite—" (a shrug).

George Jonathan put the monocle in his eye and said, "Marriage is a convenient arrangement for those who're no longer in love."

"For heaven's sake," I said, "cut out that foppish married-man talk. After all, we know very well there exist enduring love relationships."

"Indeed," Jonathan said, "some women do possess that sort of genius."

"What genius?" Kvaale yelped.

"It's a question of feminine tact," Jonathan remarked, smoking agreeably through his nose, "an innate ability, which incidentally is not very common. Modesty, milords! Just the right amount of reserve—as far from prudishness as from the contrary.

"You see, the husband must," he went on, "be kept in a state of uncertainty. He must have the illusion of conquering the beautiful one, of gaining her favor, of seducing her—constantly; he must feel like a conqueror, the favored one, the one who is continually chosen afresh among so and so many rivals. If he feels secure, the game loses interest for him, and if she trails after him she arouses his pity. A woman must never allow her husband to entertain this thought: Poor thing, she has nobody but me! 'If one wants to be prized, one must maintain one's price'; the women who rightly understand this saying make the grade."

"Those who have a knack for coquetry, you mean?" I said, by way of interpretation.

"Yes."

"Our Nordic women are really too good," Kvaale said, smiling.

I did not like them. All things considered, what wretched cowards these men are, not even capable of managing a marriage.


## XII


We were taking our most common walk, out along the Ljabro highway.

The fjord is frozen. Nothing but snow. The vast snow basin gapes at us, huge and empty, through the dim light of dusk.

"That's just like life," I said, "an open, empty frozen chasm of snow, with the waning light of dusk and a gray, snow-filled sky. How sad to be a lonely wanderer through such a wasteland."

"Yes," she exclaimed, "nice to be two!" Adding quickly, "Alone, you see, I wouldn't go for walks; I'm afraid of the dark, among other things."

"Yes, you women have a tendency that way, don't you. I suppose it's the need for a protector?"

"I don't know what it is, but I always think I might come to see such visions—what are they called: hal-le-lu—"

"Hallucinations, yes; ghosts as they used to say in the old days."

"Yes, but—are you so sure, incidentally, that there is no such thing as ghosts?"

"Hmm. I wish there were, I almost said."

"Oh, dear; why?"

"Well, every once in a while the world becomes all too patented for me. Everything is so terribly rational and correct. Nothing but mathematics and horse power. Well, that's nice, but . . . it's awfully nice. . . . Anyway, you have nothing to fear—after all, you have God."

"Yes. But what if he, too, should be lost!"

"Oh no. Hold on to him. Who knows, in a decade or so maybe he, too, will become fashionable again."

SHE. Wasn't the one you said hello to Blytt—the painter?

ME. Yes.

SHE. He's a fine one, isn't he?

ME. What do you mean, "fine"?

SHE. Such a one—a Don Juan.

ME. Oh, yes. He has a sense of beauty.

SHE. Pooh, some expression.

ME. Quite correct, as it happens.

SHE (*ready for battle*). Well, I suppose there could be more than one viewpoint on that subject.

ME (*indifferently*). Hmm.

SHE. Those he has made unhappy can't take it so easy, can they?

ME. Hmm. Unhappiness, you know, is such a difficult notion. I too have experienced unhappy loves. But I must confess that of the few "happy" relationships I have had, none has absorbed me so much, or been sacred and precious to such a degree, as those "unhappy" episodes. Such an unhappy love—*that* can really make your soul resonate; you can live on it for years afterward. Love *is*, everything considered, unhappy love.

SHE (*curt, sullen*). Queer talk.

ME. Still, that's the way it is.

SHE (*after a few moments*). You weren't left in shame, with a child, were you?

ME. If a woman is ashamed of having had a child, then she deserves to go to hell.

Silence.


"Optimists—what are they, exactly?"

"Well, people who believe in the goodness of life, the victory of good, and so forth; who on the whole think that the world is good."

"Then I'm an optimist—just now anyway. Aren't you?"

"O-o-h! I suppose the world could be even worse. I keep my wits about me, at any rate. Oh, dear! Well, in short, it's either/or. Either you say goodbye to the world, or you adjust to it; it's no use whining. 'Sniveling,' as George Jonathan calls it."

"I think that's true."

"These optimists, well. . . . They're very fine people. Useful people; we wouldn't get far without them. But—oh well; they are a bit shallow, of course, don't exactly think very deeply; sometimes a little narrow-minded too, perhaps. They are often people who lack the courage to look reality squarely in the eye and who therefore get wrapped up in all kinds of belief and hope and love in order to put it more at a distance—that is, like religious people in general."

"Yes, but—one has to believe in something, right?"

"We have to believe in ourselves, as far as it goes."

"Yes—if one only could."

"We can what we must."

"Perhaps."

"But if God didn't exist, why should people have come up with the idea of believing in him?"

"Hmm. Sometimes I think we have invented God to have someone we can be sincere with. That is, someone we don't have to playact with."

"Oh. So you think we playact with everybody else, do you?"

"Naturally."

"What if you, for example, had someone you really cared about—?"

"Then I would lie to be interesting; and when my love was over, I would lie because I no longer felt like undressing before that person."

Pause.

"Of course," I added, "we lie to ourselves most of all. We simply have to. To see ourselves 'as we are'—that would be too hideous. Then we would go downright crazy, see. No; but to set up such a figure outside ourselves—a 'God,' a being who knows all, so that it just is no use to playact, and a being who understands everything, so we won't actually be in any danger if he finds out about us—that is, indeed, a quite cunning idea."

"If only I could find out for certain whether he exists or not, otherwise it's no use."

"Well, as to being certain—. It's quite unimportant whether God exists or not, as long as we manage to be convinced about it."

"Oh dear—can't you understand that you make me completely lose my faith when you say things like that?"

A shrug.


"I wouldn't mind if you told me a little about all the remarkable things that science has now discovered."

"Hmm. Well, now that you ask the question—you don't want me to tell you about the telephone and spectroscopic analysis, do you?"

"No, that's not exactly the most important, I should think."

"As far as God, virtue, and immortality are concerned, science no longer concerns itself with such things. Those are questions for peasants."

"Hmm, yes—perhaps."

"When you ask me like this in general what science has discovered, I guess I'll have to answer sort of negatively: it has discovered that so and so and such and such—is *not* so. And that, you know, is in itself just as important."

"I don't understand."

"Why, each time we discover such a new piece of ignorance, we scrub off another layer of stupidity, you see."

(Laughter.) "One could end up getting quite thoroughly scrubbed off that way!"

"Yes, one does come to feel rather stripped."

## XIII

February '85

Why do I keep tormenting her with these inquisitions into her previous life, and so on? God only knows. It's quite ridiculous. I have no right to, after all. No purpose. But I just can't stop.

And the less she tells, the more curious I get. It's clear there are some episodes that she hides from me—and why in the world shouldn't she hide them? But, you see, I *must* find out about them. I ask and pry, examine and cross-examine, using moral thumbscrews and all sorts of mean tricks employed in judicial interrogations. It's shabby, it's contemptible; but what am I to do?

You see, she's quite astute, the little one. Tells me every imaginable thing that *doesn't* interest me; slips behind her story of relatives and acquaintances, about tomfooleries in the Women's Club and so on; evades the little traps I've set with a nimbleness that amazes me. Either she's supremely innocent or—since this is unthinkable for a girl so grown-up and no hothouse plant—more experienced than I like to believe.

Does she know, for example, to what degree something like that excites a man's curiosity, stimulates his fantasy—this uncertain something, half-dark, half-dubious, with possibilities in every direction?

Most cunning of all perhaps is the "naïvely" openhearted way in which she tells about her many "friends" and "companions." It is obviously unthinkable that there shouldn't be something more behind these companionships with young men, with whom she has wandered about in field and forest here and there—just like now with me. Yes, but our relationship, God knows, is proper enough, isn't it? Oh yes; but what if *I* deserve the credit for that! Not all those young men were as old and as good as I have been.

Do I know how she would act if I suddenly assaulted her with my love in some lonely spot? It's in poor taste, this secretiveness of hers, basically nothing but cheap coquetry.

She believes in the Ten Commandments on two stone tablets. Especially in the sixth naturally, which to these young girls is simply the fullness of the law.

In these "Bohemian" times, by the way, it's this commandment that is constantly brought up for discussion. I excuse the men as much as I can, saying it's not all that easy; and, good heavens, she's willing to allow for a great deal. But her basic principles are those of Dr. Martin Luther's small catechism. Monogamy was established by the LORD GOD in the garden of Eden, and ever since that time all human beings have lived nicely and contentedly, each of them with his own wife or her own husband—aside from some unmentionable and insane exceptions, who have all received their well-deserved punishment in the torments of hell.

"I know, of course," she says, "that there are a great many coarse fellows who go to such—who step out; but that men who wish to be considered cultivated, who later show up in respectable company and talk with . . . the rest of us, and . . . shake our hands, that they can undertake to—that they can . . . bring themselves to enter the house of such an individual, that makes me feel like vomiting!

"We women have a self-respect which you men don't seem to understand, a directly physical self-respect, so that much of what *you* can do is quite unnatural for us, quite . . . insurmountable. And these tarts, whom you are practically defending—well, they must have so quite destroyed . . . so completely suppressed all that was human and feminine and clean in themselves that there is absolutely nothing else left than this . . . this . . . cadaver; and then to be prepared to—ugh! No, you must *not* try to 'explain' such things, Gram."

She teases me with her evangelical-Lutheran notions until I get irritated and let her have a dose of the history of morals. Afterward

I'm annoyed that I told her about all that filth; you can't tell what impact such violent truths may have on an unprepared spirit. They could certainly ruin a great deal for her. Altogether truth is often so sordid, and finer natures ought to be spared it. But what is one to do? When those finer natures thank you for sparing them by becoming excessively stupid?

It vexes me—almost like an impermissible technical flaw in an otherwise excellent painting—that she has been so little chary of herself, has shown so little feminine delicacy. Imagine roaming about with one man after another, exposing herself to all sorts of suspicion, all sorts of vulgar language, giving up her good name just like that—what in the world is a woman without a good name? Good heavens, as far as I am concerned her "chastity" may be as unassailed as you please, it isn't particularly relevant to the matter in hand; but how about the feeling of certainty, the guarantee, that great, sacred trustworthiness? An intelligent man can calmly live with the certainty that his wife was married before she became his, but uncertainty, doubt, an uncertain possibility, a perpetually rankling question—no, that he cannot negotiate. Am I wasting my confidence on a dissembler who betrays me in her heart? The male who is forever utterly decent and childish will always find his mother in his beloved: the holy woman in whose arms he experienced absolute security. The young girl who has no inkling of that is not capable of marriage; she is a noxious animal and can only give rise to unhappiness.

People ridicule conventions. And they ought to, insofar as they have in mind the rule that forbids a young girl to love. But insofar as convention aims at safeguarding her trustworthiness, safeguarding her against the possibility of suspicion—to that extent its rules and absurdities are some of the most precious things in existence.

When (as in France) the young girl must always be guarded, never dares go out alone, and so on, we damn democrats and boors should refrain from laughing; there is something very serious behind that farce: her own happiness, and that of her prospective husband and future children, are thereby safeguarded from some terrible possibilities. A young girl who has been alone with a man for half an hour is, as a rule, very chaste and honest, but it *could* be the case that she belonged to those who sought freedom to misuse it. She is *not* proof against doubt anymore; she is *not* prime quality, not first-class A-1*. I may believe in her, but my belief, you see, is nothing but a belief; the most trifling incident can foster my doubt, and suddenly we're both unhappy. Despite all her chastity! It *is* conceivable, after all, that she had a knack for playacting! On the whole, something will stick to her after an affair of that sort, something that cannot be removed for lack of witnesses—the *possibility* of a possibility, the *conceivability* of the inconceivable, the *shadow* of a shadow. And where there's love, deep, tender, sensitive love—plus, of course, a bit of nerves—that will suffice.

For me, at any rate, this alone will be sufficient to exclude all thought of marriage—with Miss Holmsen, for example. It may turn out the same with her next eventual suitor. And so this fine girl, who in all probability is perfectly honest and good in every way, may remain unmarried all her life—or have to throw herself away on some cad or other—just because she imagined that, for a woman in this world, it was enough to *be* honest.

I want to stop this. After all, I'm right now compromising her in my turn. Compromising her worse than any of my predecessors. Evidently she has absolutely no idea of these things. So it's up to me, with all my wits about me, to use them. To let her go and ruin her reputation for good, deprive a good woman of her sole possession, all her prospects, her entire future, and doing so without either being able or willing to offer any compensation whatsoever, that is simply not to behave like a gentleman. I have felt it the whole time; now I see it clearly. Ergo . . .

## XIV

Hopeless—even if I were stronger than I am. Suddenly I meet her, and the game is up; there's certainly no reason why I should be discourteous to her. And if I bring up that bit about her reputation she'll get annoyed. "Calmly leave it to me to take care of my reputation," she'll say, not without a certain contempt in her voice and glance.

Then, when I come home after such a walk, I sit here till late in the night, thinking, dreaming, dissatisfied, sick. What shall I do? Eventually I must have her. Marriage is out of the question. In which way, then, can this other thing be introduced, so it won't be too ugly?

The same thoughts over and over again; the same thoughts whirling around and around at increasing speed, until my brain aches. The question is always just as interesting and just as hopeless. I'm aware neither of time nor tide; my whole being is absorbed, as if I were God and sat here ruling the world.

Marriage out of the question. I don't love her sufficiently. She's not first-rate enough. Besides, different levels of education, different dispositions, different lifestyles and living conditions. Everything, everything.

Consequently, the other thing. But how? She shows such tremendous trust. An idiotic, childish trust that keeps the gentleman in me on the qui vive, makes me start thinking, hinders me from surrendering to my mood. Not a trace of challenge from her.

And, God knows, she may love me—really love me. She looks up to me as something better, higher, absolutely reliable, something she can depend on. How could I then respond by offering her what she, with her half-educated, evangelical-Lutheran notions, will look upon as an expression of contempt? So *that's* what he's been thinking! *That's* how he has understood me! Women in love can take such an affair with idiotic solemnity.

It could become downright vulgar. I could risk all sorts of things. The devil knows what she's really like inside. If only she'd been in a different position, a bit more protected, a bit less "defenseless." She will think I want to take advantage of her defenseless position, and so forth, in the manner characteristic of bounders and big merchants—bah! If only she'd been a woman of good family! Or if she'd been one of those who *know* they have to be prepared for offers of that sort. This intermediate kind is dangerous; an extremely embarrassing situation.

We know women. They can say any number of emancipated things, but if you come and ask them—in the most considerate way ever, so that all they have to do is say "no," quite simply and calmly, and the man will make a bow and beg pardon—oh forget it! She lets out a yell like a servant girl, "Are you mad! Do you believe I'm one of those!"—and escapes into the bedroom and throws a fit.

And in my mind I make hundreds and thousands of drafts for a letter, which would tell her in the most unequivocal way that this is not meant as a lack of respect, on the contrary—.

These completely loose relationships are nevertheless, when all is said and done, those that entail the least suffering and least nonsense.

Her whole frivolous, raffish little face lights up as she throws herself around my neck and laughs, saying in her impishly gay, naïvely jolly girl's voice and Stavanger dialect, "Why, here you are just in the nick of time! Believe me, I was getting so bored with myself, I didn't know which way to turn. Well, now we'll have lots of fun, won't we?"

"Sure, baby; just let's have something to drink, Mathilde."

"That you shall have, my boy. So you haven't completely forgotten me, after all! You come so seldom now. We always used to be so happy together; don't you think so? Ha-ha-ha, you rascal. Well, now you shall have a beer. Or wine perhaps? Hah!"

I sit down on the sofa and she brings me the goods, humming some comic song or other. Whereupon the gossip gets going. God, how she talks! And this naïve, soft, childish dialect of hers—how damned well it goes with the more or less brazen stories she serves up! I let the mill run and just sit there taking a rest; I find the dialect so amusing. "Why, now you aren't listening again!"—"Oh yes, I am; go on with your story. So you really made it to the station, all of you?

"How are you, anyway? And how are your friends?"—"Fine, thank you. But don't imagine I have that many friends! There's no-body except that graybeard, and then my good old acquaintances of course, who remember me from bygone days—I can't say no to them, can I? They're such sweet boys. But they're very fickle, a bit like you. Why can't you come more often? You know I'm fond of you; you're so nice, and kind too, at bottom. Well, the other boys are nice too, don't get me wrong; I won't have anything to do with someone who's not a proper gentleman, you understand."—"No, of course not."—"Yes, don't you agree? Well, perhaps you don't believe me, but I've always, you know, been one to look out for myself a little."—"Absolutely sensible. Cheers, Tilda!"

There's no nonsense. We have no claim on each other, and so nothing to blame each other for, nothing to bother each other with. We both know we have only one sincere purpose: to help each other kill an evening, that and nothing more. And you make merry and let tomorrow take care of itself. She has nothing to lose, and I know what I'm doing; it works out just fine.

But, of course, at the back of my consciousness those hidden but not forgotten worries keep gnawing at me, like little sharp-toothed mice. And every once in a while something or other turns up that reminds me of . . . the other one. Then I become depressed and can't quite enter into it, and Mathilde is displeased and says I'm boring. And so a lot of drinking is necessary—until you have reached that acutely alcoholic state in which you love any specimen of the sex whatever—without regard to the individual.

This evening, for example, there suddenly turned up a chic little girl who waited on us a bit, lighted the fire and so forth (a daughter of the "landlady"); and why shouldn't this little girl be called Fanny? Anyway, her name was simply Fanny. I grew so sentimental when I heard that name that Mathilde finally asked me, very much in the manner of women to be sure, if I had been in love with someone called Fanny.

Afterward I found it impossible to get up my gallows humor again. I left quite early.

And now here I sit—so strangely, painfully smitten that, God knows why, I want to break down and cry.

## XV

I must have offended her. I cannot find her anywhere. Obviously I have offended her.

The thoughtless old flapjaw is not yet dead in me. When I'm preoccupied with something I'm capable of forgetting my surroundings, regard for others, everything under the sun; I just rush thoughtlessly off after that one thing: to get hold of my thought. I'm capable of saying the most impossible things in the middle of a ballroom. (No great matter, insofar as I'm not troubled with invitations!)

I have obviously gone off and told her, too, something terribly tactless and nasty. Frightened her, as I frightened Elinè in times gone by. You see, I have such pretty thoughts about her off and on; so noble, so lofty! About her, who in this particular respect has such a remarkable aura of purity—.

In her simplicity she assumed that as long as she was an honest and fair comrade, I would be the same. Yeah, some nice comrade's thoughts I have many times!

No, no, I just cannot be her "comrade." And when she now withdraws, I ought to make use of the opportunity. Put a stop to it. That's the best, most sensible, simplest, and safest resolution of this whole complication. Her disappearance means one of two things: either that she's tired of the affair, or that she's become afraid of me. In either case the situation is clear.

*Iacta est alea.* I shall overcome the temptation. I am overcoming it. I have overcome it. The earth is round. Period!

He knows how to be elegantly silent, George Jonathan does.

For example, I'm fully aware of his relations with Mrs. Bøck-mann, and he knows I'm aware of it. But not a word! He will suddenly get up and say, "You'll pardon me, I'm taking my walk." He knows he might as well have said, "I'm going to Mrs. Bøckmann's," but he doesn't say it! And his face doesn't register a flicker, his eyes not a smile, that could be understood as a confidence. Damned elegant! Every inch a gentleman.

I bow to him with genuine recognition. Glory be to the intelligent man, who knows how to keep his private life holy!

Mathilde has gone downhill quite a bit since I saw her the first time—when she was still a chorus-singer in the theater.

But it looks as if the dirt doesn't rub off on her. She's so light-hearted and has such a short memory. To her, a lover is nothing more than what an ordinary admirer at an evening ball may be to a lady: tomorrow he's forgotten.

Only by her language do I perceive her decline once in a while. She will use expressions that have to be washed away with lots of alcohol. On the whole—on the whole . . .

It's no use anymore. The more I wallow in drunken merrymaking, the more wretchedly sentimental I become; I yearn with tears in my heart for the vanished one—as for a bath of purification and renewal. I'm awash in painfully delightful fantasies to the effect that, if she would take me into her arms and kiss me, I would be as a child again, pure, healed, blissful.

Why should everything be so impossible?

Why am I not like other people? Here I go about afflicting and torturing myself with an affair that—a sheer absurdity that wouldn't even suffice to make a proper comedy. Tortured, worn down, I can no longer sleep, and shortly my headache will set in. And within three months I shall be mad. For nothing!

I'm becoming a pessimist. A misanthrope. All my famous resignation goes by the board; life again lies before me like a glacial desert, a black, frozen heath with snowdrifts and ground ice. Not a human being, not a cottage, not a lighted window anywhere; and, above it all, nothing but a monochrome winter sky gray with snow, without stars, sun, or moon. But from far out comes the roar of the ocean, and that's where the road leads; sometime I'll drown in that ocean.

And it seems to me that, if I could come to an understanding with *her*, everything would suddenly be different. The spring sun would break through, with a south wind and mild air, and the glacial desert would be relatively pleasant.

Come now. Buck up, damn it. Stuff and nonsense—.

Write to her? Explain myself? Ask what's the matter—if something is the matter?

It won't work. I can't find the right tone. I become bitter and mocking and sentimental; and I always write a word too many.

But if I do *not* write that word too many, I cannot bring myself to send the letter; it's positively one word short.

Anyway, what tone should I adopt? I don't know. I don't know her. Instead of using the time to get to know this young girl, I've walked around talking about the immortality of the soul. Is there a more stupid animal than a male who endeavors to behave sensibly?

Is it my guardian angel who wishes to warn me? Or my demon who's afraid that I might perhaps still act resolutely for once? Or is it telepathy? One thing is certain: wherever I go these days, marriage is criticized.

Maybe husbands always talk about marriage, you just don't notice it until you are in the midst of it yourself. Just as old bachelors always talk about suicide—or young bachelors about you know what—only that you have to suffer from those manias yourself in order to become aware of them.

This morning Jonathan and Dr. Kvaale vied in mockery, worse than ever. I fell quite silent from distaste; I'll write down some of the most characteristic exchanges for the novel (possibly for a play: *Husbands?*).

DR. K. Marriage is in general two illnesses that join forces to produce a third—and a fourth and fifth—an entire family of illnesses. Domestic life always smells of medicine.

G. J. To be married means: to be obliged to like empty talk.—He who wants to get married should go to a surgeon and have his sensitivity extracted.

DR. K. If only one could be brutal and take females for what they are, and throw them aside when one's through with them. But we men are so weak and sentimental. All such relationships invariably go on for too long. We aren't able to quit before someone gets hurt; we stick with it until the whole thing turns mushy.

G. J. Man despises woman because she's so physical. She's like a bundle of nervous cuddliness, itching to be touched; her love is a dream of some bearded mouth that will kiss her, and of sinewy arms that will squeeze and crush her. She's sheer body. A delicious body, by the way! But still, in the end a man gets tired of that sort of juvenile game.

DR. K. To us the physical is subordinate, something second-rate, in reality something disagreeable which we . . . liberate ourselves from; we yearn to go back to higher, more human things—and to work.

G. J. Or to our indolence.

DR. K. Alas, yes. But, damn it, she doesn't want to be free, she wants to stay put. She likes it well enough where she is; it's her element, you see! *(Smiles all the while a disagreeable, witheringly cynical smile, with a shrewdly satisfied expression, as if he thought he was witty.)*

G. J. Yes, she always wants yet another kiss.

G. J. *(continuing)*. Anyway, she's a funny creature. An outright wood nymph: beautiful in front, but behind . . . Difficult to tame; in a domesticated state, a splendid animal. Special characteristics: most beautiful at a distance.

"Nonetheless we prefer to have her close to us," I countered.

G. J. Yes, we despise her and thirst for her. In one moment we flee like Joseph, who let her have his cloak when she wanted yet another kiss, and yet another, but we always steal to her bed afresh, humble as dogs and court flunkies. And why shouldn't we humble ourselves? Our spirituality is, when all is said and done, worth less than her corporeality. The brutal fact is that spirit and body go so poorly together. Face to face with Venus, every man is a helpless graybeard. And therefore women despise men.

DR. K. Yes, as I've said: Monogamy is the vilest invention ever.

G. J. Easy, Doctor. All evolution moves in circles. Someday we'll again return to barbarism—civilized barbarism—and then we're saved.

Whereupon they start discussing social questions.

## XVI

The only one who faithfully sings the praises of marriage is my excellent colleague Markussen.

He has a wife and three children and toils night and day to provide food for the nest. Many a time he's so exhausted that he falls asleep at his desk.

"You feel sort of sorry you got married, don't you?" I say to him.

"No, no," he grunts, with his usual little toss of the head.

"But sitting here as you do, figuring and auditing till well into the night. . . . Bank business and commercial affairs, and one thing and another—it can't possibly be much fun."

"Oh yes. It's nice. I never get tired.

"She needs a lot of sleep," he adds seriously, in confidence, "and so she mustn't have any worries. She must know that I can manage. And I do!" he nods triumphantly; whereupon he laughs, as if begging pardon.

I'm downright fond of that boy.

\*

Yes, thank God, there are several good husbands. Comically touching in their naïveté; genuine homebodies, happy people.

And when the chips are down, isn't it happiness, in all simplicity and modesty, that we all desire?

Like, for example, my old acquaintance Klem, the editor. A man of refinement, he never speaks about his private affairs. But if you can get him to drink a toddy and a half some evening in select company, then he'll take you aside and say with quiet conviction, "My wife, you see. . . . Well, she's simply unique, there's nothing else like it . . . in the whole world. What a woman she is!"

And his small, good eyes shine with rapture.

I nearly gave him a hug this evening. So it cannot be completely impossible. Mrs. Klem is an excellent woman, to be sure, but "unique"? You only need to find someone whose nervous system is tuned in such a way that it chimes harmoniously with your own. "Only" that, sure—thanks!

Oh Fanny, Fanny, if I just could retune you a little!

Anyway, it's over. She avoids me. I've seen her twice in the street; she walked calmly past me, didn't see me.

Goodbye, you fool—.

Anyway, it shouldn't be such a big deal.

How do these marriages come about? As casually as possible. You live in a small town where there exists only one non-impossibility, so she'll be the one, though you've seen a hundred you liked better.

Your social life centers on a specific circle for a fairly long time; you are exactly at the right age. Within that circle there's one who "appeals" to you. All at once it's decided—though a year ago your eyes were drawn to an entirely different quarter.

You live at a widow's who has some daughters. You live at that widow's for a long time; little by little you discover that the youngest daughter isn't so bad, after all. One fine day the engagement is in the paper, though you hadn't had the slightest intention of getting married.

That's what happened to my old friend the musician—let's call him Brun. It was a rather risky experiment; he's a good but nervous person, and she was quite ordinary, not at all specially refined, sired by a veterinarian.

It was Sunday today, with clear, glittering frosty weather. I awoke early and was just lying there thinking about this, when it occurred to me that I had an invitation to Brun's and that I had neglected the honest old bandit scandalously during the three years since he'd been married.

I was smitten by a desire to go see him and his family. There he has lived in a quite exemplary marriage for three whole years despite everything; I like such people. I jumped up with uncharacteristic energy, made myself ready, and went to the station. Brun is doing his composing in Sandviken at the moment.

This time, however, I had bad luck.

I found the missus alone; the master, hmm, was still in bed. We sat and chatted a bit; but ah, there he was all of a sudden. Half-dressed, raging, with a vest in his fist, he goes straight for his wife, then discovers me; a "devil take" flits like a nervous twinge across his face. Restraining himself, he nods good morning and shakes my hand, hastily and brusquely. "Oh, how nice," he says; simply translated, "Go to hell!"

"You'll excuse my getup," he continued, "that's life when you're married, you see." (Abortive smile.) The missus tried to save the situation in a hurry, "Oh dear, those buttons; I forgot about them yesterday, after all. . . ."

He went on, addressing himself to me, and I could distinctly hear his enraged heart hissing under "the joke": "Well, if you get married, Gram, you'll have to be prepared for such things: three tall females loafing around in the house and still total disorder—missing buttons in shirts and trousers and the room freezing cold in the morning when it's time to get up. . . ."

"Isn't the fire lit?!" the missus cried.

Forgetting about me, he rushed savagely toward her: "The fire lit? What's the good of that? First, a woman simply *cannot* light a fire—as little as she can make a bed—and second, it obviously never crosses her mind to go in and check if it's really burning. She simply walks off, and one, two, three—the fire's out!"

"Yes, Severinè is a bit careless," the missus said soothingly; "now I'm going to—"

"Don't bother," he says crossly, "I've managed by myself, as usual. Has Gram had anything to chew on? Try to remember your visitors at least. . . . Sit down and take it easy, Gabriel; I'll be with you presently. (To the missus:) Quickly, give me needle and thread, I'll do it myself, then I know it's done."

She snatches the vest out of his hand with a jerk that is more venomous than all his scolding and disappears into a side room.

Slightly embarrassed, with an uncertain attempt to change the tune to one of cheerfulness, he turns to me. "Well," he says, "that's how it is; one has to yap at them once in a while; otherwise they aren't happy. . . . You, as a bachelor, get alarmed of course, thinking it means a scene. . . . Only the necessary pepper in the salad, you understand."

But once more he's overcome with rage, and he rushes up to the door and bellows into the kitchen as if he wants to raise the dead, "Severinè, the clothesbrush! My black coat hasn't been brushed in two weeks! (A protest is heard.) No, damn it, it has not! Hand me the brush; in this house you have to wait on yourself. My boots haven't been shined either!" He slams the door shut so hard that I have to scratch my ears. "I'm sorry, Gabriel; but shuffling about among women like this *can* drive a man insane!"

The missus brings the vest; she acts jovial, throws her arms around his neck and kisses him. "Now you'll be sweet again, won't you, darling!"—"Yeah, sure, sure," he defends himself. I see how sickening he finds this playacting in front of a visitor. He tears himself away and manages a strained smile: "Excuse me a moment, Gabriel."

The missus smiles unnaturally and talks about her husband's morning grumpiness. "At other times he's as good as gold, but in the morning, before he's been given his coffee and his pipe. . . ." I put up my most innocent smile. "I know all about it, madam, believe me. I'm so angry in the morning that I could eat babies. It's simply a kind of madness; one is quite irrational."—"How true! So you get it, too? It must be painful."

Phew, a scene like that can scare even the most courageous. That hissing undertone of long-saved-up, painfully suppressed irritation . . . my God, what suffering this kind, nervous fellow must have been through, from all those millions of pinpricks, before he could bring himself to make a scandalous scene like that—in the presence of a bachelor to boot!

No, it's best as it is. I'll swallow my infatuation, even if it's going to cost me a brief stay at Gaustad, the asylum.

It will work out, all right. I'm stronger than I thought.

She is there of course, deep in my soul, behind my consciousness, all the while, like a secret stinging pain; but that's where she's going to stay. And if, in an unguarded moment, this huge, heavy wave of emotion washes over my consciousness, like the ocean when it breaks the embankments of a tideland, then I'll force it back again and repair the bank.

And then I pay a call on Mathilde. I sit there and listen to her talk—well, not so much to that as to her carefree voice and that naïve, childish dialect, soft as a lullaby. And her laughter, in which there are no undertones, no quivering echo of grief overcome, only unabashed, depraved banter, only the gypsy-like recklessness of a jailbird. Well, she does have a sense of humor, the genuine earth-dweller's humor—that of the savage and the satisfied, playful animal, gypsy humor—while we, heavy, dismal Nordic souls, really belong only in heaven, or, since we would be as bored there as at a Salvation Army meeting, in Nirvana.

Her round, ruddy, cherry-like face with those small blue rogue's eyes often appears to me like that apple on the tree of life about which God said, "Men will lick their chops for that one, you bet!" Indeed, by everything that I hold sacred, there are evening hours when I love her. Then she laughs at me, but she likes it. "But how on earth did you get the idea of calling me Eve?"

I hate scandal.

It would be bruited about on every street corner: Gabriel Gram has shot himself, Gabriel Gram has taken poison; and all those revolting customers would stand there shrugging their shoulders and remarking, "The d.t.'s. . . . Quickly done, by the way." Ick.

It would have to happen "by accident."

To freeze to death? That's just *too* disagreeable. I can't stand cold. I would get on my feet again and go home and light a fire.

You could perhaps incur a sufficiently severe case of pneumonia in that way. Sure. But then some decent fellow, a doctor, would come and "save my life."

Wait till spring. Go swimming early. "Be seized with cramp" and go to the bottom. . . . But when the good Lord realizes that you *want* to drown, he always sends someone who pulls you out again.

Take a trip to Hamburg and "fall overboard" some really dark night?

Somebody would always notice. Such things always fail. Someone or other discovers that you go around scheming something of the sort and alerts the captain. Suddenly you're surrounded by an army of spies, and no sooner are you overboard than the ship backs up and some humanitarian soul is right there and grabs you by the hair the third time you come to the surface.

Capsize? That's better. I'll wait till spring, borrow Jonathan's boat, and sail down the fjord all the way to Færder—past Færder—and look out for a moment when the horizon is clear. I'll have to choose a day when there is a fairly strong wind, of course.

Yes, that's possible. I see no difficulties with it. So I'll have this thought to console myself with for a while—till the day comes.

Without her I don't care to live. Anything is better than to live with this wastage, which sucks my head dry of wit and my bones of marrow. But I can't live with her either. I love her to the point of distraction, but not enough. In two weeks it would be over again, and then, in whatever form, there would be hell to pay.

ME. You are lucky to have all those interests.

G. J. If one wants to live, one has to live extrovertly. A robust will is always directed outward, and without a robust will *(shrug)* one either ends up in the lake or at the pastor's.

Oh yes, a "robust will"—bah, that boring middle-class "robustness."

There's only one thing that interests me: this agonizing struggle inside me, this sickness whereby my being is split in two and my will divided against itself—*that* is my life. Consequently I live inwardly and introvertly, and consequently I'll end up in the lake.

## XVII

For a while now I have fought quite bravely—a nasty fight in which you lose even when you win, an obligatory fight in which you quietly pray to God to lose. Because victory means that a great possibility of life is lost.

But I fought and fought; I was weak in the evening, but got up each morning with a new resolution.

And then, today, we meet on the street, and pst! My resolutions are as fluff, a speck of dust—all gone to hell. I take her to a pastry shop and sit there and flirt with her for half an hour. Then a walk, everything back in the old groove.

I feel like a fallen Good Templar—very happy and a bit embarrassed. Actually, it didn't taste *that* good. I could have abstained, after all. The whole long struggle wasted. But thank God, thank God, all my torments are over for the time being, I can look forward to an agreeable time.

How, exactly, it will turn out? I have no idea.

She's no child. It's up to her to look out for her reputation. I have given her more than due warning; she knows what risk she runs. So that is really not my concern. She also knows full well that I do not intend to indemnify her. My conduct is open and clear, it can't be faulted.

All the same she believes that I'll marry her in the end; women have their own logic, don't they?

Or is she playing *va banque?* Let come what may? She wants a better-class husband after all, and he can be procured only by getting a decent fellow to compromise her, so that, as a gentleman, he will be forced to stick around. Eh?

If so, she will be fooled. She's no threat to me except at a distance.

*

*Why* does she refuse to open up?

Considering how intelligent she is and how well she knows me by now, she ought to realize that such a confession couldn't do her any harm.

There must be some *extremely* bad things, since she doesn't dare come out with them after all that I've said. Or it's just that she looks on me as a stranger who has no business with that sort of thing.

—??

We walk around talking about indifferent things, with long pauses in between. We may both be having one and the same thought, but one of us doesn't dare, and the other doesn't know whether he wants to. . . .

Every now and then a renewed attempt to get her to talk about herself. Always to no avail.

"So who was your next . . . friend . . . after Aas, I mean?"

"Uchermann, a student."

"Was he, too, in love with you?"

"Yes, unfortunately."

"Unfortunately? Did you feel . . . wronged, wasn't he—"

"He was the best person I've ever known. He was the last person I would wish to cross, but it couldn't be helped."

"And the next—?"

"The next? Friend, you mean? He was the last one. The rest are only 'acquaintances.'"

A long pause. Does she also count me among the latter sort? Anyway, I'm not the "best person" she's ever known.

How tremendously easy it is to fool people! Just put up a face and they believe you.

She thinks I'm so awfully superior. So sure of myself, so on top of things, so clearly aware of everything. "Are *you*, really, in doubt about anything?"—"Can *you* really feel stumped?"—"Is it possible that *you* can be bored?"—"*You* don't know how to occupy yourself?" and so forth, one astonishing question after another.

So I, who fill my idle hours with thoughts of suicide, can be taken for someone who's sitting pretty just because I have a little tact: not wearing my heart on my sleeve every day. I, who could have bet that my mask was quite transparent!

But I guess that's the way things are. We are all mistaken about one another. Who the hell can bother to check what there may be behind this or that mask! So we accept the mask at face value, and even feel grateful that people lie a little to us. Just think what a hellish doghouse and loony bin the world would be if all of us started wailing to our heart's content!

What we know of people is sheer surface. Under these surfaces there lurk all sorts of strange animals, repulsive and vile animals, insane creatures, criminals, suicides, savages. . . . Who knows, for example, what hides behind the mask George Jonathan? A skeptic, maybe, when all is said and done; a misanthrope? Maybe every evening before going to bed he does his devotions in front of a vial of morphine. Who knows?

Many sad and terrible things take place in all those closed rented rooms where the isolated, weak individual suddenly realizes he's shut up with himself and his own fearful conscience.

Dear, dear Fanny,

I cannot live without you. But knowing myself, I'm convinced it will only lead to unhappiness for both of us if we make a stab at marriage.

I tell you this so plainly in order that you should understand that I respect you and have confidence in your intelligence, and also that I don't intend to deceive you or engage in any kind of dishonorable game. I lay all my cards on the table and say: this is how matters stand. You will understand.

The question then is whether your feelings for me are such that you *want* to—and think about love in such a way that you *can*—do something other than break off our relationship after this declaration. If you break it off, this is to say goodbye—and to express my thanks for an interesting and agreeable interruption in the monotony of my so-called life. If you show up for our walks as before, you will make me happier than I have words to express.

But take careful notice that you can win nothing, but have *everything* to lose. And remember that some fine day, perhaps exactly at the moment when to you it seems that it goes swimmingly, I will come and say: I don't want to anymore. *Do not agree to what I propose* unless you, like me, have the courage of despair, which says: my life for but a moment of bliss.

G. G.

Thus read the latest letter I burned.

"Certainly not—emancipation is not dangerous. It's a new kind of coquetry, a new way of drawing attention to oneself and making oneself interesting. When the lady in question has found a husband, I dare say her zeal will cool off considerably."

"Not always!"

"As a rule. The only trouble is that the members of the Feminist Association learn to be so ungracious; the ballroom is, after all, a better school for a young girl. But again, there is the advantage that in the women's association they acquire greater respect for us men—"

"Well, that—"

"Oh yes. In the ballroom, you see, you meet us mostly in our shabbiest manifestations, at least in our silliest moods, I can safely say, and accordingly you develop a deep, quiet contempt for us, which is not wholesome. But in the association, where they shut themselves up and seek to master a few of the things we thought out and invented when we were in our rightful domain, our sphere of activity, there at any rate they get a certain idea that man is entitled to respect. Does the advantage offset the loss? Doubtful. However, it's all merely a passing phase, naturally."

"Yes, but tell me. . . . Of course, woman is to be wife and mother, we know that; but tell me what, precisely, you want all those of us to do who do not get married."

"Be on the lookout at the right moment and get yourselves a husband."

(Laughter.) "Yes, but—what about those who don't find a husband even so, do you really mean they should sit out their lives quite idly, maybe starve as well?"

"They don't have to starve, do they, just because they don't get a job in an office? What does a man do when he can't find a job? He finds something else to do. Good God, eventually there's always some way out."

"As time goes on there will be so many unmarried women that they may very well need access both to office jobs and government positions."

"Yes; but what about the men who will be forced out of their jobs that way? Is it better that they should starve? Besides, that will only lead to there being more unmarried women; for an unemployed man always means one marriage less, while a woman with a job is not one more marriage."

"Well, not all men are so sensitive that they wouldn't let themselves be supported by a wife!"

"No, no. But the point is that neither the government nor other employers will be well served by employees who have to take a nine-month leave every once in a while. You women teachers, for example; I believe I've heard that a woman teacher cannot keep her job if she gets married."

Pause. Then she says, "Oh dear; you can tell that the good Lord is a male."

Shrug. Long pause.

She hasn't had a home, so she's not domestic. And I am a persnickety fellow, to the point of absurdity.

I can see it, of course. If only from the way she throws her clothes around when she enters a place: some on this chair and some on that; the parasol in the sofa, the gloves on the console table. O-o-h, children's toys would float around in every corner; sewing things, newspapers, and hairpins would be all over the place, together with wilted bouquets, knickknacks, used collars, ribbons, and ties—I would simply lose my appetite.

No; for these professional women, these women with no home, these bachelor women, it's either/or: either they have to go in for sexlessness definitively, or they have to live like bachelors in earnest. Life without a home makes a woman unfit for marriage. She loses her equilibrium, her bearing, her center; develops a strained, restless, disjointed, unreasonable air; loses her feminine self-assurance and superiority, and becomes nervous—tense, harassed, torn.

A woman without style and without grace, what should one do with such an animal? She will have to sit in that office, which was supposed to be so grand, or pace a schoolroom yelling and nagging. In a home—. Almost all men have a sense of beauty.

And as for the future Mrs. Gram, she would, among other things, have to understand the art of conversation. Light, unaffected, smooth; without strain and without pretension, without the least hint of a possibility that she might say something—untrustworthy. I, who am such a homeless person myself, cannot do it (without plenty of help); few Norwegians can. Our strenuous, democratic life only teaches us to make speeches or to argue. She cannot do it either. She's too much of an autodidact; she has presumably also been silent for too long. The polished lightness, the controlled, smooth naturalness, the art of gliding quietly and freely on the current of a conversation, being able to say good things without underscoring and the necessary trivialities without being boring—that art requires schooling. Between husband and wife, who are to live together daily for years, the possibility of cultivated conversation is a necessity if the relationship is not to turn into a sheer horror.

In my weary head a Sisyphus works day and night at the moment. He ceaselessly rolls the rock of one and the same thought, rolls it and lets it go again, rolls it and lets it go, always without a break, till my brain is on fire.

## XVIII

She introduces me to odd company. Schoolmasters, schoolmistresses, graduates from teachers' college, art students, all nice people but unfinished, inferior, as a rule with a touch of the subaltern, which accompanies the consciousness of not being quite tops.

A deplorable tribe, this intermediate breed. Not ignorant enough to be happy, and not knowledgeable enough to be able to resign themselves, they whine and writhe in a sort of intellectual hysteria. They rave about "big ideas" and "great truths," which they believe hold bliss for the initiates but which they themselves—due to an unjust fate, namely, lack of money—are excluded from, for which reason they consider themselves entitled to hate God and men and the whole world.

It would seem easy to explain to them that the happiness of those with knowledge is extremely problematic: that to "be tops" means to know how infinitely little can be known at all; that "the holy of holies" is a *camera obscura;* and that the latest and highest finding of science is the great question mark. But it's no use. It's not understood. You simply become a suspect if you tell them something like that. It is a difficult realization to make: to realize that nothing can be known.

A certain Ebba Lehmann is a remarkable person. Her pessimism is truly hysterical. Actually, she's not unintelligent. And yet disagreeable. Its cause is all too clearly evident: namely, that she hasn't had sufficient initiative to get herself a modicum of children.

A woman must be extremely careful in choosing her company. If she associates with people who are superior to her, she easily gets lost. But if she is with people who are considerably beneath her, she gets sort of dragged down.

It pains me to see Fanny in this company. Among them she herself becomes—so disagreeably like them.

Headache.

Some friends she has; real, true friends, all right!

I'm tormented by my doubts, they leave me no peace. I stoop to spying, try to make her acquaintances talk, since she refuses to. They all say, "Oh yes, Fanny is a good girl . . . as far as I know."

They hesitate a little. Even good Mrs. Markussen: ". . . I don't *know* of anything wrong, at any rate." There "was some talk, to be sure, about her and this fellow Uchermann"; and besides, it was said there had been something with a young man in trade. "But it wasn't that sort of thing, apparently."—"And as long as one doesn't know something definitely wrong about a person . . . ," and so forth.

Is there a more ridiculous and impossible situation than mine? She's not my fiancée, nor is she my mistress, and in all likelihood she's not going to be either; nonetheless I'm being consumed by the thought that she may possibly have had an affair—*I!*—who to this very day go to see Mathilde and suffer all the torments of hell for doing so!

What a dreadful misfortune to fall in love outside one's own circle. In the other social strata another language is spoken; other notions prevail, even other feelings. For her it may be a matter of course, a right, a duty of self-preservation, to keep quiet about everything that could damage her in the eyes of her suitor.

What is jealousy? I dare say not even a Frenchman can be found who is capable of giving an exhaustive definition. I cannot on my own explain my state of mind to myself. I only know that I suffer—senselessly and indescribably.

It's not jealousy. The whole business doesn't really concern me, after all. It's just that I feel so sorry for her. It's a pity, it's a great pity, if such a nice, pretty girl should have been stained and ruined in that brutal struggle for existence which rages down there in "the lower depths," where people simply cannot afford such luxuries as tact, purity of soul, truthfulness, pride. Abominable! Outrageous! George Jonathan is right: society must be overturned!

But the most tragic thing of all is that this same girl possibly—and in all likelihood—has fought a most courageous battle to keep herself clear of all filth during her entire youth and that, in fact, she *has* saved her purity. But when she now stands there as a fully mature woman with the palm of victory in her hand, worthy of marrying a prince, there is not a single human being who believes her.

Oh conventions, sacred, foolish conventions! It *is* necessary that the young girl be accompanied wherever she goes by an elderly, virtuous duenna. If she's able to fool the duenna—*tant mieux!* At any rate, that future jackass of a husband has his "warranty."

\*

It can hardly be in doubt any longer. She's in love.

But of course!

What shall I do now?

O-o-h, not onto that whirligig again. Headache. Headache. . . .

Those dreadful headaches are starting again.

That awful, paralyzing pressure above the eyes. It's as if fate has placed its finger there and says: so far and no further.

Courage, will, thought, ideas—all droop limply and, dejected and listless, I sit staring at some point or other, which invariably turns into the muzzle of a revolver.

However, it's not worth taking the trouble. Tomorrow or the day after I'll fall dead anyway. Like an ox with the butt of an axe planted in his skull.

Those mad pranks of youth.

You go around looking for a woman, but on the way you commit so many follies that when you finally find the object of your desire, then—well, you'd better let her go again.

Ruined lives. Ruined lives. Get out the mourning colors and the mourning crepe; this is more than just a funeral.

## XIX

Miss Berner has come to town; I met her during a Sunday visit to Klem, who seems to be a sort of cousin of hers.

She will be living here. With Pastor Løchen, who is married to her female cousin or something.

I was quite pleased to see her. She's a lady at any rate. Indisputably so. A being from a higher level, where there's sun and clean air. If *she* has had an affair, you can be sure it's one she can acknowledge . . . or one that's sufficiently hidden.

Light, clear air! Assurance! That great feeling of security! It's awful to sink down among the lower depths.

Away from all that. Up to the surface again; up toward sunlit shores,

> where the wave sparkles so clear and warm . . .

26 March

I strike her out.

There's only *one* explanation. She's the wiliest playactor imaginable.

What I've heard tonight has ripped all benevolent feelings and all respect for her out of my breast with a butcher's grip. It hurt, and it aches and burns in there still. I didn't know she had become that dear to me. It's ridiculous and desperate. But it's a good thing it's over. How could I fail to understand! After all, it's as easy to figure out as a problem in rule of three. A man who knows the circumstances in those circles set up the arithmetic problem for me. Eighty kroner a month barely equals a respectable woman; what does forty kroner equal?

Ha-ha. Now I understand all that used to be difficult. Her poise, her experience, her calm "playing with fire," the boldness with which she allowed herself to be dragged around by a bad character! Naturally—she had nothing to lose! What does it matter to such a person if she becomes the victim of an indiscretion? She's an old hand at it. She knows how to manage a situation like that, there's just one question: the price.

My goodness, how her entire person changed in my eyes—to something at the same time ugly and sad. She's dead to me, and in her place there's nothing but a cadaver.

She has, however, preserved an appearance of honesty, and so there might still be a possibility of finding a simpleton of a husband. And, of course, she has long practice in playing virtuous. (Genuine virtue makes a less strong impression than the imitation, just as imitation diamonds exceed the genuine ones in brilliance. As for me, she figured I was sufficiently naïve and far removed from her previous life to make it worth the gamble to set her cap. God, how she must have laughed in her heart at my respect for her.)

But am I, the buyer, any better than she, the seller? Empty phrases. A gulf is fixed for all eternity between the one who uses someone else and the one who lets himself be used; no talk can cover that up.

I'm so limp and cold and dirtied inside. I'm done for. The hand withers on its handle; my handwriting is becoming paralytic.

Ridiculous. Disgusting. Damn it all, what business is all this of mine? A regular whiskey and soda——.

## XX

I didn't know she had become so dear to me.

I walk around as if stupefied, like a man visited by disgrace. At one moment I feel like howling with grief, at another shame overwhelms me with its clammy chill.

An unpleasant tangle of feelings. One cannot free oneself either by grief or by contempt. I suffocate, my soul gasps for air inside me. A battle with serpents under a woolen blanket. A fever in my consciousness, sweaty heat alternating with frost.

I do not dare look people in the eye. Ha-ha, there's the fellow who had that affair with the beautiful demimondaine! Ha-ha! He was already about to ask, *in optima forma,* for the kept woman's hand and heart, ha-ha. Ha-ha, those old bachelors.

I cannot refrain from whipping myself with these scorpions. It is a ripping, burning, odious pleasure—like someone who suffers from eczema scratching himself till he starts bleeding.

A nice stroke of luck that Miss Berner came. I seek her out as a kind of rescue. She will pull me up again to a level where there's air, open air.

She knows how to converse, she's tastefully dressed, she plays Beethoven, she uses fine perfumes. Assurance, harmony, purity are hers; it would never occur to her to tremble in fear that there might be a wine stain on her dress. . . .

I cling to all this with both hands. Compare and compare and bring out all her good points, by hook or by crook. That she's not young and not really pretty, I forgive her; in the end, what value does that sort of thing have? What I set store by is dependability, confidence, pure chords; I'm disgusted with beauty without poise, beauty without fine perfumes.

I was plagued by hate, contempt, rage to such a degree that I decided to see her again and tell her the truth.

And I met her. And felt my heart flutter. I grew anxious and afraid, and ashamed of what I wanted to say; anxious and ashamed like a thief, though actually I was a judge. And as she approached step by step and her face cleared by degrees and changed into a smile, a delighted, blushing smile, my suspicions evaporated along with my decision, and to my amazement I tried in vain to hold on to them.

This was *not* the "Miss Holmsen" I had dreamed up during those awful days! This air of having a good conscience, her confident self-respect, that familiar, naïve expression of a comrade's unlimited trust, completely disarmed me. I suppressed my emotion and acted as if nothing were the matter.

Cowardice. Male cowardice. As she stood there before me with those large, sad, brightening eyes, and that pale brow with all its brown whorls and intricacies that not even her wide-brimmed hat could give the lie to, I felt weak and touched, as if facing a beautiful child that comes jumping along with an unsuspecting smile on its face, when by rights it should get a spanking.

But I was annoyed by her being badly dressed. A dreadful jacket made her droop-shouldered and flat-chested, and an enormously wide brown straw hat squeezed her flat. And she immediately came out with her complaints about boredom, despair over life, and so on; it suddenly sounded half-educated to me. Inferior. Good Lord, that's the way life is, after all; there's nothing new to be said about the misery of life. So we had better be adults: adjust to things as they are or, quietly and proudly, go and hang ourselves.

Moreover, what can such a girl of twenty-four or twenty-five have gone through in life? I fell into a bad humor, and once again my evil thoughts reared their head.

What do they mean, these lamentations of hers? Now she's dissatisfied with school, she won't be able to teach religion—some twaddle about being "true," about how awful it is to "lie," "play the hypocrite," etc. Good grief, to hammer into some street urchins a few ideas that, while muddle-headed enough, are at any rate infinitely superior to the notions that the above-mentioned urchins bring with them from home—that shouldn't be so terrible, should it? If she herself has an even higher standard, well, so much the better for her; but she should still be able to help those Hottentot brats reach that relatively high standard represented by Luther's catechism. But, of course, complaining is *de rigueur*. Is this a quasi-covert appeal to me to liberate her? Turn her into a wife, with a maid? I became cross and fell silent. And since, after all, it had been decided that the acquaintance should be broken off, it might just as well occur at once. But that was no reason to serve up every thought in one's head; a form could be found that was less brutal.

I introduced the matter by warning her against her friends. Poor dear, it hit her hard; and cruel it certainly was. After fighting all your life to preserve your chastity and honor, suddenly to see yourself defenselessly at the mercy of, and cast doubt on by, a few indifferent, garrulous male and female "friends"! I felt in the position of an executioner. But, you know, people *have to* be rescued from that sort of friendship; she *had to* be told in what hands her well-being and honor lay. I ended by gently hinting how impossible my own situation was vis-à-vis a person I knew so little, and managed at last, not without effort, to come out with what basically had to be said: "Get married . . . with some good man whom you know and who *knows you*." She grew ominously silent and quickly took her leave. I remained standing outside her entrance for a moment, with a feeling like that of a murderer after the death-dealing blow, and I thought I heard a violently suppressed sobbing from up those dark stairs.

Gloomy and listless, I went home. It's all so terribly, terribly ugly and brutal and painful. Here I sit, my mood strangely broken, soft. I feel a boundless desire—a peculiar, idiotic, but almost irresistible desire—to write her and say, "Dear, lovely Fanny, I love you beyond all bounds; give notice to the school and all your 'friends' and marry me in a week."

## XXI

3 April—or rather 4 April—2 o'clock, night
Reason is not really fixed very firmly in the head of a human being.

A strange anxiety overcomes me when I come home after a rough night, automatically walk up to the mirror to see how I look and, noting that I'm extremely pale, otherwise *all right*, chance to look into my eyes.

They are good-looking, those eyes, brown and sincere, with a tinge of wistfulness and resignation in their gaze; they draw me in. And once they get hold of me, they draw me more and more forcefully, until I'm seized by a kind of vertigo. The things around me disappear, I'm dismally alone with this silent being that bores its pupils into my brain, deeper and deeper, more and more forcefully; it feels as though I might lose consciousness—I have to *pull* myself free, as one has to pull oneself out of a nightmarish dream.

The mirror is an uncanny instrument. You sort of stand face to face with your Doppelgänger—feel, maybe, a vague urge to fall upon this fellow and strangle him, for what the hell does he want?—or face to face with your soul, a phenomenon that fills me at once with religious dread and a desperately brazen curiosity. To find out, at last, about this specter that is behind my whole existence but that I cannot possibly get my hands on—not even get proof that it's there at all! That is, there must be something, an agency, a driving wheel (which in all probability is connected to the transcendental world machinery by some sort of endless drive belt), and why can't it just as well be called soul? Perhaps it is the world soul herself, sitting behind her screen like the director of a puppet show and pulling the strings that bring my flesh-covered skeleton to jump and dance and perform all these absurdities, which she enjoys with such divine childishness?

Talked all evening about "woman." Obliged with all sorts of theories, accused and defended her by turns. Nobody understood what was at the back of it. Agent Lunde, who of course drinks, like all failed husbands, informed me in his cups that he had actually divorced his wife because she "smacked her lips when she ate." I can well believe it. A repulsive elderly bachelor whom I met for the first time related that he was such a good friend, he lent his pals from the provinces his mistress when they visited him, which caused merriment in the young men's camp, mingled with a certain surprise.

"You do, really?" they said, gaping. They hadn't thought there could be found that much friendship in Israel.

And they sat there smoking and tippling, with hot, poached faces, like those you see in a railroad compartment on hot summer afternoons. A young, green literary man was a spokesman for woman and defended the ideal marriage with toddy-inspired enthusiasm. "The two of them should do everything together, share *everything!*"—"Perhaps you want her to go on a spree with her husband too?" the agent asked. "Yes, of course! That would be just fine!" said the young man, slightly taken aback. I supported the young fellow: "When a woman comes along, the spree is more civilized." The agent gasped.

"Oho, those bachelors. Oh yes, women in pubs! At nine o'clock the missus starts yawning. At half-past nine her eyes are small and red, and she looks so pale and distressed that out of sheer anger the husband orders yet one more of the same. Then there comes a whimper from the petticoat side: 'Why, you really want to drink more?'" He imitated the ingratiating, martyred voice in such a horrible manner that I could suddenly look down the throats of the whole gang on account of their wide-mouthed laughter.

Depressed, my breast filled with anguish and woe, I got up and staggered over to Mathilde's place.

Nothing is more banally true than the fact that life is suffering; therefore it is also in such bad taste to talk about it.

I feel no pity for those who complain. Their suffering cannot be very deep, as long as they can still bother to try and find words for it.

For convenience' sake, Miss Berner could well be a few years younger; anyway, she's all right. There is a certain genteel air about this seemingly insignificant face, which improves on closer acquaintance; and her eyes, which are neither large nor morbid, have the firm, discreet look of the cultured person—without shyness, without ogling, and without currying favor. You can safely look through those windows, you won't see any further than into the drawing room. The inner chambers are sure to be closed off, with doors and portières, as in every respectable house.

Nor does her mouth gossip. It is suitably large, quite well-shaped, with a perfectly controlled expression; doesn't smile without sufficient reason, which strikes one as civilized. God, how tired one gets of these perpetual charming ladies' smiles—with or without false teeth! Her voice is confident and firm, her delivery muted and calm. All told, she is—"considering our circumstances"—an exceptional, wholly cultivated human being; she gives an indescribable and inimitable impression of having grown up in spacious, harmonious surroundings, in wealth and luxury governed by taste.

She also gives the same impression intellectually. Her views, or rather opinions, fit in perfectly with the established order in every respect, and with a sure instinct she shies away from any aspect of a modern woman that might appear disharmonious. In regard to me, she practices a well-bred woman's thoughtful tolerance. As far as her personal life is concerned, she is quietly conventional, conservative, correct. Puts on an excellent act of being ignorant of *les affaires d'amour*—suitably ignorant.

I catch myself trying to keep her entertained. It's passably boring but agreeable. It makes you feel you're sitting pretty: intellectually well-dressed, impregnable. When I get home I don't remember what we talked about, and it certainly wouldn't occur to me to write it down; that's how a cultivated conversation should be.

With great tact, she acts as my guardian angel, drawing me into circles that may have a corrective effect on me. I let myself go along everywhere and bear my boredom valiantly; perhaps these small diversions can be a sensible expedient in my miserable struggle. That is, all my energies have finally pulled themselves together to retrieve my freedom. I jabber and argue, even dance, managing that way to banish *her* for an evening; I only feel her as a burning emptiness in my innermost heart.

But when I sit here at home again over my last cigarette and my last glass—.

What if, in spite of all, all, all, I should risk the leap? This one time? My misgivings come to seem so small, such petty bachelor's crotchets. What if I should risk it all the same? Finally? Soon the hour of grace will be no more. Most likely I'll never again be so much in love. And Miss Berner can say all she likes. . . . I can easily sell my life for a month's happiness with the woman I love.

And I succumb to my yearning and agony and pick up my pen and write—not studies and impressions for my "novel" but a three-page letter to her. I implore, scold, whine, being rude on one page, ironic on another, sentimental and dying on the third. I write the first page over again, the second page over again, the third page twice over again; finally the first page over again one more time and yet one more time. . . . I go to bed with throbbing temples, trembling nerves, and a lump in my throat.

As soon as I've had my morning coffee I burn the letter in cold blood. Damn it all, we are agreed, after all, that we won't give any more thought to that business. . . .

## XXII

Oh Schopenhauer, Schopenhauer.

To suffer is to live, to live is to suffer. These two are one. Loss, loss—that's the fire that burns and burns and all the while surrounds itself with a phosphorescent sheen; this phosphorescent sheen we call life. Loss, loss, wearisome, unappeasable loss, gnawing, glowing, consuming loss. . . .

And the gratification? A moment's bliss mingled with pain, and afterward the emptiness, the disgust, the weariness. Would I take her here and now? Yes! But not for the sake of the joy she could instill. Only to extinguish this burning loss.

Death must be a glorious moment. A wonderful, infinite moment of rapture mingled with pain. The blissfully agonizing extinction of all losses, of the consuming fire of life itself.

The old myths speak of Satan. Schopenhauer discovered what was at the back of this myth and, instead of Satan, installed the "genius of the race."

He's the one responsible for all suffering and all evil. To him there are no individuals, only specimens. He drags he-specimens and she-specimens together with harpoons and ropes, so that they may produce new specimens, whom he again can pull together with harpoons and ropes. And once his purpose is achieved, he forgets the old for the new, and they lie there squirming among his ropes for life, until they become so venomous and evil that they murder one another.

But he who wishes to tear himself away from his harpoon is left to sit as I do here—with the harpoon deep in his flesh and the long rope tugging and tugging.

I must have a God. A soul center no. 2. . . . A burden is easier to bear when it's divided.

I need a God, therefore I invent him. And I pray, pray: God, give me the madness it takes to believe!—or to die.

You have to fight fire with fire. The devil casts out Beelzebub; woman banishes woman.

Mathilde on the one hand and Miss Berner on the other, the earthly Venus and celestial friendship—shouldn't the two together be able to banish an ever-so-slightly pale face with a mop of brown hair?

If only it weren't for the eyes—those large, melancholy eyes. But *enfin*—they too. They too, naturally. One day they will sit on the retina of my soul like two dying, disappearing stars. . . . No! I *won't!* Shut up, you fool. You *will*, all right.

Yes, this Miss Berner is not so bad at all. She's in possession of what I need more than anything else, something soothing. Calming. Cultivated. Being a good listener! No screaming, no loud laughter! She's this maxim personified.

Her eyes pose no danger, and her pitch-black, lackluster hair sits straight on her head and sets no snares. She's what I need, and what I need now. And on the other hand Mathilde with her frivolity.

Goodbye, siren, who popped up from your depths, with long brown hair and deep, dark eyes!


And now, George Jonathan to the rescue. He incites my thought and stimulates my pride.

And enlivens my imagination.

Naturally, I don't believe in his utopias; but at least I believe as long as he's talking. And that dream of "humanity's progress," which one has to keep alive within oneself to be able to exist, draws so much nourishment from his bold fantasies that it doesn't completely die out.

"According to my calculations—and I'm not sanguine!—in a hundred years Norway will have twenty million inhabitants. Overpopulation? Sickroom chatter. At that time countries will be cultivated in such a way that one square foot of ground will suffice to feed one human. And, mind you, feed him like a king! They have already succeeded in producing wheat seeds that yield over ten-thousandfold—but that's just trifles. The main thing is that in a century or so we shall have made ourselves independent of the climate. All the arable part of the earth's surface will have been provided with a glass cover. The necessary heat will everywhere and at all times be produced by electricity, and then we can grow dates in Bodø and grapes on Spitsbergen. Norway's valleys will be roofed over with glass from one mountain to another, and there, underneath, the glory of the South will flourish to the full. In three hundred years the country will feed one hundred million, and, mind you, not peasants and slaves but gentlemen. Hanging on every wall in the country will be paintings for one million kroner, and every square kilometer will have a theater playing Shakespeare. And obviously, among so many cultivated people, everyone will find friends, the kind of friends he needs, and women who will befriend him and send his hypochondria to kingdom come with a kiss.

"Why I am an altruist? From ego, naturally.

"I hate the poor, the down-and-out, the shabby; they offend my sense of beauty and spoil my appetite. Therefore, away with them! The sight of misery and stupidity humiliates me as a human being. Why? We claim to be rational beings and yet can't keep free from vermin! Rational beings—living in the middle of a swamp! No, that won't do, you see. It's just too wretched. *Homo sapiens, my* class, cannot be more stupid than other beasts of the field. Every fox has its hole and every bear its cloudberry bog; we human beings must accordingly each have a palace, and each a goose on our dinner tables.

"Not until all that is in order will life be possible for a proud man. Only when there's free competition can the superior person shine. Then all will be so strong that it's worth while to be a champion, and all women so beautiful that possessing the most beautiful will mean something."

"Yes, but what about equality?" I ask.

"Equality? (Shrug.) Consists in equal weapons. We don't need to have equally long noses, do we?"

"No, but—granting equal weapons to the rabble goes a bit too far, doesn't it?"

"I'll feel superior to the rabble even when the weapons are equal."

And on the other hand, Pastor Løchen. A whole army against a miserable young girl.

A comic constellation: the bandit Gabriel Gram and the penitent thief. But the pastor is not exactly stupid, and there is something about his piety and his clerical manner that soothes tired nerves.

Of course, I can't refrain from teasing him a little, quoting Tolstoy to him, and so on. But the hairsplitter inside me is pretty much dead. I can't bother. It's just the old absurdities, every candidate for confirmation sees through them. Criticism is too easy, the jokes too hackneyed. However, once in a while I discover that the above-mentioned tissue of absurdities can be beautiful; and who will bear his lance against an elfin world, a fairy-tale play? Only upper-class schoolboys make the objection: "But there are no fairies."

What is beautiful may very well be nonsense (*must* be nonsense? Truth is ugly!); even so it has its justification.

Mathilde is deteriorating more and more. She knows how much I appreciate illusions, but as soon as she lets herself go she nevertheless oversteps the mark.

This evening, however, it was something else that drove me away. I had an attack of sentimentality and couldn't keep myself from asking about Fanny—"the little one who turned up here off and on, the daughter of your landlady."—"Oh, she," Mathilde answers casually. "Well, she's in business on her own now."—"Which? What? On her own?"—"Yes. There are many men, you know, who like them at that age."

I grew silent. A kind of horror or shame came over me. Mathilde began to talk offensively, and to stop her I asked what the parents thought about their daughter having already started out that way. "Well, they should be only too pleased," Mathilde said. "That Fanny, too, has begun to help provide." Then she laughed, threw her fattening self into my lap, patted me and said, "It isn't everybody, you know, who is as decent as you are, fatso, dear!"

I put a few coins on the table and made off. Ugh!

Oh well, what can you say? That's the way it is, there's nothing can be done about that. Unless you want to "overturn society" after the fashion of Jonathan. But that won't be tomorrow. And in reality it's good Christianity, after all: the masses must go to the dogs so that some can remain on top. We simply must have a higher stratum, a finer public; but no fine public can exist without ladies, and ladies cannot exist without a certain degree of chastity. And so, it is obviously a must to have such a Salvation Army of tarts, and that army has to be recruited. If you accept the goal, you have to agree to the means. It would be nice, of course, if the children could be spared; a child is still always a possibility. But—. Daughters of seamy innkeepers—for them it's probably the natural way. A little earlier, a little later . . .

What makes me so sensitive in this particular instance is obviously the coincidence that the little one is called—well, has this name. If her name were Mathea or Indiana . . .

Poor dear.

Oh well, how does it benefit my Fanny to have chosen the path of virtue? There exists at the moment one human being whose opinion she cares about, and this human being needs just a couple of skeptical insinuations from some complete outsider in a café to go off and use expressions like "kept woman." I hereby spit in my damned face!

## XXIII

"Yes, you men of the church have an answer to everything and a remedy for every case. But when I consider that the best brains of humankind have been sitting for seventeen to eighteen hundred years, actively engaged in working out that system of yours, then it is not really that remarkable. The system is fine, indeed."

Pastor Løchen smiled quietly. "Yes, but isn't it really remarkable," he said, "that the best brains of humankind have been able to sit for seventeen to eighteen hundred years working on that system, as you call it?"

"Buddhism," I parried, "is also a very ancient religion, which many good heads have occupied themselves with throughout so and so long periods."

"There's much truth in Buddhism," he said evasively. "But it's interesting, from a purely historical viewpoint, that Buddhist Asia stagnated already a long time ago, while Christian Europe has constantly advanced."

"Europe advanced in periods when the Church had no power over men's minds."

"Well, yes, the Church loses its power once in a while—which as a rule is its own fault. But note that people have returned to the Church after these long periods of decline—which suggests that it is still capable of accepting progress. It also suggests that people, however much they grow, do not grow out of religion. You will have noticed that even now—after this latest and most massive period of decline—a more religious trend of thought is awakening in the great civilized countries; it's quite natural. The more development forges ahead, the greater grows what we call ennui, worldweariness, cosmic despair. And for that sickness, which must be the most severe and terrible of all sicknesses, for that there has only been found *one* physician, namely, he who said, and who really could say, 'Come unto me, all ye that labor and are heavy laden, and I will give you rest.' "

Rest! A lovely, alluring word. I let the conversation, conducted half in jest, drop and said, "Hmm, who knows; anyway, I quite understand."

It amused me to tease George Jonathan with this business of the "religious reaction." He shrugged his shoulder.

"All right," he said. "People are beginning to take an interest in that sort of thing—witching sticks, hypnotism, necromancy, and I don't know what. Marius Tullius Cicero is conjured in between two sheets and speaks English; Julius Caesar taps a table and tells Paul Petersen that his brother, Lars Petersen, has died of cholera in America. And played-out ladies and elegant pox sufferers sit listening devoutly to it all, intoning rapturously through their noses: '*Enfin! Voilà la vérité, la grande renaissance!*'

"The old bourgeois culture is about to enter its second childhood, you see. You've whored around so long, in London and Paris, that you're done for; and then, naturally, you send for a man of the cloth. Unction and chrism and incense and morphine—sick people must have it all. When ancient Rome started rotting, people also got into the habit of running after miracle mongers and mysteries. When everybody has been taken in by this nonsense, so that they can no longer look after their earthly concerns, then the time is ripe for the Huns and the Teutons, anarchists and miracle men, to come and sweep away the filth, gods and ghosts included. *All right!*"

"Well, it can't be that serious," I said. "The Romantic period went through something similar, and yet the old culture prevailed. It probably just boils down to the fact that people are beginning to get tired of this never-ending horsepower jargon."

George Jonathan gave me a cold, searching glance, which made me smile.

I wonder if we "freethinkers" would tolerate any *freethinkers* in our midst.

"Have you read Strindberg's *Creditors?*" Miss Berner asked today. We were sitting by ourselves with a cup of coffee on Pastor Løchen's veranda. "It's the title that is so good," she went on; "I think it could stand as an inscription over many love matches. I have a friend with a husband who is very much in love with her. Actually, she's fond of him too, but I can very well understand how it makes her suffer. True, he is a very considerate creditor and not at all pressing, but still, she does have these loving eyes spying on her, and it makes her terribly nervous. I can easily imagine how it feels to have this mute claim lurking about you all the time. There is a special, unpleasant tension in these homes, and if you've lived in one for a couple of years you almost develop a kind of aversion to love matches."

"But love will have its way, that's its nature, so what should one do?"

"Love will certainly have its way," she smiled discreetly. "I simply do not deem it necessary to have it wither away in a marriage."

"That sounds very nice," I said, "but then we must have more freedom—that is, women must."

"Women have the freedom they need—if only they had sufficient tact to use it," Miss Berner said. Incidentally, I believe her face turned red. And she continued hastily, "For them it will be happiness enough to preserve the experience of their youth in a faithful heart, so they have something to live on however much they may be married." Now her face was certain to be red; she had taken out her embroidery to be able to sit with her head sufficiently bowed.

"You're getting quite romantic," I said. "You once loved—with a grand passion? And you haven't turned bitter because he chose someone else?"

She shook her head.

"At the moment I'm glad he did," she said. "If I'd acted like Emilie, he too would probably be a worn-out, nagging husband by now, and I would be left with nothing. But today I remember him as he was then, and I'll (smiles) keep him till I die."

"Even if you get married?"

"Oh, come!"

"And your husband?"

(Smile.) "At least he would—avoid having creditors."

"But he could become *your* creditor, couldn't he?"

"Then I wouldn't take him, you see."

"Ah, that's true. . . . Marriage of convenience."

"Yes, just convenience. So as for *that*, no fear! May I offer you a little more coffee?"

"No, thanks."

"A drop of liqueur? You should be rewarded for your patience."

"You think I've been bored? Instead you should watch out; one fine day I'll come and ask for your hand!"

"Because of my solid principles?"

"Because of your liberal principles."

"If you're deeply in love with someone else, I might accept you!"

Laughter.


Loving and having one's fling while young, and afterward a marriage of convenience befitting one's station. . . . Our elders are right.

There isn't very much left of my youth. I'm celebrating my last love these days.

Why not go for it, then?

Offer myself to her? Unfathomable weakness!

Unfathomable strength. We men are supposed to be the weaker

sex, they say; and even so I, the weakest of the weak, go around setting myself veritable tests of chastity. Unfathomable.

It's because love transforms us. When a woman loves she becomes
weak; if a man loves he becomes strong. If a man finds himself in a
situation where he *can* seduce a woman and he doesn't do it, you
can be dead certain that he loves that woman.

But everything has its limits, and I'm no longer able to be strong.
I *cannot* leave her in that way; we two *must* be young together for a
while. Just think how much suffering could have been avoided if I
had pulled myself together and made up my mind earlier!

I'll tell the truth. I'll be a gentleman. She'll have every possible
opportunity to say no. If she still says yes, if, that is, she does so of
her own free will—well, then I would commit a veritable crime if I
cheated her out of the adventure of her youth.

The saving decision at last. However she feels, it's my duty to let
her choose. She shall have the opportunity. I'll go for it. Happiness
comes to the brave.


To write is senseless. If you want a woman to come to a decision,
you mustn't give her time for second thoughts. That takes away her
ability to make up her mind. She's willing—no, she's not. She
needs a push from outside to do even what she herself desires to do.
Never once in the history of the world has a woman reached a
decision on her own.


I look for her and cannot find her. Alas, no; after that last time . . .

Shamefaced and miserable, I seek out the "friends" in whose
company I can forget. What kind of crazy idea is this whole thing
anyway: to offer her a "relationship"—.

Maybe, if I had taken care to choose the right moment. But now
I've frightened her. She despises me now. I'll never see her again.

Yet once more I felt happiness treading on my toes without being able to go for it. I stepped politely and shyly aside, bowed, and said, "Pardon me, miss, that I was in your way."

I see her disappear over the hills like a white cloud. Her smile is mocking, bitter, and sad.

That was the third time she brushed past me. And she won't be mocked. It was the last time—"this Thursday evening still, and then never again." She's no hussy, that she should be trailing after me.

Poor fellow. Go to your "friends"—and to those women you can drop and pick up again. You're a wreck, washed up onto a stool in a government office; there you'll hang until you rot.

»»»» «««

# Part Two

*I*

26 July '85

Here these notes end. An eloquent silence follows. I dreamed about the happiness of the brave; in reality the story turned out to be about folly and defeat. I chewed my tongue with vexation for several days. Something so unbelievable, so oafish: to attack the young girl with banal, sophomoric platitudes—"friendship forever," "share everything," "stick together as long as it works out"—scaring her away like a little boy who scares the bird he wants to catch, instead of simply. . . . Well, hindsight always knows better.

Man is a ridiculous animal. He can tame the lightning and figure out the orbits of comets, but to figure out how one catches such a stupid little bird of a young girl—.

If it's someone you don't care about, all right. But what if it is a wild, free bird, rare and precious—then the hunter gets heart palpitations and loses his head. He sees the bird sitting up in a tree blinking its eyes, then he rushes off in confusion and shakes the tree, thinking that the bird will fall into his lap, like a ripe fruit. When the frightened bird disappears in the thicket with a cry, the fellow just stands there, intelligent as he is, biting his tongue.

The infatuation itself was extinguished for a while by the terrible, cold shame that ensued. You have to possess a certain degree of vanity in order to love, a belief in the possibility of being loved in return. But in those days I had no more vanity than a wet dog. That is, I felt she despised me with her and my own contempt combined, which added up to a triple contempt. That left no room for any fine feelings. I walked around like an outcast, an impossible person, someone who didn't count, an outsider. Such a fellow is ridiculous, prowling about with his tail between his legs on account of something he did because he couldn't help himself. Surely, a man who has made such an attempt and been turned down must be the most pitiful creature in existence.

Naturally I sought out Miss Berner. I needed a woman who respected me; and I attached myself to her with a certain sincerity, like a wounded man in need of nursing, a homeless person who begs for a place to stay. Then my moral courage lifted its head once more; I rose above my defeat and felt at my proper level again, on the heights, up among the chosen. Whereupon the infatuation reappeared—worse than ever before.

In the meantime I had managed to send off a letter, a cursèd letter in which I assumed a supercilious air—going on about my "idiotic idea" (it was to be passed off as a momentary thoughtlessness, naturally), telling her an exquisitely indifferent goodbye and informing her that I intended to marry someone else, an "intelligent" woman. There was in this—besides the lie—a good dose of mean revenge. Can there be anything meaner than a male who has been humiliated in his masculine vanity?

One idiocy worse than another. With that letter I blew up the last bridge between her and me, barring my retreat as thoroughly as possible. It's like the hunter who, in his annoyance that the bird has flown, discharges a shot after it, though all he accomplishes thereby is to chase it even deeper into the woods.

Today I heard through my friend Mark-Oliv that she has gotten engaged, she has "sold herself" to a prosperous old man. An absolutely sensible thing to do, of course. More sensible than I had expected. They certainly do not die of love these days! Nonetheless, here I sit, my face so long that I can feel it myself. A peculiar, helpless shame. And underneath it a repressed, furious pain.

It's over.

I hate Miss Berner. She was the witch who charmed me to sleep;

had I not been hindered from waking up that Thursday evening, never again would the princess have been allowed to leave me.

A highball, another highball! Liquor and marriages of convenience, that's your field of expertise, you oaf. The great rapture, perfect bliss—I'm not made for that. I am half a man, a "man of the future," too much brain and too little blood. When my princess comes, I pick up my pince-nez and examine her; and if I discover a flaw in her hairdo, or if a cobweb sticks to her dress after she has groped her way through the cave that leads to my castle, I crinkle my nose and let her go. The devil take Miss Berner and her marriage of convenience!

And so my adventure ended. Skoal! Edite, bibite, kollegiales, post multa secula pocula nulla—.

I can't be bothered to write. There certainly won't be a novel. What a humiliating ending!

Only to relieve my heart now and then, perhaps. After all, you do occasionally feel a certain urge to laugh at yourself. Thumb your nose at yourself. Scream.

Evil times are imminent. Now that she is irretrievably lost, she's becoming my be-all and end-all—.

And existence is nothing but this black glacial desert: the Grim Reaper waiting behind a rock. Utter darkness, where there shall be weeping and gnashing of teeth.

My "hallucinations" are almost uncanny. Every evening, after the house quiets down, she comes stealing up the stairs. I hear her quite clearly. First on the stairs, then in the hallway. She doesn't knock. She simply stands there, listening, waiting, choking her tears. I feel her so intensely that sometimes I take the lamp and rush out to check. But when I've gone to bed, I hear her breathing, here, in my room.

## II

8 Aug.

Bjølsvik celebrated his wedding today. He and his young bride boarded the ship for Le Havre directly after dinner. The happy couple will live in Paris.

All the same it's sad. True, our friendship was lately somewhat besotted, preserved in alcohol, but still it was a solace, a rescue in the hour of need, a last resort. It's getting more and more empty around me. Soon I'll be alone.

Lucky old boy who's married! The only friend who doesn't skip out in a time of adversity is one's wife. The bright young being he welded to himself today so he'll never again be alone with himself—reminded me a little of Fanny. I grew sentimental. Sat at the banqueting table pretending to eat—swallowing and swallowing my tears, an old bachelor's bitter tears.

The ceremony itself moved me. These old things aren't that stupid, after all. Charming old Sven Brun spoke simply and prettily, and the marriage formula itself is beautiful. Naïve, honest, and trustworthy in an old-fashioned way. Those old verses from Genesis sound like childhood memories, like a quiet, sacred voice from faraway times, from the forefathers, from old, wise forefathers. It's all said in such a deeply sincere way, so stern and gentle; your heart is stilled and touched and purified. "In the sweat of thy face shalt thou eat bread. . . . Thorns also and thistles shall it bring forth to thee . . . till thou return unto the ground; for dust thou art, and unto dust shalt thou return.—In sorrow thou shalt bring forth children, and thy desire shall be to thy husband, and he shall rule over thee." It's God the Father speaking from up the high choir, calmly, fatefully, irrevocably. With a kind of moral indignation I was thinking that perhaps the little modern lady-bride stood up there grumbling to herself at this ancestral wisdom. These shallow-pated modern people with their lack of piety are just insufferable.

Then the organ joined in, soft and solemn, respectfully answering God's lofty speech. The song of millions of souls, the song of centuries, our forefathers' faith and reconciled, resigned understanding of life—it all surged forth, filling the vault with simple, grand chords. I felt uplifted and pure; a powerful, gentle emotion filled my breast; all sorrows and burdensome thoughts were left behind, far behind, and became alien and small—quaint, stupid freaks and petty demons who were passing out of sight and disappeared.

I'll be going to church off and on—a Catholic one preferably. It matters very little whether you "believe" in these legends—we can't do that anymore, of course. I want to hear the song of the centuries, to swim and drown in its waves, feel uplifted and pure. And I'll fold my hands in humility during the confession of our forefathers' faith—and *wish* I could believe as they did.

"He that believeth shall be saved." That is, *is* saved. Happy elders!

In the end there is only one friend who doesn't abandon us in times of adversity.

One's wife? A modern woman? When things look bleak she applies for divorce—.

The following day

Today Miss Berner mentioned her for the first time.

Namely, to tell me that she—"isn't she called Holm?—oh, Holmsen—boarded the ship for Le Havre yesterday with her mother and her somewhat aging fiancé—to go to Paris."

I hate Miss Berner.

### III

Only one thing in the whole world is fun: to sit here writing letters to her. I know I'll burn them. Tomorrow or the morning after. I know it's stupid. Unmanly. Idiotic. Perhaps softening of the brain is setting in. It began around this time with my uncle; maybe a bit later. But all the same. All the same. It's the only thing that gives me peace of mind. The only thing that can occupy me. Maybe I'll eventually even knock off something I can send.

It's an odd, intolerable torment to feel that you appear in a dubious light to the one person you care about. I must, *must*, explain myself to her.

And still I know that I'm nothing more than a half-forgotten nuisance to her. She has crossed out my entire account—bah, *what a fool!* At the moment she's getting ready for her marriage of convenience, which perhaps I and nobody else forced her into.

Ha-ha! Write your letters and burn them, you old bachelor! In any case, you cannot find any better use for your leisure.

You can have your highballs at the same time, of course. Some day they'll take you to Gaustad. I'm a reservoir of every imaginable inherited family sin and sickness. It manifests itself in my case as dipsomania.

Thank God I was strong enough not to lead the good girl into a marriage with such a cadaver.

What consuming agony! Its paralyzing pain reaches down to my very fingertips, so that I have difficulty holding my pen.

If I marry it will have to be with someone who cares for me only to the point that she can send me to the hospital without a sigh when the fateful day arrives.

Without a sigh and without fuss. One who can use words like

"depression" and "nervousness" with the right conviction—or whatever other euphemisms are used when nice people catch a grave illness.

In short, someone getting along in years and sensible, like Miss Berner.

She takes care of me. She needs someone like me to nurse and save. Unmarried women are like that. Dogs, cats, or old bachelors. *Prosit die Mahlzeit!*

Oh God, the whole world seems nothing but a big, black hole.

## IV

October

Headache. That tight, painful pressure above the eyebrows. The beginning of the end.

One must fight fire with fire. Not a trace of love anymore. A nurse—that's the word.

How disgusting—when you're sick you lose your energy. Right now I care so little about life that I could easily undertake what is needful. But I'm too weak. Absolutely done in. To hang oneself, for example, requires such a lot of energy that the mere thought— phew!

Or to ask Dr. Kvaale for morphine—phew! Putting on an act like that—can't bother. Besides, the thought of somebody being privy to—.

Antipyrine . . .

I have associated with too many physicians in my day. I have too little faith in that humbug.

The only thing would be if the doctor had such a personality that he could hypnotize. Get the patient to swallow all those pointless pills, etc., with the necessary piety. But when you know the physicians and their tricks—.

I'd better stick with my old cure. Walking and walking. My fortunate habit of taking a cold shower every morning makes me quite resistant; and when I then drink plenty of air—and no cognac, only an absinthe now and then in order not to go instantly mad—.

The worst of it is all these rankling, tormenting thoughts that frazzle my nerves, until I'm gaga and frightened, afraid I'll see visions and hear voices. Every bird that darts out of a roadside bush throws me into paroxysms of fear.

One should have someone pleasant—oh Fanny, Fanny! All the others bug me. Especially that infatuated old spinster whom Miss Berner drags along when she goes for walks. That mademoiselle makes damn sure she never takes a walk alone with a disreputable man; she knows the way of the world better than poor Fanny.

By what can one recognize a truly cultivated man?

"By this," Miss Berner said, "that he conducts himself like a cultivated man also toward *older* unmarried women."

There was an edge to her subdued smile. I must at some time or other have been guilty of a faux pas vis-à-vis her spinster friend. Good heavens, I have all possible respect for that lady, but—.

"Why it is so difficult to make up one's mind to die?" said Dr. Kvaale on the way home from Jonathan. "Well, I suppose this urge to live that we have refuses to die until it has run through, tried, all possibilities. It would, I assume, be quite easy to croak the moment you could tell yourself: now I've tried everything, it's all over, the world has nothing more to offer."

"Or if one knew one would live on?" I hinted. "Then, presumably, it would be as easy to cast off this bodily form as changing one's shirt or coat."

"I'm not sure of that," the doctor said. "It doesn't matter how immortal our soul might be, it would still be bound by this miserable body. . . . There are so many undersouls, you see, body souls: the nerve soul, the blood soul, the souls in the abdomen and all the other concavities. The moment the oversoul realized that it wanted to throw away this body, those body souls would pounce on it and overpower it, as sailors do when the captain gets the d.t.'s and wants to strand the vessel. They simply tie him up and shut him in. Oh well, we shall see. If we live, we live."

He appeared to sigh.

"It's repugnant that one shouldn't be master of one's own life," I went on. "When all is said and done, I suppose nobody kills himself until he goes mad, and then it can't really be said that he 'himself' did it."

"There *are* those who kill themselves in their right mind," Kvaale said.

We entered the cabinet at the Grand and continued talking. In the end, of course, about marriage. I defended it, he attacked. "Such a husband is just like the dragon Fafnir in Wagner's—I believe it's *Siegfried:*

> Ich liege
> und besitze,
> lass mich schla——fen!"

### V

At Pastor Løchen's for tea. After the tea a very discreet toddy. He sincerely endeavors to lay aside the clergyman in my presence. But whether it's my fault or his, we're steeped head over ears in religious drivel.

He refuses to admit that he hates the "modern atheists." "Rather," he said, "I have a certain respect for these tough minds who are able to recognize the emptiness of a godforsaken existence—and able to endure this terrible recognition."

"Sure, it does require strength."

"But," he said—at once making some reservations—"I must add that when I read those people, I nearly always have a certain feeling of dryness, of shallowness—I mean a sense that perhaps they haven't quite realized the full depth of 'the world's suffering,' at any rate not felt the depth of it."

"Why," I said, "even if one both recognizes and feels it, one has a certain pride, after all, a certain morality; it won't do to give one-self up to something that's owned to be idiotic—pardon, *known* to be idiotic—simply because one finds it hard to look truth squarely in the eye!"

"Well, no," he mumbled, "and as far as that goes, all due respect. But," he continued, "when you fail to understand that modern people— like those members of the English aristocracy, for example— can return to Catholicism, then I must maintain that precisely this recognition of the meaninglessness of secular life is one of the mightiest schoolmasters to bring us unto Christ. Once the impossibility of a scientific explanation of the world has been recognized in its full depth, there will eventually come a moment when one must choose between madness and Christ. And many a tormented soul will then throw its 'pride' overboard and seek salvation where it can be found."

"Weak souls . . . oh well."

"Even if they are. A soul like that will perhaps be weaker than usual. But it could also be a strong soul, one that has known world-weariness at greater depth than usual."

"One prefers to include oneself in this latter class, naturally."

"I for my part must admit that, unfortunately, I have to count myself among the weaker souls. I have, as you may remember, a somewhat aesthetic disposition—maybe I have an essentially aesthetic disposition; and aesthetic spirits are not among the strong. But for me this very desire for beauty became my schoolmaster. When one day the world dissolved in my eyes into a single deep, glaring disharmony, there was only one thing I could do, namely, to go where there was at least harmony, and that was with Christ."

"I see."

But these English aristocrats interest me. I myself may have felt like taking shelter behind old church walls and altars many a time, but to actually do it! To conquer all one's modern skepticism and knowledge and really find peace in something so outlived! I can't understand it.

But perhaps it's not "outlived." Solomon wrote: no new thing under the sun; he ought perhaps to have added: and no old thing under the sun. Maybe the "new" thing is merely that which we need at the moment; the "old" is that which we have just used. That people who are weary of thought go in for mysticism is no more remarkable than that a meadow becomes thirsty for rain after a long spell of sunny weather.

Miss Berner is musical. A lucky thing in case she should marry; music is such a fine family lightning rod.

"I, too, am a bit thirsty for tunes once in a while," I said. "In my youth I even wrote some music. There's no illness I haven't gone through; I had a rather bad case of musical measles.

"But in the end it became too monotonous for me. So poverty-stricken. Just the two wretched keys, major and minor, minor and major, two sharp contrasts without reconciliation; can you imagine anything more inartistic? I bored and bored to go deeper, eager to find a 'third key,' the one which, according to legend, makes everything dance and tintinnabulate. But those two were the only ones.

Waltzes for those who liked to dance, and hymns for the laity. And so I became bored with it—as with everything else."

"A typically youthful thing, I'd say."

Well, yes, of course it was.

But I still sometimes dream about the deep keynotes, those which dissolve all existence in vibrations and sound. If I had those—what bliss it would be to play them and see this heavy, gray world evaporate in song, first into luminous clouds, then into a fine bluish smoke, and at last into a grand, cold starlit night.

## VI

Religion "old"? "Contrary to reason"?

These are probably just empty phrases.

For example, is there anything older and more contrary to reason than love? And yet it's real to the point that I, a grown-up modern man, am wasting away with yearning for a young girl whom, when all is said and done, I won't have—.

February 1886

The modern investigations of hypnotic, magnetic, and other nervous phenomena are in the end perhaps the only things that give us some hope. If that path won't take us to "the soul"—this remarkable unknown that makes the cadaver strive and struggle—then there isn't any path at all.

There *is* more between heaven and earth than the physicians apprehend.

As long as there is no explanation of how vibrations of the air become sounds in our brain, the staggering dualism of "matter" and "spirit" will remain; and our nerve strings are nothing but telegraph cables that take care of the communication between these two worlds. To find out how these telegraph transmitters function must therefore be the first step.

I borrow books on hypnotism—and even spiritism and the like—from Dr. Kvaale, who just asks me "kindly not to go crazy." Well, no fear of that; there's too much palpable nonsense in them. But strange and mysterious things do exist, all of us experience them without being aware of it; and I cannot understand why action at a distance—real, not just imagined—between her and me should be "impossible."

How gamely men speak about women and love when they're not in love!

George Jonathan, who was once very honest and naïve, married his mistress, the reason being that he was afraid the wench would go to the bad! (Good grief, if a tart goes to ruin, she doesn't deserve any better, and if she deserves better, she simply won't go to ruin. And anyway, "go to ruin"? Aren't they bound to anyway? Aren't we all bound to? Is it so much better to go to ruin in boredom and propriety and in the end go waddling about like a fat, yellow goose of a philistine missus, than to live at full speed for a few champagne-crazy years and then die the death with a bang and without any nonsense, in a hospital or in the gutter?)

But that time, you see, he was in love. And he who is in love wants the girl for himself. My hatred of the old geezer who has run off with Fanny is, in its quiet way, so venomous that I fancy it would be a pleasure to plant the heel of my boot on his neck and stamp him to death like a snake. So now it's me who doesn't like joking about such matters.

"So it didn't come to anything this time either?" Jonathan smiled somewhat ambiguously.

"With what?" I grew hot.

"You understand what I mean, I see," he nodded. "Congratulations, by the way."

"So? You know the woman?"

"No, but I know you. You're not suited for monogamy."

"So?"

"You're deficient in humor. One must be a humorist to pull through marriage unhurt, you see."

"Anyway, you are on the wrong track, insofar as I never intended to marry that woman," I said bravely—all lies are half-truths. "However, she was a sensible young girl and I very much enjoyed walking around with her; there was nothing in the relationship of what you are likely to . . . assume."

"It was a platonic relationship, sure; I know that."

"Know it? Why, you can't really know it—"

"You were too elegiac the whole time, my friend. One can tell at once whether a lover is in possession or not."

"Oh well, lover—that's another false expression. There were too many things about her that . . . I didn't go beyond developing a certain interest."

Suddenly ashamed of my cowardice, I added, "Well, she did finally take hold of my imagination. That kind of weird, fantasized infatuation, you know—love at a distance—with inevitable melancholy when the object is absent."

"I noticed," he said, in a tone of understanding, which was unexpected and therefore touching. "You should free yourself," he added.

"Ah; more easily said than done."

"More easily done than said—after she's married, I mean."

"Rubbish." A vigorous shrug of denial.

"She's awfully chaste, is she?"

"Chaste? It's not that. Every woman can obviously be seduced, there's only the difference that—well, it's only a difference in price.

But this one, you see, belongs to those who take it seriously, and you try to avoid such ones as long as possible. I'm nervous about things like that."

"She will take it less seriously after the wedding, you'll see. Marriage is a clever arrangement. It deprives the little girls of their bashfulness and disappoints them, whereupon they easily fall prey to a Don Juan. The more so as marriage provides a certain safeguard in regard to the offspring. So make sure to turn up at the right moment. She will give in at once, and with a fury that will frighten you—you good old maid."

I hated him as he sat there. "What sort of French novel have you been reading?" I asked arrogantly.

He gave a shrug—even more arrogantly.

"A novel of real life," he said. "You know it too. You must be very much in love, indeed, if facts of that kind are offensive to you. We cannot make use of free marriage; well, then, we'll manage with broken ones."

Actually, I don't much like the guy. In my future novel he will appear as a typical representative of that cold, boring time, prosaic and matter-of-fact, which is called the present. In general, of its shallow optimism and positivism, without imagination and without religion. I find Dr. Kvaale much more likable; I sense depths within him. With all his doctor's materialism he's a man with soul; he has suffered and suffers still. He looks deeply into the eternal night, and he has learned *resignation*.

It *is* her. It's enough to drive you crazy.

She's beginning to haunt me during the day. No sooner have I appeared on the street than she's there, instantly, ten or twenty steps behind me, staring at me with sad, alluring eyes. I instinctively turn around; naturally there isn't a trace of her. But she's there all the same.

How much basis in reality may there be to such a perception—? Without a doubt, I have a psychic talent; I have experienced similar things before, naturally without taking notice of the fact. We have so far had only one word for all such things, the big, crude word "nervousness"—just as in the old days doctors gathered together all sudden attacks of illness under the concept "apoplexy." It's about time that these areas should be investigated.

It's worst at night. After I've gone to bed and put out the light, I feel her presence quite distinctly somewhere or other in the room; she's there, I can hear her breath. Last night it became so clear that I lost my head, made a light, and began looking for her. Completely crazy! But as soon as I had gone to bed again and turned out the light, it began afresh, and I heard her breath as distinctly as the pounding of my own heart.

The associated insomnia is awful. I'm loath to begin taking chloral. Hssh, there she is!

Later the same night

I'm afraid of ghosts. There's something wrong here. She's dead—in her despair she has jumped overboard, to avoid the graybeard's revolting caresses; it's her spirit that's here. . . .

Dear, beloved Fanny, if you're here, then say so; do you want something? Do you have something to tell me? If you can't speak to me, make some sign or other. . . .

## VII

I had a rather serious talk with Dr. Kvaale today. He gave me some potassium bromide and asked me to return his books on spiritism.

Perhaps he's right, I'm too nervous right now. It's taxing reading. Cosmic despair and potassium bromide should suffice for one person. There's no need to summon any additional powers of dissolution.

The steady nervous pressure on my brain makes me anxious. My soft-headed uncle haunts me all the time. Better not sit inside and read now; walk furiously, chase away all anxious thoughts—and all ghosts.

My best company these days is, in short, the pastor. His broad, blandly serious clerical manner soothes me. I have a kind of superstitious feeling that I won't so easily be attacked by mysterious powers when he's near.

He offered to take evening walks with me, and I said, "Thank you, yes," with real pleasure. "I'll leave the clergyman at home," he added with a smile.

And so the clergyman and the atheist walk side by side like friends, talking nonsense. His calm, reconciled view of people and things pleases me. It's naïve, of course, this thing about a God sitting up there and looking after us, but I like naïve things at the moment. Whenever I feel a bit low, this religious fancy invariably turns up. "The sick have need of a physician," says the pastor.

Miss Berner usually comes along, and I find myself in a sort of good, safe family circle. We talk about music and literature. The pastor has a literary taste that doesn't displease me at the moment; he claims that Norwegian "secular" literature has only *one* author worth reading, namely P. Chr. Asbjørnsen. "That is to say, privately I'm really more enthusiastic about Welhaven and Moe," he adds, "but maybe it is the religious vein in their work that I find so exceptionally appealing."

I can't get him to talk about hypnotism or spiritism and that sort of thing; he changes the subject to ghost stories and tales of the old manse, which are actually every bit as interesting and, besides, have all that glimmer of poetry about them in which these modern "isms" are so sorely lacking. I say to myself: even in superstition our elders have the advantage.

Only one thing is missing the whole time; that is, there is a gap in our circle. The fourth party is with us, but all too spiritually—.

"We shouldn't blame the ages of reason," Løchen said today in his conciliatory way, "they are needed; they have their definite and necessary place in the process of development. They elucidate and purify, and produce a criticism in all areas, not least in the religious one. But you may be right in not finding them particularly interesting; after all, they are characterized by a certain dryness. And that, of course, is why there comes a reaction, the reaction or breakthrough of feeling and of the heartbeat in the great periods of renascence—if I may be permitted to use that expression in this context. Those periods, I mean, when people live more fully, not only with their intellect but with their whole being. That religion, too, comes back into greater favor in those periods is natural enough, considering that humans are also beings who have a consciousness of the infinite. One would think, when reading the penetrating, learned, often witty critiques that in ages of reason are directed against Christianity, for example, that the latter had been overthrown and could never again be revived; but when all is said and done it is not the intelligence that is our fundamental faculty, and hence that which is rejected by pure intelligence can nevertheless be a vital necessity for a human being—viewed as a whole."

"Yes, if only *that* could prove anything!"

"It still is, when all is said and done, the sole criterion of truth we have," he replied. "Anyway, what right would we have to try and suppress this element of feeling? We cannot even do so: *naturam furca pellas ex*—. More than one great skeptic have in the end had to recognize that they had forgotten *la partie religieuse et sentimentale*."

"He was a broken man, then, Auguste Comte, as everyone knows."

"That may simply mean that he had a deeper experience of life. A sick man knows many things that a healthy man has no inkling of."

"And that a healthy man is therefore unable to understand."

"Sooner or later we all get sick," the pastor said.

A shrug. A rather long pause.

Alas yes; you can get sick just from a little miserable love affair.

You miss so grievously and for so long this woman who was to complement your being that you end up feeling you must die. Then you become modest and seek remedies. If you can't have the best, you take the next best. In the absence of woman you content yourself with God; in the absence of happiness you are satisfied with salvation. It's the old myth. You cannot embrace Juno, and so you kneel before a cloud.

I wonder if someday I could bring myself to propose one of those "marriages of convenience" to Miss Berner.

It's definitely the best I could do. She knows all about how to treat such a weary man, talks away my anxiety when I'm nervous, and understands how to "converse" alone, so that I can sit in silence and take it easy while at the same time having the illusion of participating—well, even somehow feeling reassured that she finds me interesting.

Simply brilliant.

I'll see how things will be when I've gotten over this period of weariness and can think of the other one with a little more detachment—still a little more. . . .

"It's purely a matter of will," the pastor says. "If one wants to believe, one can."

Oh sure, that's true. It's simply a matter of autosuggestion, after all. Of suggesting to yourself, with sufficient energy, the idea that you are in the grip of the devil and can be saved only in this or that specific way.

But that, you know, requires a greater energy than is at the disposal of yours truly.


## VIII


Poor, kind Brun—he has looked very much askance at me since last we met; he understands what I think about his marriage, and so he has vacillated between two things: breaking with me or making me his confidant.

Those poor husbands! They all begin by acting superior: they "no longer need" their old friends, and so they become aloof or make a clean break. But who knows? In a couple of years they may come back; after all, they must eventually have someone "to talk to."

Brun came. He needed all too badly to get something off his chest, most likely. So why not just as well come to me? I already knew beforehand—a bit too much.

And I felt sorry for the good musician, whose life had turned into discord, and accepted his invitation to "a regular bachelor evening" at Ingebret's.

No sooner were we through with the necessary preliminaries and the inevitable diffidence than it started.

She was the most gorgeous person in the world, and so on. On the whole they were quite happy together, and so forth. There was, of course, one or two things; it happens in the best of marriages, etc. "By the way, how is Bjølsvik doing?"

"Well, let's hope all goes well," he went on. "But that's the way things are, you know, with us artists: we don't quite know how to cope with these everlasting nuisances of everyday life, and so it's usually the old story of the drop that hollows out the stone."

The ice was broken. He breathed more easily.

"Well, yes," I said. "In general, I suppose, marriage becomes harder the more nervous people grow."

"Exactly, exactly. Brilliantly said." God, how touchingly grateful such a husband can be for a tiny word of sympathy which has no hidden sting in it.

We had finished our coffee with chartreuse and were pleasantly settled over our second toddy. He was going to spend the night in a hotel, could come home whenever he liked, and was happy.

We jabbered away. The incipient alcoholic paralysis opened our hearts and loosened our tongues; he already risked—in jest naturally —congratulating me for having avoided all "dangers": "You were in a precarious situation again, from what I've heard, eh? Oh, indeed not? Only such a—. Really, not even that? Well, in any case. . . ."

At the third toddy he told me the tragicomic story of how his love had received "its first jolt."

"You see, I was so head over heels in love, quite naïvely; she was simply my ideal, and so forth. And she was lovely, after all. Wasn't she? I'm sure you remember—I went around shaking hands with people, telling everybody that I loved them. Well, I really did love everybody that evening. You know, one gets to be like that when one is very contented.

"And she, of course, was also in her element, felt satisfied and free, a wife, an artist's wife and all—great; she was gay and let her hair down, drank toasts with her friends, tasted the punch too in the end, and everything was going magnificently. At long last we were in our bridal chamber, and I committed every possible stupidity—knelt and declaimed and I don't know what. Suddenly she turned pale and sat down. I was terrified and asked if something was wrong. She asked me to go out. 'Shall I . . . send for the doctor?' I asked in my fright. 'Please go out, quickly, quickly!' she implored. I didn't know what to do; I had to get out but didn't dare go

far. Suddenly I hear some strange, moaning sounds. My hair stood
on end, I rushed back in, frantic with despair. There she stood in a
corner behind the bed in her full bridal finery and—the poor thing
hadn't been able to deal with those few drops of punch—delivered
the entire wedding feast in the happy bridegroom's presence.

"Ah, you can laugh. But I—well, I put the best face on it, of
course, said it didn't matter in the least; that the punch had really
been too strong, that many of the women had drunk just as much as
she. But—well, I somehow felt so embarrassed inside. An ideal that
vomits, you see—all of a sudden she seemed to be someone else
than she had been."

"I can imagine how you felt, sure."

"I forgot about it, of course, but still; once the violin has got a
crack—. It's silly, I know, to bother about such a little accident.
Now it just seems ludicrous, funny. But she must have noticed that
a certain coolness had come over me, and so she felt disappointed,
no doubt—alas, yes! These are difficult matters. It's like when you
try to write something: the most trifling detail can upset your
mood, and so it goes poorly."

He took another swallow, enjoying the triple happiness of toddy,
freedom, and fellow-male understanding, and then went on, probably a bit more open-heartedly than he had actually intended:

"Oh well. *Commune naufragium.* We aren't the only ones, I expect. And so we quite wear each other out, it makes us so nervous
and so. . . . The worst of it is that she doesn't understand anything;
she has no idea how I'm feeling, doesn't even try to find out. And
so you grow weary. I often wonder if there's really anything left of
the whole business. There's no longer a stab of joy in my breast
when I think of her, and no longing, only a tired, empty feeling of
some sort of obligation—"

"Creditors," I cut in.

He gave me a blank stare. He probably didn't understand but said, "Exactly. Brilliantly put." Whereupon he emptied his glass and continued:

"She isn't capable of putting me in a good humor anymore, I mean. Consequently, I'm not often in a good humor. And then I also put her out of humor. But when I see her in a bad humor, I get annoyed. That makes her nervous, and so she cries. Then I get irritated. And she gets angry. It's just ridiculous; it means nothing, but——. I sometimes get furious if she simply forgets to sew a button on a vest"—the mere thought made him furious—"damn it all, for thousands of years women have had nothing else to do but sewing buttons on clothing, and now they aren't even good for that anymore!" It dawned on me that he must have had another scene today, most likely one of the nastier sort.

"But she's so thoroughly decent, you know," he continued in a sentimental tone, "and I wouldn't even consider living without her; one has to put up with these squalls. After all, she's still my best friend, don't imagine I would want to be unmarried!"

He regretted his candor, I could see. I soothed him as best I could, but thought to myself, Good nonetheless that I was sensible.

Well, God knows.

They want us to believe there is nothing more between heaven and earth than a few huge rocks. But what if, with these my own hitherto unpunished and unindicted ears, I clearly hear her tapping on my window at night—as I do, though I live on the third floor—?

Or what if I wake up from a dream and feel quite distinctly, in both my arms, the pressure of her body, which at that very moment rested there—the pressure, the warmth, everything, with the same complete, unerring distinctness as one generally feels the pressure of a warm female body—!

Then I have to ask myself what, precisely, I should believe.

I think I could bet my life that she was here last night—in person, bodily. When I awoke, I remained in bed awhile, my eyes closed, blissfully happy, holding her tight, tight. I *was* awake! Only little by little did I notice how my arms became empty, how the pressure ceased, how she slowly and quietly vanished. I caught at her—she was gone. But the sheets were warm beside me—with a special, pleasant warmth—that is, exactly where she had been lying.

Is there any other reasonable explanation of this other than that she dreamed, dreamed about herself in my arms, and so vividly, with such a magnetic intensity that her body—her spiritual, "astral" body, the psychic or dream body—really rested in my arms for a while?

It's enough to make you daft.


## IX


Today was payday; at such times I usually take in a small lunch with Markus Olivarius.

"Well," he grunted suddenly, pushing back his mop of hair, "were you at the wedding?"

"What wedding?"

"You weren't *there?* How strange."

I suddenly understood what he meant, and a couple of sharp, electric currents passed through the region of my heart. Then I suddenly went cold.

"Hm, hm, it hits home." Mark-Oliv nodded. "But maybe you still want to deny it, eh?"

"What should I deny? Oh, that nonsense. Good heavens, one doesn't love more than half a year at a time anyhow. By the way, was there something strange about the wedding?"

"Nothing else than that it was a clandestine wedding. Ah-ha-ha-ha!" he exploded. The waiter dropped the serving tray on the floor in fright.

"Oo, don't laugh like that, man! Clandestine, you say? What sort of expression is that?"

"No banns, and no invitation to a single person, at any rate not to *her* acquaintances. My wife, for example, who really has been a very faithful friend of hers (tut-tut! I thought)—she didn't have the faintest idea of it, either. And you were also one of the forgotten ones. Oh well, that's the way of the world. I'm glad you take it so calmly."

"I think it's nice when such women get fixed up. It was high time. And she knew her stuff, this one—an affluent old man like that. . . . A widow's pension and everything; so there! Altogether nicely pulled off, as we say in Bergen."

"Yes, she's quite comfortable now. A villa at Nordstrand: six rooms, kitchen and bath, servants, horses and carriages, and a host of admirers—ah-ha-ha!—plus a henpecked husband."

"Really."

"When he sits in his room and feels an urge to sneeze, he must first send a servant to the missus and ask if her grace grants permission—ah-ha-ha-ha!" Another six plates on the floor. All the guests in the room roar with laughter.

I shift the conversation to other matters; suddenly I recall I have to mail a letter before 12:30, and we leave. Mark-Oliv is truly happy that I "take it so calmly." "I was really afraid you were rather smitten!" he says admiringly.

"Then I would obviously have married her," I say.

Not a word. Not a sound. Not a hint that might eventually enable me to . . . Simply gets married, just like that, without even looking around for the other one she was trying to entice.

If the fish refuses to bite,
just send it out of sight.

Typically feminine.

Ha-ha! And I who for a moment believed she was in love, who even went around having scruples: how horrible it would be to make such a defenseless young woman unhappy! Ha-ha, you knucklehead, you prize sap.

Imagine going around all winter and—bah, about time I got cured, thank God.

She has stood in front of my door sobbing, has been here so intensely in her mind that I've heard and felt her physical presence—ha-ha, ha-ha. Oh, you bachelors! There's only one remedy for this everlasting romanticism about women—to get married. Married men know women, and they're not sentimental, by Jove.

The truth is simply this: her maternal instinct having some qualms about the old gentleman, she sets her cap for a younger man one last time. After all, it might be well worth trying! True, I was just a junior clerk, but a junior clerk can advance, especially if . . . well, a young, attractive wife can certainly help—in different ways, who knows! And then, of course, I was twenty years younger.

But she understood at last that I was too sly for her. So, *que faire?* You simply let go of the fellow. The old gentleman is also good. *Nur rasch heran!* The requisite youth can be had—on the side. Poor good, defenseless girl!

And she marries her graybeard; within a week she has the whip hand of him so that he dare not breathe a word. Then she beckons forward her young admirers.

Have I learned something, finally? I wonder.

*

I'm happy—so free, so cold, so pulled together. A cold shower like that was just what I needed.

And if every once in a while I still happen to hear padding and sobbing out there in the hallway around midnight. . . . Well, all I need do is to picture her in the old man's arms, stained by his disgusting, toothless kiss—no thanks, madam! I decline the honor of sharing my bliss with your young admirers.

Was it reasonable to expect that she should maintain any kind of "friendly relation" with me after what had passed between us? Would it have been correct?

No. Neither reasonable nor correct. But that is precisely why she would have done it—if her love had been something other than playacting.

She feigned being in love. The more I think back, the more certain I feel about it. The very fact that she became a strange man's companion—without ever betraying or intimating in any manner even the possibility of other intentions—could be understood only in one way. And then all those thousands of little things, those fugitive glimpses impossible to retain, even less translate into words: nuances of voice and glance; soft, warm, adhesive, virtually naked handshakes which only a woman in love could produce; spontaneous exclamations and words; her magnetic urge toward physical closeness—not to mention all those flowers she picked for me in field and forest, those eloquent blue anemones and forget-me-nots. . . . And then that last meeting: that softly falling, blissfully swooning way in which she half slid backward into my arms, her eyes closed and her warm body shuddering all over. And she let me kiss her! At any rate, the playacting was mixed with some genuine elements. But of course, at the crucial moment she remembered her reassuring position as the future Mrs. Ryen and tore herself away. The following day she got rid of every trace of sentimentality and laughed at the whole thing, kicked me away, embraced her old man, and said, "Okay, honey bunch, how about the two of us teaming up with each other, anyway!"

And since then she has been cold and clear and correct. No sudden outburst of suppressed feeling has carried her away to as much as a note, a greeting, or any sort of feminine thoughtlessness; for there was no feeling. Maybe she has done the same as me: written letters and then burned them? That's what a man in love does; a woman writes and seals the letter and puts it in the mailbox—and then has second thoughts. But not a single instance of such thoughtlessness, not a trace! And the decisive thing: imagine not even giving me an opportunity to do it all over again, to explain myself, come to some understanding; a woman in love doesn't give up hope so easily! Oh no. She could see that it wasn't "leading anywhere," not to anything "real"—in a reasonable amount of time; it seemed to her she had made sufficient efforts on that score, she couldn't bother any longer, gave up, and let things take their course.

Playacting, playacting! Cold, clear, correct calculation from beginning to end. Such and such a long time and so and so much love will be spent on that fellow; if it works out, fine; if it doesn't, I'll fall back on my graybeard.

Typically feminine. Goodbye, madam. To be sure, I was naïve—ridiculously, unforgivably naïve. But fortunately not as stupid as you imagined.

If only I could sleep at night. The bromide no longer helps.

I'm getting to be so listless. Walk around all day in a somnolent daze. Miss Berner holds forth to me about some bathing resort or other. It's too expensive. And too boring. I tried Grefsen once; but *whoever that country has seen will never go back—will never go back again.*

I've got to talk with Kvaale.

*Now* we could perhaps "find each other, we two," she and I, now that we are less sentimental. I at any rate.

I wonder what kind of prudishness it is that causes someone to have qualms about making the woman he loves his—"mistress."

Anyway, this has turned out to be my most painful affair.

I crossed this meridian twice before (aside, of course, from the many times when I was more or less near it). Both times the illness dissolved into one and three years, respectively, of quiet sentimentality, which may not yet be completely cured but that, in any case, was not dangerous.

This time the sickness is taking a nastier turn. Maybe I have less resistance nowadays. Maybe, on the whole, late loves are contrary to nature. The sad, autumnal feeling that this is probably the last time, that the great Pan will never again stir within me, must also be a factor. It's so cruelly hopeless.

Well, to put it simply: this affair is turning out to be the worst because it was the silliest.

Dr. Kvaale wants to send me to the mountains.

"You live too strenuously," he barks, "and sit too much indoors daydreaming; that won't do. Out and perk up, old man. Mountain air, that's just the thing for you, fresh as champagne compared to this dead, stale air down here in the plain. Not to speak of the garbage-can smell that people call 'air' here in Kristiania!"

Well, I guess I'll have to get hold of some cash and go, then. True, I have grown lazy and, true, I've become rather chained to the cobblestones and to my corner at the Grand, etc.; I've turned into a flabby, balding middle-aged figure on Karl Johan Street. But—. Well, it may do me good to get away from all this for a while and receive some "new impressions," to live under the influence of nothing but new suggestions.

I'm enticed more and more by the romantic memories from my youthful hikes and summer-dairy visits: shepherd's horn and tinkling bells, wood nymphs and dairymaids. And when I come back again, I'll have forgotten . . . *all.*

## X

On board the steamer, 2 July

Lovely to get on board. To cast off from everything around you, say goodbye to the whole world. To feel the sea breeze sweep over your weary brow—and then, on the open sea, to spew up Kristiania.

If only I could sail to the world's end. This bit of a coastal trip is just a parody.

But in Hitterdal the air is pure. And I do have this idea, after all, of wanting once again to hear that low, broken, naïve, trusting ting-a-ling-ling of the bells at the old church.

The Langesund fjord cleared.

I stood and vomited, thinking about immortality.

Immortality? These waves that rush along over the deep of the waters—they must feel that their existence is extremely meaningless. But what if the individual wave should conclude from this that it will go on rolling on a transcendental sea when some day it lies broken and shattered against the rocky shore?

Hitterdal, the hotel

The traveler resembles a man sitting down on a stone. He has a "double pleasure": first, when he sits down, and afterward when he gets up again.

A trip has two beautiful moments: when you step on board with your suitcase, and when, tired of rolling and of the smell of machine oil, you step ashore again.

How does one recognize an unhappy person? By the fact that he's always so glad when he's packing his traveling bag.


Norway, like ancient Greece, is not a country but a continent. Every parish is a kingdom. Now the ocean dominates, now the mountain, now the forest, now the green, cultivated field; now a larger or smaller number of these basic themes unite to form more or less rich or meager harmonies.

The landscape east and west of the mountains is as different as major and minor. You can travel through entire scales of landscape tones in a few days. From the blackest gloom and the most desolate waste to the softest grace and the brightest light.

The population is similarly varied.

The old division into petty kingdoms was the natural one. What concern of Telemark is Numedal? It's as far away as a fairy tale. Or what does Telemark have to do with Setesdal, or with Hardanger? Kingdoms, kingdoms; distances where princes and princesses can wander about, "far and farther than far," come upon trolls, witches, *hulder* farms and palaces, and finally arrive someplace where all is sheer wonder.

Strictly speaking, it was a crime, the feat that began in Hafrsfjord in 872. First, all the individual kingdoms—*Kopf ab;* then all the great families—*Kopf ab;* at last the final consequence: *Kopf ab* for the last great family and, with it, for Norway. Now this once so aristocratic country, so rich in tradition, lies adrift like a miserable, democratic flat-bottomed boat, filled with penny politics, Stavanger piety, bluestocking prudery, and posting-station culture.

\*

There should sit a king on every headland.

Not a "constitutional monarch," who is a model for the male head of a family, just as his queen is a model for the mother of a family; they should be sea kings, pirates, warriors, noblemen, *grands seigneurs,* who would know how to set store by power and glory, know how to enjoy the world's pleasures and terror, wine, blood, naked bodies.

Heroes would gather and skalds flourish among them, and beautiful, proud, wanton women would fire them with zeal for heroic deeds and love, for song and crime.

Dreams, dreams. Piracy is prohibited. It is also prohibited to wage war—without the consent of the Storting. Consequently, no heroes. And as far as the skalds and the women are concerned, they sit harmoniously side by side weaving homespun and teaching Sunday school.

And instead of a king, a lay preacher sits on every headland.

I take a daily walk to the old church.

I sit there dreaming and grow romantic again. Such a small funny old church, where every form is bursting with childhood faith, barbarian fantasy, and strong, simple feelings, and where legends, ghost stories, the romance of funerals and weddings, of old clans and families, have a nest under every rafter—that, finally, is something. Even an old dyed-in-the-wool rationalist like myself is properly moved. "Come unto me, and I will give you rest," says the old tarred rural church to me; and I come and find rest.

If only there was a really old and really bearded wild man of a parson, one from the time of Kristian V or thereabouts, a former pirate or brawler, or even a small, round, jovial, sodden one from the Zetlitz period.

I do not enter the church, by the way. It has been restored, you see. The poor-relief authorities have been at work; all that was old and quaint and funny and nonlay has been swept away. The church has been dechristianized. I have seen a photograph of its present interior: it is as brushed clean as a bourgeois coat, as naked and empty as one of those hicktown churches in Kristiania.

And then there is an album. A book where the tourist rabble from all over register their idiotic Persen or Pålsen—as if they belonged here. It's disgusting. As if it weren't enough to be pestered at one's hotel by these irreverent gray-pants, the church itself smells of tourists. Of tourists and the present. By God, if such a Pålsen or Persen was so eager to see the interior of the Hitterdal church, he could come up here some Sunday for the scheduled service, walk in, and sit humbly down by the door doing penance, because he had dared enter God's old sanctuary.

Our elders are right. Reality contains nothing that we can build on: honor, wealth, glory—all is trash. And love, woman—oh, go to hell!

Upshot: to build oneself a dream kingdom where there is eternity and peace. Build oneself a church.

Jesus, Mary, pray for us!

Toward evening—up in the woods. Sunday Quiet. Not a sound. Only, off and on, far away, the sound of bells dying away, carried here by a puff of wind.

Bright, peaceful, holy quiet; a Sunday quiet.

A squirrel jumps up a tree trunk without a care in the world, sits down on the lowest branch and munches.

The sun is slowly sinking. Red, warm light along the lush dark green of the mountainsides; the pale golden light of the sun washing in toward the yellow pine trunks. Long blue shadows settle on the lake and the floor of the valley.

I become so wonderfully still, hearing only my heartbeat off and on. And then this faraway sound borne here every once in a while—an echo, a resonance—perhaps of a shepherd's horn or of a cattle call. Who knows what kind of freshly blushing dairymaid is walking about up there calling her flock. Perhaps the wood nymph. Though at this time, during the summer, she probably keeps herself farther up in the mountains.

The sun sinks more and more; its golden light washing over the world becomes paler and paler. The shadows grow longer and deeper, the stillness so still that one has to hold one's breath.

> There is in the woods a darksome copse
> where the elves are ruling the ground.
> There, seal your lips when walking around!
> Even the nixie when he stops
> gives to his harp a softer sound.

What a blessing to be released from the rack for a moment.

Every day constantly the same impressions—that's what drives one insane. It's the drop that continually, again and again, falls on the crown of one's head—at mercilessly regular intervals. My soul has become overly sensitive. Constantly the same streets, squares, people, vistas—they have injured my retinas, turned into ceaselessly repeated pinpricks in my brain.

This clean, free, quiet nature cools my heart like a cold compress. Everything is agreeable to me; I even love the fantastically clad peasants—they contrast so refreshingly with those Kristiania fools. And their language—it has an infinitely finer and purer and more aristocratic sound to me than this brutal East Country language. I'm still enough of a West Country man to hear the hoarse crudity of the "Viken" intonation. Besides, those dry, bleating bureaucrat voices that engage in polite conversation in the drawing rooms of Kristiania can in the long run wear out the patience of an ear that makes musical demands.

Whether it is the mountain air or all the "new impressions," or the inevitably restricted use of liquor, one thing is certain: I'm calmer. I'm not plagued so constantly by the same thoughts. And I have powers of resistance.

I can actually walk about thinking of other things. Without any special effort. And when *she* comes, I chase her home again with her whisk broom of a husband.

Well, *naturam furca*—. It's worst at night. I dream that she has gotten married, that she lives extravagantly in order to forget her marriage, that suddenly one day she sees that it won't work and escapes from the whole thing, flees back to the only one she loves, makes off after me—by rail to Kongsberg, traveling post to Hitterdal—looks up the hotel, the room . . . knocks, rushes in; tears, embraces: "Here I am, take me!"

But I can go to sleep after drinking a quantity of beer.

They have two big nuisances here: the tourists and the papers.

The latter are the worst, insofar as one can't avoid having something to do with them. And so it is the same boredom every time.

Politics and politics. Now a certain conservative has compromised himself here, now a certain liberal has suffered a fiasco there. And when it reaches a very high level: a serial article about women's liberation.

Nothing ever comes to an end in this country! Once we have gotten hold of a bit of an "idea," we chew on it until it starts smelling.

Strange animals, these emancipated women, by the way. They hate man and all his being, but strive at the same time with all their might to copy this detestable man. "Woman always acts illogically."

Only in one respect do they require that man should be like them, namely, in regard to chastity. It annoys them that they must themselves be good, while he, that lout, takes it so lightly—it's enough to make you have kittens. He shall convert and become like one of us, the bluestockings say.

I've put together the following mystification, which I'll have printed when opportunity offers:

"Saint Augustine says that a woman ought never to have more than one husband; however, it is only natural that a man has intercourse with several women. The church father justifies this in the following manner:

"The man is woman's God; but to have more than one God is not admissible. It's different at the other end. For man, woman is at best his angel; but that a God has several angels, well, even thousands of them, in no way conflicts with Holy Writ; cf. Revelation. . . ."

But I forget: the bluestockings don't even have any respect for the church fathers anymore.

Up here one becomes so poor in spirit that one even finds time to concern oneself with women's liberation. If I remained here another couple of months, I would start taking an interest in politics as well.

What is "femininity?" A certain newspaper bluestocking let it be understood that she had no idea. I can well believe it.

"If only you gentlemen would someday define for us the concept of 'femininity'!" she sighs. And she adds with knitting-needle sarcasm, "Or perhaps you can't?"

Yes, that's just it. We can't.

To wit: "femininity" is *that* about woman that makes a man fall in love with her. And what is that? Why did I fall in love with a woman I only liked halfway, and whom I scarcely had any respect for?—Silence.

Femininity is the sum of all the qualities and peculiarities, merits and faults that make woman desirable to man. What sort of qualities *are* they?—Silence.

Similarly, masculinity is that about man which causes a woman to fall in love. It can be qualities or peculiarities, merits or faults; all of it is "masculine"—if it is attractive to woman.

That means: "femininity" is, like "masculinity," the—undefinable. The mysterious. Emotional concepts, concepts generated by the racial instinct. Women's maternal instinct says: Such and such shall be the father of my child; and she calls that man's nature "masculine." The paternal instinct says: That woman shall be my son's mother. If you ask that same man why, he replies: Because this woman seems so feminine. Period!

How painfully characteristic that a bluestocking wants to have these concepts "defined!"

Every story of seduction falls into two parts: 1. The story of how she captivated him. 2. The story of how he, caught in her meshes, did what she wanted, in the belief that he was a hell of a lady-killer, quite irresistible.

"Egoism" is not evil; *woman's* egoism is.

Man wants simply to be happy himself; woman can be happy only through others' unhappiness. Only then does she find life worth living, when she has ten desperate admirers chained to her triumphal chariot. And if one wants to give a woman a *really* pleasant surprise, one should, as everyone knows, hang oneself and let people know it was done for her sake.

The best thing is to row out on the lake and lie there in a boat, adrift. Then I feel safe.

The lake gleams blue around me on every side in the trembling sunlight. The hamlets rise softly and undulatingly with their green bosoms, wrapped in the hazily blue summer air as if in a veil. A thick, sweet fragrance of new-mown hay, evergreens, aromatic mountain flowers, libidinous and heavy, sensually intoxicating like the very breath of life. I lie down in the stern with a cigar and dream and rest; I'm Buddha sailing about on the silver waves of Nirvana, released and free.

I found a quaint old book in a farmhouse where I dropped in to light my cigar: Thomas à Kempis. I read it from time to time and lose myself so deliciously in it. Everything becomes God, he in me and I in him. The sun's light is his eternal love, which permeates the universe with warmth and life; his creative essence can be heard breathing and throbbing throughout existence like a faraway, quiet soughing. I am thrilled by pantheistic rapture.

Only one thing awakens me now and then: the idea that she— *she*—might come swimming here from the shrubbery over there, like a fair, fair mermaid, her tresses glistening down her lily-white back. . . .


                    The Hotel. Rainy weather
I'm not a rationalist. Only my intellect is; but what is intellect— other than a tiny, miserable lantern in the middle of a big, dark, labyrinthine attic?

The part of me that feels and perceives, that is me. That is my depth, the sea, the infinite in me. Down there is the surge of forces on which I depend; but at the bottom of this ocean there are underground connections to the oceanic universe.

George Jonathan seems to me like an English tourist dressed in gray, driving up through dark valleys with a pince-nez on his nose and saying, "There is a waterfall; there factories can be built." Then he doesn't look anymore. When the sun shines strongly, he says, "It must be possible to collect all this solar heat and turn it to some use." That's the only thought he has apropos of the sun.

But the waterfall is something other than the amount of latent horsepower it contains; the sun is more than a steam boiler.

This spreading reliance on reason as the be-all and end-all kills and denies something in me: the finest part of me and the deepest.

"But in any case the most useless!"

Usefulness—to whom and for what? Nothing is as useless as love. And yet it takes only the sight of a certain style of hat to make my whole being revive, like a mimosa beneath a ray of sunlight. "Usefulness" is a dogma like "happiness" and "truth"; it's important that it be properly understood, and not too narrowly.

Useful is what helps us live, feel alive. A dream is useful if it's beautiful. As for truth, it cannot be found; and the truth that can be found is useless.

Imagination, a life suffused with color, rich perceptions, existential depth. Why should we let ourselves be frightened by the word "illusion"? Almost everything that incites us to live, to feel life, is or is based on illusion.

The misty hillsides, the lonely lake with its mermaid dreams and its Nirvana stillness. Science comes along with its lantern and says, The mist is water vapor; the forest is nothing but ten thousand pines; the lake consists of so many kilos of hydrogen plus so and so many kilos of oxygen. The existence of mermaids and Nirvana stillness has not been demonstrated. But how does that affect me?

Anyway, to me "truth" is the misty hillsides and the lonely lake with its mermaid dreams and Nirvana stillness. The hydrogen and the oxygen leave me cold.

I *want* to dream, I *want* to have illusions.

Up above, white clouds drift by.

Up there it's peace. Someday my soul will be sailing there, just as I'm now floating along in this heavy bucket of a rowboat. My soul will imbibe sunlight and inhale ether, and its kingdom will be the endless ocean of light where the fleets of the sun are sailing, and in whose clear waves the liberated spirits are frolicking like nereids and dolphins.

Is there a God?—"We don't know."—Is there a soul?—"We don't know."—Will we live or die?—"We don't know."—Does life have a meaning?—"We don't know."—Why do I exist?—"We don't know."—Do I exist at all?—"We don't know."—What, then, do we really know?—"We don't know."—Can we know anything at all?—"We don't know."

This systematic we-don't-know is called science. And people clap their hands together in admiration and rejoice, "The advances of the human spirit are just fantastic and incredible; from now on we need neither faith nor gods anymore!"

For science has discovered that when a kettle boils strongly, its lid is lifted by the hot steam. And it has learned that a straw is attracted by a piece of amber rubbed with wool—without, incidentally, being able to explain these phenomena otherwise than by a jargon that changes roughly every tenth year. Accordingly, we no longer have any use for gods.

I rather wonder what's the use of such a "science"! Good Lord, these telegraph wires are quite astute and the steam engine is clever. The speculators on the exchange can commit their thefts of millions more easily than before, and a bank teller can quite easily take off with my savings, if I have any. Good heavens! All due respect, but—.

What concern is it of mine that the earth is round (which it is not, by the way)? Or that the world may have once been fog (which is dubious); or that the fetus in the womb at certain times resembles a canine fetus—as long as we "don't know" what has given a fog bank the idea of evolving into a world?

Oh, vanity, vanity. Oh, this aching weariness in my head. Old Dr. Faust was right.

> Wie nur dem Kopf nicht alle Hoffnung schwindet,
> der immerfort an schalem Zeuge klebt,
> mit gier'ger Hand nach Schätzen gräbt
> und freut sich, wenn er Regenwürmer findet!

Wouldn't the selfsame Dr. Faust have done better to empty the cup of poison than listen to the Easter Sunday hymn?

"Jesus, the soul's bridegroom."

A strangely naïve, strangely profound idea.

As a matter of fact, the religious *unio mystica* contains exactly what we also demand from love. Infinite devotion and tranquil happiness. A blissful fusion with and passage into the other being, in which our own finds its complement and consummation.

The way of faith: "from clarity to clarity, from light to light; from blessedness to blessedness."

The way of knowledge: from clarity to clarity, from light to light; from despair to despair.

You work yourself up the long ladder, liberate yourself from one cloud after another, one superstition after another, one belief after another, one theory after another—until you are at the top and see that everything is emptiness and a dizzying abyss. Then you understand that what you used to call clouds and beliefs were friendly tears that wanted to conceal the abyss from us, so that we shouldn't feel dizzy. If you try again to catch these mists, they flee from you. You cannot get back down, and up above is the emptiness; you stare and stare with frightened eyes—until you fall down.

## XI

"Viel Geschrei und wenig Wolle," that's the name of woman.

Just watching the commotion caused by a woman before, say, she can get herself maneuvered into a cariole, or before she is ready to go—the coachman still has to run back for her shawl, her red shawl!—is enough to make you sick.

And all in all. Two ladies on the stairs, for example, blocking everyone's way—they have nothing to talk about, they hate each other, can't bear each other; but fifteen minutes at least! Such a terribly interesting conversation: Mrs. Dahl's little girl is sick, she's *so* sick, it's *so* sad! And can you imagine, the doctor thinks it's diphtheria! For the last half hour I've had two such females standing here in front of my door; and they'll keep standing there for at least another twenty minutes. I had meant to take a nap, but I'll obviously have to forget about that.

> Wenn Männer auseinander gehn,
> dann sagen sie: auf Wiedersehn!
> Wenn Weiber auseinander gehn,
> dann bleiben sie noch lange stehn.

And the same in everything. When they love, for example. They make a lot of noise, wail and weep, so that we, who judge by ourselves, think it's a matter of life and death. At least! If I can't have *you*, my darling, I'll jump into the Kattegat—at the very least!

Well, she cannot have the above-mentioned darling, and what happens? She marries Mads Madsen and has children and grandchildren and great-grandchildren; and when Mads Madsen asks her, "Weren't you madly in love with Johan von Ehrenpreis that time?" Gretè answers with a warm smile, "Oh, pooh, just a ballroom infatuation."

\*

A woman never kills herself for love.

If she really jumps into the Kattegat, then it's either in the hysterical hope that it will make "him" extremely unhappy, or it is for fear of "the shame."

At the autopsy all youngish female suicides are found to have been pregnant.

August

I'm sitting all the way up in Meheien Heath. A rainy mood; mist-wrapped ridges and hills; autumnally romantic.

### Song of the Hulder

My dairy sits high by Hulder Peak,
where the wet wind blows like a streak.
And the reindeer roam in the rocky bourne,
nibble the lichen and flee my horn.
But in the dwarf-birch copse the snipes alight
and cheep away each rain-heavy night.

I took my herd there one night, to a dell
beside Svarte-tjern by Munkestofjeld.
A cooling fog hovered near the crest,
and the crag and sky became one black mass.
And the cowbells tinkled and sang ding-dong
with a fleeting sound as we ambled along.

There I saw my boy. He was weary and spent,
had been lost in deep night wherever he went.
But a breath of wind makes the fog banks part,
and mountains can't capture a peaceful heart.
They take flight and run. It's cold on the moor.
And downhill they go, by an easy spoor.

He saw not her who sat there by stealth
and listened quietly to his breath,
bending toward his tawny face
and giving his eyes an ardent gaze . . .
And the fog clears away, the sun makes you see.
No one in the world dreams about me.

Now a song is borne from Hulder Peak,
as we bring the herd underneath the rock.
Behind the foggy pass my farm sits lone;
they won't track it down, the trail is gone.
I've longed for years, endless and slow;
but summers come, and summers go.

*(Calls.)*

Oh hoorooleehow!
Come goat and cow!
For mountain flowers
and billows steep
must sleep.

And the wind blows cold through the long nights.

Strangely enough, the mail brought me a letter. I pounced greedily on it and tore it open—(from her?!).

Far from it. A couple of engagement notices. Who? What's that? My old boon companion Blytt, Don Juan, the painter?

Good heavens! Even he.

"You lose them like the hair on your head," or like bad teeth. Loneliness is getting stretched tighter and tighter about me. Before long I'll be locked up in it as in a cell.

A strange feeling. Alone. Quite alone. Like a mountain peak; face to face with God.

I can't stand it. I'll go mad. I'd better risk this marriage of convenience all the same, to have someone around. Not to be alone in that dreary apartment throughout long, stormy nights, when ghosts sigh and spirits knock; marriage is probably still the best one can come up with to protect oneself from eternity, which, dark and cold like an October night, will descend upon a tossed-about soul in the wilderness.

Almost *too* correct? Almost *too* irreproachable?

Nothing that's mysterious, nothing to stimulate your imagination—a good, cultured, respectable, well-bred lady. Nothing special.

The "mermaid" from the "lower depths" wasn't domestic enough for me; this one here is perhaps too much so. I couldn't mention my headache without receiving the formula of a household remedy, or make a hint at my nerves without being burdened with instructions about cold baths and a regular life. I see myself in my mind's eye as a husband with warm and cold compresses both here and there and become very uneasy.

And her ideals of domestic happiness! Peace and quiet, tea and sandwiches. *Aftenposten* and porridge for supper—"And, you know, one *ought to* get used to going early to bed." O-o-f!

And besides, no longer young. Skin color a bit indeterminate; on the verge of graying.

Nothing young and round and soft and developing anymore. Everything so ripe, so finished. The only prospect hereafter: the overripe, the angular. The long, sad process of decay.

Not a fresh breath anymore. No spring. No promises.

It's strangely sad.

All possible respect for every imaginable good and excellent quality. But that power which led Eve to Adam and said, Love her! didn't give a thought to those excellent qualities. Only *one* absolute requirement did he plant in the man's breast: your son's mother must be young—young!

I should by rights go into the church and look at that old Bible; but then I remember that all sorts of tourist rabble have turned its pages and defiled it, and so I lose my desire.

In my decadent periods I always get so sick with longing for what's old. The thought of my mother's old Voss Bible once made me pay out four kroner. I went to the bookseller and asked for "a Bible" and got it, wrapped in pretty blue paper; but when I came home it was a nice new, boring book from just a few years back, printed in boring modern type on boring white, unmysterious paper. Hell, it wasn't the Bible at all; I put it on the shelf and haven't looked at it since.

Here, however, there's really an old Bible; but it's "public."

Such a book has to be sacred. It must be accompanied by a quiet family tradition of two hundred years. An old pair of granny glasses must be hidden among its pages, and slips of paper with notes and references by white-bearded grandfathers. But in the most beautiful places there are traces of sorely tried mothers' tears, and under the profound, enigmatic words of the prophets or Christ are seen lines left by the awkwardly wielded pencils of men engaged in an earnest search.

I'm leaving. I long to be in the city again. Here there's nothing for me. The peacefulness of the church and the quiet of the forest weary me; I must have the chatter of the tavern and the hubbub of the street.

I have tried to lull myself into faith and romanticism, but it won't do. That ability is lost. Devoured by gray, busy rodents of reflection and the clammy, dank mildew of doubt. I must get back to my milieu. Romanticism belongs in the woods, contemporary man in the city.

Miss Berner shall be my solace. At least she's a woman. She has the maternal instinct. She will help, alleviate, relieve, soothe; in the end she might still perhaps put the ghosts to flight and make me a home where I could be happy.


## XII

Kr—ia, August

My first evening turned out to be rather wild, and around twelve it was clear to me I had to pay Mathilde a call.

She had moved.

An unpleasant, righteous-looking man came out in his underpants and barked in an inimitably Norwegian manner that here was no—cathouse, and that "the female in question" was presumably to be found in the Mangel building. Bang! The door shut! Not even good night.

I left. On the way I was overcome by melancholy.

I have no idea why. Because of the transience of all things or—?

And here I sit feeling blue. I'm all but hearing someone stir in the hallway.

Outside it's dark and autumnal. A wind has sprung up, a proper wind with rain, making doors and chimneys produce howling noises. If you emerged from the night for me now, you pale mermaid from the lower depths—.

Gone, gone—it all goes. Gone, for example, are those pleasant "burgundy evenings" at George Jonathan's.

He can't afford the time anymore. He's becoming more and more busy. Partly with public affairs, but especially with his business.

He works like a horse, speculating in houses, timberland, and so forth, while his partner "fattens himself with decedent estates and unjust lawsuits." George Jonathan intends "to get rich," you see; he comes "more and more to the conclusion that life is unlivable unless one can sleep in silken beds."—"But you are a democrat, aren't you?"—"Sure, a true democrat."—"Aha."—"There's a bad democratism that wants all people to be cotters; there's also a bad aristocratism that wants the majority to be cotters. We true democrats want as many as possible to be lords and masters."—"And to begin with, you want to be a lord and master yourself?"—"Sure."—"Even if it must be at the expense of others?"—"At the expense of stupidity, sure; those idiots *want*, after all, to pay dearly for their education. But when they have forked out a bit of money, they will say, 'Why are we paying for these attorneys and this legal business, anyway?'—and one fine day they are bound to discover that this lesson was worth the money, after all."—"Very clever."—"Sure."

"From now on," he said this evening to Dr. Kvaale and me (the most steady partakers of his "bachelor sprees"), "from now on I can only allow myself one rational hour in twenty-four; the rest must be devoted to the idiots. But to avoid turning into an idiot myself, I must have this opportunity to hear George Jonathan speak for an hour a day. You ought to provide me with this opportunity, milords. Therefore, if possible, show up here in my tent, University Street, at five o'clock every day. Mrs. Jonathan answers for the coffee, I for the liqueur."

We laughed and thanked him. Dr. Kvaale cracked a joke. "I too appreciate hearing George Jonathan speak," he yelped with his good-natured, ugly smile, "and so I'll come, as long as no other candidate for Gaustad claims my attention." (Dr. Kvaale, you see, is in the habit of maintaining that Jonathan suffers from megalomania.)

George Jonathan bowed. "You too, Gram?" he then asked.

"Sure, seeing that you serve such good liquor."

"All right."

"And these exceptional cigarettes—"

"*If you please.* So that's settled."

"Good night, you revolutionist in silk stockings!"

"Good night, you pricey tutor of idiots!"

"Goodbye, milords."

By the way, he won't make it. True enough, they use him to some extent, and he's not without esteem, but he'll be kept outside politically. He'll be forgotten when the quarry is to be divvied up.

He playacts quite well. But he doesn't act well enough. He's too odd for them and always will be. Too much Jonathan.

Already the many paintings and the exquisite comfort scare the Kristiania hucksters, when they step across his threshold. "Humph, I smell the blood of an Englishman—it smells positively European!"

The idiots aren't as stupid as he thinks. They have an instinct at least. They sense it very well: Attorney Jonathan with his stiff neck and his white hands is not a member of our flock. He has a chilly air about him in their eyes; they suspect that he mocks them in his heart. At a small semipolitical soirée I heard one of the leading master shoemakers say, "Jonathan is a very able man, but I don't know, I somehow can't get to feel any real confidence in him." A rural Storting deputy and lay preacher who was present said, "He's an intellectual aristocrat." They have an instinct for it.

## XIII

I'm overcome by emotion each time I take leave, for good, of a pair of old boots. These twins, which have followed me so silently and faithfully from birth on until now, carried and supported my person on all its ways, and that are now simply dismissed—without ceremony, without a pension, without a decoration—they become so strangely sad to me.

There is *Weltschmerz* in their downcast faces, reproach and bitterness in their drooping ears. "So *that* is the end of the story; *that* is the gratitude! Simply casting us aside, as you kick out old mistresses. And then exchanging us for those boring, fresh, soulless products from a shoe factory, that commodity that's nothing but a copy of the cobbler's last. . . ."

"True, true, my friends," I sigh. "But that's life. We even change our skin—our own earthly skin, which was once muscle tissue, nerves, blood, soul—simply throw it off as it gets worn out."

And with thoughtful gentleness I put the old, lopsided boots, which had become a part of my self, away in an attic, or some other place where they can be safely hidden. I can't give them away; it would be abominable to let the old faithful creatures change their soul, to have me traded for any old tramp or gandy dancer. But I don't want to see them again either. That would be like seeing ghosts—skeletons with broken skulls and large, empty eyes.

If it weren't for this hideous city life with its permanent homelessness—nomadic life without the freedom of the desert, without the freshness of the mountains—I think I would establish a shoe cemetery, a boot mausoleum. There I would gather, to stand side by side, arranged in sections and chapters, all the shoes I've worn out; and every Sunday I would go there and do my devotions. And when I died my sarcophagus would also be placed there; for what is a coffin other than our very last pair of boots?

"You don't have much respect for literature, Jonathan, do you?"

"Even less for the litterateurs. A writer seems to me to be like the young whippersnapper who steals out, his heart going pitapat and his cheeks looking pale, in order to make conquests on Karl Johan

Street. Sure, all's well; the girl smiles charmingly. He discovers that she's not an ordinary girl; quite the contrary, she's a lady, a woman, a real woman, someone who has fallen in love with him at first sight. He's favored by fortune, he finds himself in the midst of an adventure. And he's happy and enchanted, squeezes out all his pitiful seventeen-year-old wisdom for the woman and shows off his ounce of callow wit; for she must be educated! He's already making plans for how he's going to 'raise' her, develop her into something higher, a being who will be worthy of him. And she smiles and smiles and is extremely amenable. Meanwhile he is in her room, and the conquest is accomplished. Hmm, just dandy. But in the morning he steals out of her den with his tail between his legs, for now he knows that she was, after all, nothing but a tart, who come evening will smile just as graciously to the next idiot."

"So, that woman is the public?"

"Sure. Today she rejoices in your book, tomorrow she sheds tears over a putrid novelette, and the day after tomorrow she applauds a play in the theater that preaches the opposite of what you tried to instill in her. Surely, a *man* wouldn't propose to such a woman!"

I rather thought he was right. "However," I said, "for want of virgins, you know—"

"Yes, that's what the writers say, and I despise them for it."

Phooey, yes. Me too, all things considered. There won't be any novel, damn it. It's all nothing but plain rubbish.

Jonathan didn't like me today. I told him about the scenery up there, about the solitude, the old church, the farmers with their strange costumes and beautiful old language, until he said I was a wretched romantic.

"We won't have any of that," he said. "The church will be converted to a theater; the solitude will become an industrial town of half a million people, and the farmers with their old breeches and country dialect, and so on, will be replaced by intelligent people who speak English."

I berated our practical, boring age of reason, without imagination and without soul; he berated the "periods of reaction." "Those cowardly periods when people eat humble pie—!" he said. "To live outwardly, that's to live healthily!"—"Healthily, yes; but you may live outwardly for so long that all there is of soul and blood in you condenses and hardens, leaving nothing but skin and horn."

"However, it's the healthy periods that move people forward," he continued, "and we should be glad that we live in a time like ours. We now concern ourselves with questions that can be answered, and by answering one question after another we will in the end have made existence quite decent and elegant. That's the only thing that can be of interest to men. A man's pleasure is to act."

"And meanwhile the English aristocracy takes up Catholicism! And in Paris voices are raised against Emile Zola himself; they find that one side of life and of the spirit has been completely suspended during this time of health."

"*All right,*" George Jonathan said. "Those are the hysterics. When work has proceeded sensibly for a while and we have finally got to a point where we are almost ready to begin, then come these hysterics, wanting to know, first, about the immortality of the soul. We're familiar with that. For the time being we will have none of it. It's like when some chap shows up in the countryside and makes the farmers believe that they'll be going to heaven next Saturday. So they set about caring for their souls, and the field has to wait. We'll put off this business till after the spring planting, you understand. Don't you agree?"

"Oh sure. We shall have to put it off, all right!" (Shrug.)

He gave me a searching glance. I couldn't help smiling. Even freethinkers don't seem to suffer freethinkers in their midst, I thought to myself.

Miss Berner has been staying on the island of Hankø this summer; looks great. Tanned, fresh color, lively eyes, youthful movements; my making her over into an old maid during my stay up there merely proves that I was sick. Old! In Paris the women are young till they are forty and fifty (and that in a place where life is so strenuous!); it's all a matter of knowing how to keep fit. Miss Berner could certainly be a stylish young wife.

Everyone assures me that I, too, look fine. "Well, the mountain air really agreed with you!" Suddenly I, too, feel that I've gotten better. And here, where there are people and distractions (I'll lead a more active social life, for one), I should soon be able to get over my latest folly. I feel no urge to see her again. Rather fear. It would be a painful meeting.

"So she was really intelligent enough, the little one, to seek consolation for the privations of marriage. Wasn't it you who told me about it? About her many admirers?"

"Tut, tut," Mark-Oliv barked, somewhat alarmed. "I didn't mean it that way, you know; it doesn't seem to be very serious."

"No, of course not; only in all innocence, naturally. By the way, our young wives would benefit from learning a little French morality; it would ease their martyrdoms. And then we wouldn't have as many emancipated ones either."

"Emancipated? Hm, hm." Markus grew excited and gave a speech. He ended by expressing his deepest respect for Miss Holmsen—"sorry, Mrs. Ryen"—because she had so warmly espoused this important cause and everything connected with it: "She's buzzing about from morning till night, participates in everything and never saves her strength. She's a member of all sorts of committees and is the bellwether—hm, bell . . . cow, ah-ha-ha!—wherever something useful is to be started. She works so hard that she's destroying herself, goes to sleep on bromide every night, my wife says. And now she wants to come to me and learn to collect and prepare the different edible varieties of mushroom. So she may get to accomplish a lot of good in the service of her country. We must have the women with us, you see."

It came so abruptly and naïvely that I had to laugh. He delivered his lecture on the use and importance of mushrooms.

We were standing at our usual corner on Karl Johan Street and were about to part and go each to his own dinner table. Then comes, as if sent by fate, a buggy with three people in it, two ladies and a gentleman. I was staggered, hid behind Mark-Oliv's broad shoulders and thick mane of hair, and donned my pince-nez.

An elegant elderly gentleman of a somewhat wasted appearance; an elderly matronly woman, idiotically proud to be riding so elegantly; and then—she.

I wouldn't have believed it. Sallow, red-eyed, sagging, with an irritated, hysterical expression about her mouth; uncannily like the old lady beside her, but almost older; sickly, bored, jittery, overworked. I stood rigid with dismay.

And with a sudden desperate grief.

It's over. It's over. For all eternity. So it's this dreary, unpleasant sickroom creature that I have made over into a mermaid and a lioness in my fantasy. It's for *her* I have suffered all those foolish agonies and lain sleepless during so many a hallucinatory night.

I squeezed Mark-Oliv's hand without a word and made off. Cold and limp and shamefaced, stripped of my last dream; stripped, stripped. Nothing left anymore. It's worse to be stripped of a distressing dream than of a pleasant reality.

I would have given my life to see her as a bacchante, half-naked and buoyant in a high triumphal chariot, with roses in her hair and a scornful, lascivious smile, followed by ten admirers chained to her chariot, their tongues hanging out of their mouths.

This was the worst.

Not even my grief has been left to me.

Only an everlasting, gnawing question of conscience: Are you to blame for this?

But in my remorse a drop of flattered vanity. And in the vanity an atom of self-contempt.

## XIV

November

What hopeless weather. Rain and a howling tempest; a din of banging gates and tiles; shrieking chimneys, driving rain against the windowpanes. Weather to go down in, sink, fall into decay; drown—tumble into the Aker River on some pitch-dark night. Nobody would hear the death cry.

> The world watches
> a long funeral procession.
> Mephisto sings,
> like bells before the expedition:
>
> "Does nothing then remain
> for your soul to find rest in?
> Take heart, take heart, my friend,
> death you can believe in."

## XV

2 Jan. '87

I've been tippling nicely for a while; tea parties and Christmas balls. One has to put up with it.

I do have Miss Berner, after all. If it gets too sad, I can always strike up a conversation with her. She's not stupid. Thank God.

But this evening she couldn't help either. I was impossible. I was overwhelmed by boredom; the emptiness turned to sadness, to agony, to physical pain.

I had "a cold."

O-o-h, it's worse. It's worse than that. It's death and the abyss. It's amen and farewell. I'm not young anymore, I'm the old gentleman.

It is not me they are looking for, those little young things, eager to dance and to kiss. They first check if there should be one or another red-cheeked male opposite number to take up with, and only when nobody like that is to be found, or when he shows himself to be faithless and flirts with that bore Marie, do they come pouting to me. I get the sulky dances. And if they invite me to dance, I can tell from every word and every glance that they do so solely because of the above-mentioned male opposite number—to make him jealous. My time is over.

Oh, I know them. I was myself twenty once, intriguingly pale with a nice tiny mustache, blue-black and silky, just made for kissing. And one had one's little successes. But—stupid, of course. Didn't understand when they offered themselves heart and soul; had scruples, principles, conscience—cowardice. Cowardice, that's it. "Morality" is all made up by shy, scared guys who wouldn't dare lift a veil—and by gentlemen of my age.

Oh, what jackasses and sons of jackasses we are! There's one time when we could be happy, when we have illusions, warm blood, fresh nerves, and brains—all the conditions for enjoying life fully and wholly, for surrendering ourselves completely to the ecstasy of the moment, experiencing a bliss that is worth more than all the venerability of Methuselah. But there comes the moralist. Watch out! Think of your health! Think of old age! Live old to die young! And the poor young devil, who is shy enough already by nature, loses all his courage. Locks himself up in a furnished room and day-dreams. And sighs. And has a conscience.

Now it's too late. Now I can but weep over the wasted years of grace. Such things are always understood only afterward.

I'm "older" to such a degree that the foolishness of the young is already beginning to annoy me. I'm scandalized, offended in my modesty, *sittlich entrüstet*. Old bachelor's spleen, old man's grudge! It turns my stomach to see all these little dodges, all the lying and thievishness and lustful meanness they perpetrate, these young-sters in love, in order to get behind a door or into a corner and press up against each other. On my honor, they are capable of selling out their best friend, their father, their mother, so as to be able to nuz-zle one another with moist snouts for a brief moment, or to whisper sickening terms of endearment into one another's ears. I know all those tricks; and when I see their eyes as they secretly ponder wan-ton betrayal, those eyes are like thieves' eyes, yellow, sick—just like the eyes of a kleptomaniac when he has caught the gleam of a silver spoon.

When the devil grows old he enters a monastery. Awfully sensible; what else could the poor wretch do with himself?


*XVI*


Good, honest Brun is trying to worm out of me how much, exactly, he told me in confidence during that unhappy "bachelor evening." I make fun of him.

"You said your wife is a Xantippe," I say.

He turns red and solemn. "That I *cannot* have said! It's mean of you to say such things. For she's definitely the best person"—and so on.

" 'She can't even sew buttons on a vest,' you said."

"Oh, little things like that. Do you really believe you could find a marriage where they don't fight a little occasionally?"

"Uh, no. Honestly, Brun, you told me nothing other than what every happily married man relates over his third toddy."

"Oh my. You know . . . being married doesn't mean you aren't human; you may get annoyed, and there are frictions at times. When two people are going to live together, it is necessary that they have a rather resigned attitude; but don't imagine I would like to trade places with you"—and so on.

"Oh, no. Rather, I might trade places with you—by entering the married state myself. You haven't frightened me that much, no sirree!"

His whole figure looked like a sigh of relief, and he became sheer confidentiality.

"Yes, you should do that. One gets so damn tired of bachelor life. You know, in a marriage there can also be bad times; you go around being enemies, bicker over a trifle, even perhaps imagine that you're completely fed up with each other. You will have to be prepared for that. Take it from me, the worst thing is all those dumb, stupid illusions: marriage should absolutely be a paradise, and all that. I have to admit I often think it's rather horrid and unbearable; it can be really painful. But then you see how quietly brave she is about it; she suffers but doesn't let on, and she manages all those tedious everyday matters calmly and smoothly. Then she suddenly comes out with some touching little trait or other that shows she would still like to be friends with this sourpuss of hers. Well, one fine day the gloom is suddenly gone, and we sit with our arms around each other's necks, quite surprised, and feel it's just like the time we were newly engaged! Yeah."

He looked touchingly happy. There was still a gleam in his eyes from the last reconciliation scene.

"And," he continued, "you feel so safe and secure and nicely set up. After all, you know her, and know how thoroughly nice and good and trustworthy she is when you get right down to it, and know that she knows her husband and is familiar with his faults and shortcomings but loves him all the same. . . . Well, these are some things you'll never get to experience as a bachelor."

He's probably right. It's a question of trust. That great, restful confidence.


Pastor Løchen interests me. So it is still quite possible to have faith, and to find rest in this faith?

If only one could "become as a child again." "The Christian is not bored," I read somewhere. Great God, to live without being bored! I just can't understand.

But I suffer from my privations, stripped of dreams and illusions, and feel cold in the certain "realization" that nothing can be known. This *aeterna nox* can be borne rather smartly as long as one is young and has one's hopes intact, but if one gets to be old and alone it's full of anxiety and ghosts. The worst of it is that everything is so indifferent; when you're through with the little girls, there isn't much left. Nothing helps. It's all *eins Bier;* there isn't even any difference between good and evil. At this point I see only one question that might interest me, namely, how one can die in the best possible way.

"The truth"? Does there exist on earth anything more indifferent than "truth," as long as we know that nothing can be known? And if one cannot have the very best, one resigns oneself to the next best. If I cannot have truth, I'll be grateful for—*peace.*

Strange how this love seems to have been blotted out. I've turned so cold, so cold. I just ache a bit deep down, where the dream had its roots.

If there was any love to begin with. That's the question, I'm afraid. It was probably only "Pan." The great sensuality.

Poor girl. Now she struggles with women's liberation and other works of charity. It must be for her what the goblet is for me, a narcotic. *So leben wir, so leben wir, so leben wir alle Tage—.*

I visit Løchen fairly often, and people are already beginning to marry me to Miss Berner.

She knows; she is sufficiently familiar with the world and Karl Johan Street for that. And since she still shows the same unchanging kindness toward me, I suppose she can't be particularly opposed to it. She would be capable of saying yes if I offered her my hand for a "marriage of convenience."

And why not?

I have nothing against her, and I trust her. Pull yourself together this one time, Gabriel; bring yourself safely into port. She'll be a presentable spouse and wise friend, and an indulgent wife. It's what you need. Peace, security, a good home, settled conditions; oh, it's high time. At long last to belong somewhere.

She has a remarkable knack for handling me. And it's precisely that which we want when we marry: to have someone who knows how to handle us, knows how to tune the harp of our nerves. It's the bent of her own harmonious nature, the way it communicates itself. Her clear chord awakens all that exists of tunefulness in its vicinity, to consonance and harmony.

Her being religious attracts me too. It has an old-fashioned relish of something trustworthy and reassuring: "When I lay me down to sleep, angels will my spirit keep"—that's something other than ghosts and *spirits*. Such an inherited family faith is like the anchor of a reeling ship; God only knows, but she might be able to pray me to rest someday when the great terrors come.

This peaceful, comforting thought of your own home—it tempts me like a lighted window in the blackness of the winter night, luring and attracting and bewitching the lonely, half-dead wayfarer.

I don't give a damn about romance and young chicks anymore. I want to rest and dream at the domestic fireside.

Taste, cheer, comfort; an old grandfather clock and an old Bible—and in the corner of the living room a small piano where all those thousands of soft melodies are slumbering, and all those chords that bring peace to the soul.

I *will* get married.

## XVII

Happy that person whose friend won't eventually come around with a bond which he asks him to endorse.

Enemies are bad, but friends are worse. What does he want to use me for? is my one thought when someone comes and says he's my friend.

This dreadful struggle for existence makes it impossible even to be friends. We are compelled to utilize one another, use, misuse, deceive one another, and as soon as we reach thirty we don't believe a single person anymore.

Anyway, if I really were to get married, I would myself have to look up old friends bond in hand. My finances are in the wildest disarray. She has some money, people say; but no one, after all, wants to act like a bum and sponge off his fiancée.

Besides, who knows? In this solid country every wealthy person does as a rule turn out, on closer scrutiny, to own—just the clothes he's wearing.

I could risk being answered: alas, there may not be much left of that wealth. Perhaps she has—like me—an old aunt at whose death she has a chance to inherit 6,000 kroner, provided that the old pious fraud at whose place the above-mentioned aunt lives won't persuade her on her deathbed, with prayers and supplications, to change her will to his—the pious fraud's—own advantage.

"Well, well! You can always try!" Dr. Kvaale yelps. "You're unhappy as a bachelor, and the experiment might be worthwhile. You have the noose as the last resort in any case."

On the negative side, everyone is right—even the theologians.

As Løchen says: concerning "the guarantees for the reliability of knowledge," the situation is wretched all along the line. Philosophy itself, whose task should essentially be to procure this guarantee, depends on an unprovable supposition, namely, the extremely risky assumption that we can know something in the first place.

What is red? *That is the question.* The answer can't be found until the brain has become transparent to itself—an eye that is capable of looking into itself.

In the darkness that now prevails—after all, we cannot get behind our own consciousness—our only hope may still be to "feel our way" toward truth, sense it, follow our instinct—like the insect with its feelers.

These unpleasant poets, especially these Frenchmen, wretched, effete characters who stuff us with all their abominable hypochondria and all their spleen and spinal tuberculosis and old *vérole,* which they dress up with big names and call experience of the world, realism, pessimism—I simply hate them.

I'm going to get married and read Marie.

Jonathan promises that existence will gradually become "quite stylish"—if we'll be patient and moderate and self-denying and always only occupy ourselves with answering "the questions that can be answered."

I can well understand that people get tired of all this moderation. There are forces and exigencies within us that insist on more.

"Happiness! Happiness!" they demand. "As much happiness as possible," replies the Englishman.—"Yes, but we don't want that," they answer; "we demand *happiness!*"—"Well, well, as much as possible," the Englishman repeats. If they finally get mad and say: "Then rather unhappiness *sans phrases!*" I can quite understand.

Patience is a petit-bourgeois virtue. I'm tired of resigning myself.

Fanny never loved me. It was nothing but the twenty-five-year-old woman's hysterical need of a man.

Hence my coldness. At close quarters I was as indifferent as before a block of marble. Had she loved me, she would have carried me away; only vis-à-vis a cold woman does a man maintain his equanimity.

Behind Miss Berner's controlled composure there's more genuine warmth than behind Fanny's fake love.

*(Champagne mood.)* Old silver jewelry makes me go crazy. I would give ten years of my life for a collection of old brooches and filigree articles. Editor Klem gave the customary *soirée dansante* on his wife's birthday—"my wife, you see, is something quite unique"—

and there Miss Berner was wearing such a truly elegant old silver ornament, which had traveled to Norway via Lübeck four generations ago, she said. Simply gorgeous! I fell in love with her because of it; I'll marry her just to become the owner of that brooch.

Old filigree brooches—and old china—and old Bibles—and old churches—and old violins—and old wine . . . and young girls; young, elegant wives, too, why not!

> Lovely is the earth,
> glorious is God's heaven,
> fair is the pilgrim souls' blessed throng.
> From all the beautiful
> kingdoms on the earth,
> we go to—God knows where—with song.

This evening I was within an ace of proposing.

It happened so naturally in the course of conversation; the question was already on the tip of my tongue: and how about the two of us, miss—?

But at that very moment she turned her head so that I suddenly could see—thought I could see—the incipient old maid's wrinkle at the corner of her mouth.

The question faded away.

Incidentally, was she her usual self this evening? A couple of times I had a vague feeling of being neglected.

I have to pull myself together: now or never. No petty considerations anymore. A home is beckoning to me; a nice, quiet, cultivated home where peace reigns, where there's harmony in everything, in the moods of the soul as well as in the colors of the rooms. After all, it's not a mistress I'm asking for, just an elegant wife and a cultured companion. And Miss Berner is the very one I could picture in that role.

## XVIII

10 April '87[*]

Yes, Miss Berner has been different toward me lately. And this evening when I showed up at her place after two days' absence I was told that she had departed. For Bergen. There were "friendly regards" to me and to "all the other excellent friends" in Kristiania.

Mrs. Løchen (who is her sister and not her cousin) was happy and almost moved. "Just imagine—it's truly a whole novel—her youthful love was widowed some time ago, after living in Bordeaux all these years; but Elisa was not forgotten. Finally, he returned home to Bergen to see what was going on, and one fine day Elisa receives a telegram: 'I'm waiting for you in Bergen, come if you have ever really thought about me.' And, naturally, Elisa didn't hesitate a moment. Poor thing, she has probably always had him in her thoughts."

I sat there gaping rather stupidly; at last I burst out laughing. Mrs. Løchen looked at me in surprise, offended, and the visit turned out rather short.

Oh, those women, those women!

She married for love, despite everything. So this thing about "marriage of convenience" was merely an "emergency theory," invented, like all such emergency and resignation theories, for help and solace in evil days, when that which she had put her trust in gave way and failed. And love prevails and wins out right along, despite all bachelor reflections and old-maid theories, despite all

---

[*]All editions of Garborg's novel that I have consulted use an incorrect chronology from this point on. The present entry is dated 1886, whereas the context clearly indicates it must be 1887. All the necessary corrections have been made.—TRANS.

philosophic wisdom and all bitter experiences; and people keep slaving away under its yoke till kingdom come, making fools, jackasses, and knuckleheads of themselves.

But those who refuse to slave under its yoke become even bigger fools and even bigger jackasses. Now I'd better do what my dear departed father did: find myself a young girl from Voss, with whom I can do the dance of death; for with a woman a man goes to wrack and ruin, and without a woman he cannot live.

For thus it was determined by the wisdom of nature: that the former should be miserable but the latter worse, so that all can be unhappy and sigh together in pain until the deliverance, when this earthly dump shall be consumed by fire.

I had become accustomed to the thought of a home by now; I almost believed I was safely in port and that this long and difficult and dreary bachelor voyage was approaching its end.

Under what cursed star was I born? Or was there a bad fairy at my cradle who said that, sure enough, I would "reach" what the good fairies had promised me, but that the wish would always slip out of my hand when I tried to catch it?

Why must I be such a half-man? Why this constantly crippled will, this lack of ability to seize the right moment, this paralysis of the spirit? Why must I always turn away like a fool from the banquet of life, because I can never make up my mind to take a seat before all the places are occupied?

I give up. I don't have the strength anymore. It has been decided in God's council that I shall crumble away in loneliness. Drink my regular quanta and talk to myself. Tumble into the lake some drunken night, or die in my bed from some attack. Nobody is present who can fetch the doctor; the death is noted only two days later.

Then they break down the door and find me with glazed eyes, wide-open with fear.

So I just settle down patiently on my stool in the department and go the way of all born copying clerks. Turn yellow like an old tax collector's shop. Sit every evening in my corner at the Grand Café with a paper in my hand and pretend I'm keeping up with things, pretend that I'm alive. Why not? There are many who slink their way through life in that fashion. I'm not much good for anything else, and so I'll have to be good enough for that. It is, in a way, a peaceful thought: when I give up living, I won't get involved anymore in these situations that I can never master.

Take a rest, citizen; it's well earned.

## XIX

June '87

The time is gone when I drank to feel careless. Now I drink because I couldn't care less. Life is a continual refusal.

But it won't do. This accursed summertime with its warmth, and all that boring light, is no good for exercises of that sort.

In reality, each season has its vice. Alcohol reigns in the dark months. In the light season women do.

Only virtue was not assigned by God a particular month in our calendar.

I cannot find anybody to replace Mathilde. Where the hell can I pick up some gallows humor again?

All things considered, I have lately been meanly solemn.

Up, my soul, pluck your strings! "Sons of Norway"; "Last summer I tended goats"; "Smiling hopes"; "Ole Høiland has escaped"—.

## XX

September

The circles to which Miss Berner gave me access are holding on to me, which is fine. A bit of social life bucks you up, and it dulls the mind. To be sure, the people I meet there mean next to nothing to me. But I don't have anything in particular against them either. They represent a good average. Solid principles and first-class paunches. Now and then a female who puts in an appearance. Nice, fine, boring people.

But how long will I be able to stand it? It's an effort. To go there and pretend to be part of it, pretend to be interested—strictly speaking, I don't think I ever knew before what indifference is. It's not just unconcern. Raised to its proper power, indifference is a veritable agony.

I no longer distinguish between the different parties and social gatherings (balls included); it's all the same fog with shadows in it. When you can't manage to fall in love anymore, there remains in the end only one great task: to suppress the yawn. And that is best done by means of alcohol; over the champagne you may even get animated. Crack jokes and talk about literature. Then, when perhaps you're finally all steamed up, the affair is over. You take the inevitable elderly lady home, compensate yourself for a lost evening by some great folly or other, and then reel home to your den, tired and nauseous, at the first or second cockcrow.

And when you get home, everything is cold and deserted and empty and dark, like a wolf's lair, like an owl's hole. Ten times sooner a curtain lecture; in any case it would end with a kiss. And even the angriest curtain lecture only means, after all, that someone has been waiting for you, that there exists someone to whom your *Leben und Treiben* is of interest, a human heart that takes part in your life. Oh, this perpetual fear and terror: to be a stranger everywhere.

It's five o'clock. Good night, world. From outside come sounds of footsteps already. Lucky people! They have slept ever since ten o'clock and are now on their way to doing something. Something useful, something that makes sense. Oh, if only one were a factory worker. What vile, loathsome creatures we parasites on society are.

Go to bed, damn it!

"So nothing came of this marriage of yours?" Kvaale yelped this evening on the way home from Jonathan.

"No," I said. "I thought it over. That is, I thought it over too long."

"I see," Kvaale said. "Maybe instead of expressing my sympathy, I should congratulate you?"

"Well, as you like."

"You have lived a little too much," he continued after a while, "and she—hasn't lived at all, most likely. That sort of thing is always dangerous. A husband in that position usually goes *ad undas*. A fairly decent mistress—I mean one who's tolerably discreet—is the most sensible thing for men of your sort."

"Yes, if only I could find someone I didn't feel excessively indifferent about."

"Aha," he mumbled.

"No, no, don't get me wrong. . . . I simply mean that I'm not yet quite finished with my bachelor sentimentality."

"One should know how to arrange one's life in such a way that there will be a reasonable ratio between pleasure and pain," I once said to Fanny.

She replied, "Well, women can't anyway. We have to take life as it is arranged for us by all sorts of other people."

She was right—not just as far as women are concerned. She was absolutely right. It's always the child who's right, the wise man who talks nonsense. What an empty phrase anyway: "arrange one's life"!

No, life is arranged for us—by all sorts of other people. It goes with each of us as the Lord described to Simon, "Another shall gird thee, and carry thee whither thou wouldest not." I still remember how these words filled me with terror when I read them in my collection of Bible stories as a child. They weighed on my chest like asthma, I couldn't breathe. "Carry thee whither thou *wouldest not!*"

Not only is life "arranged for us," but we are a given entity to ourselves. I do not know who created me, but I do know that he who created me predestined me in all possible respects. He set such and such a definite proportion between ability and will, between desire and strength; he put such and such desires of such and such an intensity into my blood, and for master of these desires he installed an ego which had precisely this or that definite ability to concentrate on its decisions.

Then he set the mechanism running, and the longer it runs, the more it becomes what it was planned to be. What from the beginning was weak, gets worn and becomes weaker; all the more overpowering does that become which from the beginning was strong. And the whole thing runs more and more one-sidedly, until finally a spring breaks, or one of the axles.

Try as I might, I cannot change the fundamental relations that constitute the individual G. Gram; my "will" is itself, you see, dependent on these fundamental relations. To be Gabriel Gram means: not to will to be anything else than Gabriel Gram. I see my shortcomings, but my will is also determined by these very shortcomings; accordingly it is not able to will beyond them. Through powerful suggestions it may be pushed to make an attempt, but with the following upshot: the same mistakes in new forms. The converted villain is and always will be a villain, only now he performs his villainous tricks in the name of God.

If I am so morbidly inclined from the outset, so disharmonious in my basic system—nerves, brain, spinal cord, ganglia—that everything turns into suffering for me; if, that is, I lacked from the very outset the pig's and the philistine's calm, devout disposition, then I can't become a philistine or a pig however gladly I "would." In the last resort, you see, I am not capable of willing it. I can admire, I can envy George Jonathan. But to want to be him—no, I can't.

And so life for me becomes suffering—notwithstanding all possible attempts I might make to "arrange" things.

"Suffering is also pleasure," Jonathan says; "it is to life what salt is to food!" That may be true for the healthy person, whose sufferings are consequently neither particularly deep nor especially long-lasting—passing squalls, more or less violent, that only make the ensuing sunshine that much more beautiful. But it's not true for him to whom suffering is the norm. Not for him who is made in such a way that he can enjoy happiness only negatively, i.e., he feels the loss when it vanishes but not the happiness when it is present; that is to say, not for him whose life oscillates between boredom and a sense of loss. To him suffering is not salt with food, but wormwood in his cup; it's not just bitter in itself but also changes the joy to bitterness.

"A reasonable proportion between pleasure and pain," when the pain = pain and pleasure too = pain! Isn't it remarkable that a grown-up human being can say something like that?

## XXI

New Year's Day 1888

This perpetual *Einerlei*. This unchanging, uneventful grayness, which makes me go around tormenting myself with my stupidities of yesterday and the day before yesterday because nothing ever happens that marks a break, with period and finale and a new chapter, giving absolution for, and oblivion to, yesterday and the day before yesterday by forcing everybody to think of something new! I can understand someone who goes off and commits murder simply to consign to oblivion the little bit of tactlessness he was guilty of the other day; and more than once I have wished for the end of the world so that my stupidities could be destroyed at the same time.

What is the good of a year coming to an end? It ends but is still there, like the memory of a death.

Sins can be forgiven. But stupidities! What God should forgive them? They can only be forgiven by yourself, and you yourself have no forgiveness. Only forgetfulness. But forgotten stupidities are like sunken corpses, one fine day they float up again. How many a time have I not suddenly stopped in my tracks, groaned aloud and bitten my tongue: I just bumped into such a corpse, risen to the surface of the waters of recollection—an old, forgotten stupidity that suddenly lies there laughing at me with grinning teeth.

There are some people I wish were dead. What harm have they done to me? They once saw me behaving stupidly or meanly. Every time I hear that such a tiresome witness has gone to kingdom come, a stone is lifted from my heart. If people knew what favor they do each other by dying!

Damn it all, why did I have to take that glass too many! In those surroundings, under those circumstances! Scandal *vis-à-vis* a whole party—to think that I abused Pastor Løchen in that vulgar fashion! A populist agitator's chatter, like a workers' association: "Not silver, not gold, not copper in your belts"—bah! Stupidities, stupidities; forget, never see him again!

George Jonathan is right. First you systematically ruin your nerves; and when you've taken sick, you turn pessimist and say, The world is a desert. And since the world is a desert, there must be a paradise, because otherwise life would be meaningless.

But since this logic is somewhat dubious, you need some help to be able to believe. The only help that can be obtained is, naturally, other people's beliefs. Then you hire clergymen and police, and suddenly the whole world believes in paradise. "But what the whole world believes must be true, after all!" the sick person says.

And thus, by dint of their sickness, they control the whole world. And if someone looks at their weft with healthy eyes and says, "But there isn't any weft, the emperor has no clothes!" they shake their heads and say, "Out with him, he's not serious."

The sick, pugh!

We paralyze all humankind with our helplessness. Our hypochondria is to pass for wisdom, our hallucinations are to be revelations.

We sick ones have only one choice, namely, to die. The world belongs to the healthy, the proud, those with courage to face life.

I sit down with my cup of poison and hasten the process. A toast to life! *Pereant* the sick!

"You always forget one thing, Jonathan: if people get to be that happy, they're going to be bored to death! If we are to endure life, we must be slightly miserable. A hungry man doesn't easily kill himself; he's constantly hoping that he'll still have a chance to eat his fill. But the rich man, who lived every day in joy and gladness, naturally went to hell then and there. Boredom on the one hand, and a bad conscience on the other—."

"He wouldn't have gone to hell if he had worked, say, three to four hours every day," Jonathan said. "That's the issue, gentlemen. Work—in full earnest, not sport; not the way you work in the department—no, work as the blacksmith works, or the farmer, to produce, create, form, be an artist, be God, creator and slave a few hours every day. That's the only way to keep our power of enjoyment healthy, and that's the only way to keep our conscience in good condition."

Dr. Kvaale nodded. "Why, if it weren't for your idea of work," he said, "I wouldn't give a penny for your future society."

Hmm, work . . .

Very reasonable in many ways probably, but—this occurred to me afterward—who, then, will have white hands?

A long white hand is the most beautiful thing in existence. Who will have fine hands when all people will be standing in the smithy every day?

This idea about work is sheer homespun. I don't like it.

Make-believe. Putting on an act. That's the only bit of amusement a cultivated person has.

I get up, drink a cup of coffee—cold—wash and take a cold shower. Fresh underwear from top to toe. My most elegant suit. Spotlessly clean collar, bluish-white cuffs. Top hat, gloves, pince-nez, cane. Then to the barber, for my shave and coiffure; on bigger occasions to the public baths, where one subjects oneself to a thorough ablution, with a cold shower on top of it. Then breakfast with schnapps at the Grand. Afterward one lights a cigarette, steps out onto Karl Johan Street, and bows to the chaste ladies.

Who would believe, seeing this smart, elegant gentleman, that this same smart, elegant gentleman sat in a shady restaurant drinking port with a certain Marguerite at twelve o'clock last night?

The chaste ladies greet him with great respect.

"Sounding brass and a tinkling cymbal." I lie here reading a German optimist who proves that life is good and existence *sittlich* and the future a rose garden, and ennui lies heavy on my nerves, like paralysis, and rummages in my stomach as a dull, dull anxiety.

*

A pity that Dr. Kvaale should be so busy, otherwise I would spend more time with him. But he has "the most secure practice that exists": he's a specialist in venereal diseases.

Odd fellow.

I can't get him to talk about anything else than general questions—he even talks politics. He is, all in all, a sensible man. He gets along well with George Jonathan. His principal interest is "this thing called love," and he's extremely "Bohemian"—if not exactly as naïve as those fellows.

But with all his general interests he's as different from Jonathan as anyone could be. In reality, he is more akin to me. That there is more to him than meets the eye I understood only when I discovered that he has his "periods." They come with shorter or longer intervals; they do not last long, roughly three to four days. Then he's not available to anybody, he lies at home and is "sick"—that is, drinking. And when a man like him succumbs to that sort of thing, then you stop dead, afraid, as though face to face with something ominous. It means that behind all those curtains, in the innermost corner, there sits a lonely soul half-insane with fear and trembling, dizzy from staring down into the eternal darkness.

> The first thing you have to do, Sir,
> is die apace,
> when a lovely lass no more can stir
> your heart ablaze,

sang Thorvald Lammert at this evening's concert.

> For then it's over for the good scout,
>
> .  .  .  .  .  .  .  .  .  .  .  .  .
>
> for then life's flame is quite burned out,
> just ashes remain;
> just ashes remain—.

It won't stop buzzing in my ear. Ashes, ashes; die, die. . . . A dream of dust under the coffin lid. Mourning rolls on muffled drums. Vapid, flat—mush. Nothing left. Into the ground, into the ground; a big hole and earth on top, lots of earth—he smells already.

Young and lean-limbed, the white nymph skips about among fauns and goat's feet in lusty dance; half hidden behind the forest green and the morning mists, she appears to me in glimpses as she pops out of the dark to vanish again, pops out to vanish. I can see the soft curves of her lithe limbs without going out of my mind, without swooning away in Pan-intoxicated enthusiasm and ecstasy, dazed, my zest for life kindled. I can see her sweet, dangerous smile, sad and sensual, wanton and deep, without being mad about kisses or sick with longing for a wedding and wild embraces. What am I then, other than a bag of skin or a dead sheep? A deep hole and earth on top, much, much earth on top, he smells already. Oh Lord, he smells already.

How wonderful, lovely, terrible you are, you innocent self-contradiction we call woman!

Maternal womb, eternally sucking up and bringing forth; all-devouring and all-generating; life and death; the sea. The diabolic and the celestial in one person. The sinner and the mother, Eve and Madonna.

You have withdrawn from my life, and therefore it is now an emptiness and not worth living. My strings are broken, the fire put out. I adore you and hate you, but my adoration disgusts you, and you laugh at my hate, which is one of impotence. I will ask Dr. Kvaale for a sufficient amount of morphine; my life is ashes.

The more our life turns out to be a failure, the more we believe in the beyond. Fanny was right. If the first part of the novel makes no sense, we *demand* that there be a second part with an explanation.

If only it helped.

## XXII

1 May

*("Spring mood.")* A chill in my soul.

Cold, weakness, nausea of the soul; figuratively speaking, a bad taste in my mouth. Distaste. Nothing but distaste. General disgust; *taedium generale.* I don't have any better name for it than a psychic cold—a cold that has attacked the soul.

## XXIII

June

Cerebral affections. Headache and insomnia.

I take a walk in the afternoon and go to bed tired. Unpleasantly tired, tired in my nerves, listless. I actually feel sleepy, my eyelids close by themselves, and in a while they are so heavy and squeezed shut that I can't open them without an effort. They sleep on their own. But inside I'm wide awake.

Some weary thought or other starts gnawing at my brain, quietly and intermittently, like a mouse in a corner. Several such thoughts come, gnaw a bit and disappear, come and go. Finally one or another gets a foothold. Stays there, gnawing methodically and patiently; I soon realize the room won't be quiet for the next few hours.

Some daytime impression, some idea or other from my inner life, has gained control. I suddenly find myself in an argument, with Pastor Løchen say, or with George Jonathan; I become heated, eager, irate; my words glow and hit home, I argue confidently and brilliantly, more and more penetratingly, more and more convincingly, until my nerves are all on fire and my body lies shaking between the sheets. Or I remember that this or that good friend has offended me, that he has been unconscionable, meddling in my private affairs in a manner that I, as a man with some self-respect, cannot permit, and, in addition, that I gave him a piece of my mind apropos of that. I then begin to draft a letter in which I explain myself, sort out the items for him; I become more and more excited, in the end overexcited. I realize more and more clearly how I have been wronged, how crudely that well-meaning but limited fellow misinterpreted and mistreated me; I recite Knigge to him, with a vengeance. It's a kind of intoxication of the nerves, which for the time being feels quite agreeable; I'm interested, absorbed, and feel superior, noble, intelligent. I deliver myself body and soul to be harried at will by these rodents in my head—until I'm so wideawake that my eyelids open as well, at any rate one, and I see the light of morning, quiet and gray, come in through my windows. Then I'm interrupted in my reflections; I'm surprised and annoyed that I've been in bed so long. The specters in my head vanish. I feel that I've become nervous, unpleasantly nervous; there is a pressure in my temples, in the crown and in the back of my head. I'm in despair that yet another night has been ruined; I jump up and empty a glass of water with cognac or take a sleeping pill, go to bed again and feel my overtired, confused thoughts floating away in a sort of soft, woolly enjoyment. So I get a moment's rest anyway. But I don't fall asleep, not now anymore; after my rest there comes a long, irksome hour of nerves. I roll from side to side in an oppressive, woolly-warm malaise, in perspiring uneasiness; my skin and all prickle and itch and my head aches, and I'm tortured by a kind of nervous burning in my legs. I can't find rest for a second, twist and toss, behaving like someone with a fever. Suddenly a bird says something outside; he doesn't get an answer and says it once more, but still gets no answer and becomes mute. A carriage rattles down the street and disappears at the corner; footsteps are heard and die away. My ideas begin to seem faraway, to double and run together.

Then I don't know any more; the last thing I saw was something white somewhere, which was about to catch fire, I think. It fades away—my afflicted brain has found rest.

That damned Kvaale who won't give me chloral anymore!


## XXIV

25 August

Passed over yet once more.

I'll sit there as a copying clerk all my life long. Hidden in my corner. So hidden that even God will forget me.

What the reason is? I'm not enthusiastic enough, most likely. Not interested enough in the good cause. I belong to the lukewarm ones. But he who is lukewarm will be spewed out of every party's mouth. Passed over by the Conservative as well as the Liberal minister. For it is clear that, if a man is lukewarm, he lacks the correct belief that we alone—the Conservatives alone, respectively the Liberals—are the saviors of the fatherland; if he had the faith, he would join us. He who's lukewarm is dubious. The idiots scent the scoffer; the sheep, the wolf.

And besides I haven't been careful enough in the choice of people to associate with. I have followed my own taste, forgetting about those "higher considerations." At the time of the old cabinet I was dubious because I had "Liberal connections," now I'm looked at askance for the opposite reason. It's not enough to associate with the sheep, it's required that you associate with them *exclusively;* even a single connection in the camp of the wolves arouses a bad feeling among the sheep. He's not safe, we can't trust him; who knows whether his sheep's hide is genuine, or whether a wolf might not be lurking behind it.

Oh human rabble! As if life weren't sad enough as it is, we do what we can to torment one another even more. The sole possibility of escape is to shut oneself up.

But this sole escape is at the same time certain ruin.

Though . . . It would be a different matter if you had an occupation, a work to complete, something sensible to do. This could be the time to try with "the novel!" It would take lots of energy, of course, but—.

In any case, there is no other way I could make something of myself.

## XXV

October '88

*(After the ball.)* All of two infatuations.

Sure. One was really nice, you bet. Blond, buxom, childish-demonic: Gretchen. The other more of a soubrette. Brown-eyed and bright. Tomorrow they'll be forgotten.

God give them a good marriage!

One gets to be so awfully miserable from this sort of life. Everything becomes so indifferent to me that I could die.

What else could it lead to anyway, the kind of life I have led? First those youthful affairs which inflicted the initial damage and the basic neurasthenia. Then this unclean life with more or less depraved women. In addition, alcohol and nicotine poisoning.

In the end there is nothing left of the whole man except a bunch of worm-eaten bones in a yellow, flabby skin. It was surely a correct instinct that kept me away from Fanny.

God, how right they are, those moralists who warn young girls against dissolute men. There should be public inspections of males every year, and all those customers who can do nothing but damage the stock and cause their wives to become hysterical should be strangled and thrown into a lime pit. Incidentally, this is something I've heard from Dr. Kvaale, I believe. I don't have a single thought that passes muster anymore; my brain is preserved in spirits.

*(The optimist's dream.)* A well-developed species of monkey spread at the beginning of the Tertiary (?) across large portions of Africa and found at last a climate so favorable and conditions of life so beneficial that after a few thousand years had passed it produced an offspring with one more brain convolution. When, after ten to twelve thousand years, this convolution had ingrained itself and become a species characteristic—lo and behold, there was the Bushman, the first so-called human being.

By means of that new brain convolution, the Bushmen were able to throw stones and the like. Furthermore, they had the idea of protecting themselves from the sun and other enemies by cunningly constructed caves, etc. Owing to this superiority of theirs, in the course of time they pushed their forefathers back into the woods and seized the best territories for themselves. They spread across the largest and most healthful parts of Africa and finally found, up near the Mediterranean, conditions of life that favored a higher development of the brain to such a degree that, after a period of twenty thousand years and by a remarkably lucky coincidence, there appeared yet another brain convolution in their heads, and look—there was the Negro.

The latter supplanted the Bushman through his superior intelligence, spread across all of Africa and even moved into Asia. Here the race found such favorable conditions that, after a few millennia, it had developed another brain convolution: the Mongolian had come into being.

This new type spread out in Asia and produced in the course of time new variations; the most recent and best developed of these were the Semites and the Aryans.

The latter pushed into Europe and found there so favorable conditions of life that they were driven further ahead on the path of evolution. In the course of a few thousand years they produced civilized man—the Greek and the Roman. Some three to four thousand years later, the latter engendered, through evolution and through crossbreeding with other variations and types, the modern European.

And now, by means of his vastly superior intelligence, the latter is in the process of pushing back all his ancestors and spreading over the entire planet. Gradually, through continued evolution, continued crossbreeding between related races, as well as under the influence of ever more favorable external circumstances, he will produce a type that is just as superior to us as we are to the Bushmen.

This all but divine race will understand what we, at our Bushman level, still do not understand: how to transform the earth into a paradise.

*(The pessimist's postscript.)* But then the sun dies.

## XXVI

Sunday forenoon

A black-edged letter: Uncle Berent has died.

"Suddenly." "Unexpectedly." And already buried; all very brief.

Poor devil. Good, honest, deficient in energy, full of zest for life—like me; did nothing else in his youth but strut around and go on little sprees—like me. Became soft in the head and lay vegetating for a decade or so—like me??—and finally died and was buried.

They were in a hurry to get him underground, I see. Why? Well, nobody was holding on to him in any case. Just get rid of him—at last. The old wreck. That repulsive old animal, a bachelor gone to pot.

Poor devil.

All people said in my youthful days that I resembled him. Of course I resemble him. Will I still refuse to disburden my fellow humans of my presence, I wonder. I know, after all, how I'm going to end up.

I don't dare stay home today. I see this limp dead ghost hanging on every wall, dangling like a dirty towel. If only he won't visit me!

The snowstorm out there howls like dogs smelling a corpse; it's my family flocking here from every imaginable churchyard to the north, south, east, and west, with him at the head. Right behind him I see my rheumatic father, and behind him, in a whitish dwindling row, grandfathers and great-grandfathers, grandmothers and great-grandmothers, stupidly staring and adding their squeaking voices to the great song of the dead. I'm not afraid of them. I belong to that flock; I'll come shortly. I'll just do a wake for my uncle first.

Come, old boy; come comrade. I'm not afraid. You're happier than I, you're over the hump. If you really hanged yourself—I sense something of the sort behind this terse letter—then you have my respect; come and teach me to follow you also in that—the only sensible thing you ever did in your whole life. Peace be with you, my brother in sin and sorrow, the next to the last shoot from a dying stock. "We are through, we should make room." All right, I'm coming, I'm coming; some day, for sure, I'll come too. So long and good night. Peace be with you!

Peace be with you all. Go ye home to bed, each in his or her churchyard. It's not my fault that I didn't amount to much; it's your fault. But I forgive you. Ye could not help it, either. Good night. Sleep well.

Whoo, how cold and sad it is here. Out! Out and see people!

\*

Dr. Kvaale would surely give me morphine. But do I really want him to be in on it—?

Dear me, is it really worthwhile to take the trouble! Death will come anyway. Well, it would be a way of getting rid of this fear of the d.t.'s.

As yet, though, no fear! Kvaale only requires constant walks, lots of exercise in the open air. But—with the winter season and those dark evenings, I feel slightly nervous and ill at ease taking walks alone.

Incidentally, poor Uncle Berent doesn't frighten me. I see him dangling there constantly—nodding and bobbing, dozing off with a rather satisfied smile in his round mug. He's just going to take a nice long snooze, he said. The situation doesn't seem to trouble him particularly.

Anyway, I barely knew him.

This won't do any longer. I have to swallow my pride, make friends with Pastor Løchen and take walks with him.

I was stupid that time. Obviously he did it with the best intentions; why do I always have to be so thin-skinned! And he was right, after all. This eternal boozing is really idiotic.

It's just this terrible desolation and loneliness. Fanny, Fanny, why didn't I meet you earlier!

It's easy for him to talk, sitting there in a snug, secure home; everything in order, a benevolent God and a nice wife. He cannot feel my ache, this ache below the chest, this aching, deadly loss—or the cold I feel. All these happy, nicely set-up people, it's so easy for them to preach—boring people.

Jonathan is essentially of the same sort. I cannot stand his whole manner. "A proud man masters the world or abandons it"; "an intelligent man knows how to adjust to the world. . . ." Always these platitudes, these empty, rumbling platitudes.

"The world," ugh! A bin, a sewer. "Everything is in flux," said the old idiot; he could just as well have said, Everything smells!

## XXVII

God, how I envy that parson. Just imagine, having something that's holy!

Something you feel religious toward, something that has value, which endures, lives on; something one can rest in and build on, hold on to under all circumstances.

Something that is holy! Really holy! A secret hope, a blissful conviction; something one can't bear to hear profaned or sniffed at. Something that one finds to be priceless; something that one protects and worships—.

A peace that the world cannot give or take away, a treasure that moth and rust doth not corrupt.

Happiness, bliss! Sweet as a secret love, safe as a home. Ah me, homeless and lost, who not only have wasted my substance, but also the ability to find my way home again.

I lie before the rich man's door full of wounds, and yet every morning I wake up in hell and in torment.

Oh, those "great ideas" which they offer us and want us to be satisfied with—instead of religion, at that! When I think back to the many, and very great, ideas I have joined others in toasting, from Scandinavianism to free thought, ideas that have partly been realized and partly not, but which in either case have left us just as unhappy as we were before—then I have to give a fresh twist to the poet's verse and say:

> Begins as a swagger at the market some day
> and ends with a gasp in a hospital bay.
> Then it's borne in silence to the burial place,
> and the whole swindle's gone without a trace.

There is one thing that fills me with longing: the monastery.

To enter the holy Catholic church and from there into a monastery. Into the quietest, strictest cell, where I would sleep on straw and lash my accursed flesh with a whip in front of the Crucified One.

But above my bed she, the Holy Virgin, would be enthroned. The mother with the seven swords piercing her young heart. The blessed among women, the pure one who still understands, the *schmerzensreiche*, the one married to suffering, who can weep but also console. I would beg and pray and beseech until she stepped down from her niche, maternal and loving, and placed her white, healing hand on my heart.

"To love people." That is required by all ethics. Religious as well as humanistic ethics.

"To love people." How should one go about that? They aren't particularly lovable.

I don't even manage to love myself. I'm a rather nasty customer, and even my self-respect is often in a bad way. Nonetheless, from an objective viewpoint I belong to the better ones within the species; most others that I meet are even nastier. Under these circumstances to love—at any rate not hate—this breed . . .

> "Ich bin so krank, o Mutter,
> dass ich nicht hör' und seh;
> ich denk' an das todte Gretchen,
> das thut das Herz mir weh'."

"Steh auf, wir wollen nach Kevlaar;
nimm Buch und Rosenkranz;
die Mutter Gottes heilt dir
dein krankes Herze ganz."—

Der kranke Sohn und die Mutter,
die schliefen im Kämmerlein;
da kam die Mutter Gottes
ganz leise geschritten herein.

Sie beugte sich über den Kranken,
und legte ihre Hand
ganz leise auf sein Herze,
und lächelte mild und schwand.

Es spielt' auf den bleichen Wangen
das lichte Morgenroth.
Da lag dahingestrecket
der Sohn, und der war todt.


## XXVIII


Bærum, July 1889

I'm staying out here with a couple of newspaper bandits, and I'm bored.

Before noon, either a whiskey and soda or absinthe. In the afternoon I swing half-drunk in a hammock reading the decadents.

The liquor will run out in three days, that's my hope. None of us has any money, you see, and I'm the only one who has credit—which, however, I'll be careful not to use. A few days' break will do me good. This eternal tippling is unbearable.

*

Monday morning

Sundays are the worst here; yesterday we had the house full of bandits. Artists almost to a man; moreover, two newshounds and one literary man.

The latter was the worst—that hopeless whippersnapper Rygg. He wanted to borrow five kroner, which I luckily didn't have, and entertained me with his worries about finding a publisher.

"It's impossible to exist in this country for people like me; it consists only of peasants and parish clerks, don't you see. And then these disgusting females," etc. "We agree about that, all of us young people," etc. "Peasant rule must go, that's clear; we've had enough of peasant lingo and that sort of rubbish. But what the hell can we do with these three or four cities, with maybe twenty people all in all who're interested in literature?" etc. Frankly, I thought it didn't much matter whether "people like him" existed or not, but I didn't bother to say so.

"No, we have to go to Denmark," he said. "We must become Europeans. We must beg admission to Denmark, wheedle admission to Denmark—even if we have to tell a few lies and kiss the asses of all the bright boys down there. We have no other choice, you see! If there's going to be a modern Norwegian literature, then we *must* have Denmark," etc.

"Well, my dear fellow, buckle to it," I told him. "After all, it's both patriotic and—advantageous for yourself, of course. Won't you fill your glass again?"

"Yes, thank you." And then he went on about those publishers again. I had to promise to write an article, etc.

The epitome of the breed. Artists are the most miserable riffraff the good Lord ever created. They have a great many fine qualities, goodness yes, but—there's always that pettiness.

I don't know who are the worst. Musicians are bad, actors are worse, writers may be the most impossible of all. When I myself don't get anywhere in that respect, it's not simply for lack of energy, but also because I got to know that sort of people much too early. Who knows whether I, too, wouldn't become like that after producing a couple of books!

It's nothing but "me." "Me, me!" "My" castle, "my" publisher, how big a royalty, how large the editions. Every time I made closer contact with one of them, a little splenetic dwarf always sat in his inmost being, and beside the dwarf a dog, who turned into a wagging tail as soon as it smelled a newspaperman.

Even worse than the artists are the journalists, those flat-bottomed punts floating about on the newspaper ponds loaded with curiosity and unappreciated genius. But worst of all are the sobersides.

We—or rather my newspaper bandits—were today visited by one of those half-educated people, a sort of political liberal, ardent supporter of sexual purity, and lay preacher. His actual business was evidently to inspire an article. "The interests of the fatherland" were in danger on one side or another, it appeared. He drank club soda and reeled off a slew of sarcastic remarks, but didn't make me lose my temper. I said "goodness, yes" and tossed off one drink after another.

Stupid, by the way. I should have hauled him over the coals. They are the sort of people who govern us now, theologians, schoolmasters, "idealists." We are a nation of idealists, we're constantly having an eye to the welfare of our fellowmen. That is, we are small-town people who cannot help being interested in what our neighbors will be having for dinner.

Artists are like women. If two of them are friends, it is because they both hate a third more than they hate each other; and the third is always the luckier rival.

Frankly, people look their best from behind; that I've come to discover more and more. The most beautiful turn of speech in our language is, "Well, goodbye then!"

"Art," "art": what, when all is said and done, is art?

An extra tasty morsel for those who have appetite, and an extra mockery for those who are world-weary. Michelangelo, Dante, Beethoven are very great. But none of them can help a soul in distress.

I get so tired of this arty talk. My own "art reviews"—how badly they must smell in God's nostrils! Thank God, the day after tomorrow Kvaale is coming out here (after his trip to Germany); he has his summer lair on a farm in the vicinity.

And science? An excellent guide in indifferent things; a perfect Dr. Helpless, if worst comes to worst.

And love, our most grievous disease? And marriage? The cure that is worse than the disease. And the whole kit and caboodle?

It's unbelievable that people can go around with such self-important airs.

Those new Frenchmen I took along are quite interesting, especially Huysmans; he's excellent. And queer. I also like Bourget; he presents in his essays a very straightforward *philosophie du pessimisme*, which I'm going to annoy Jonathan with, and he appeals to me by his religious inclinations. This fellow Hennique is rather peculiar, preaching spiritism in dead earnest.

*Fin de siècle.* Strange times. The world is on the eve of another turning point. The more we know, the more we see that we can know nothing; all we can do is to recognize this and seek remedies elsewhere. Our soul has, after all, deeper needs than the professorial ones; and "faith," the great assurance, the great fundamental conviction we can live and die by—that cannot be replaced by a volume of hypotheses.

This is a long-standing feeling of mine.


### XXIX


"No, my practice is not pleasant," Kvaale said, "but one learns a good deal, of course. A person in my position takes no stock in empty phrases, that's for sure!"

And then and there he began riding his hobbyhorse. (In my novel he will represent contemporary pessimism—a contrast to G. J.)

"The Germans," he said, among other things, "are not as strait-laced as we are, and in consequence one needs only read a German newspaper to see what the situation is—behind the scenes. One must read the ad page. Yes, the ad page. There we find, first of all, the matrimonial ads—a dozen a day, the ads of marriage bureaus not included. From this alone one understands that there's *something rotten.* Then we have the further effects of the disorder: 'Ladies are offered discreet help by midwife N. N.'—twelve ads a day. Further, twelve licensed businessmen advertise for sale choice, inexpensive condoms for men and women; illustrated price list free of charge. And finally, twelve ads from—specialists of my sort. That gives us—a kind of map of the situation."

"As I've always been saying," I replied, "love is our worst disease."

"Your wife is ill?"

"A bit poorly, yes," Dr. Kvaale snarled.

"Sickly in general, I believe?"

"Yes." His face became sullen, almost somber.

"Then it's lucky she has a physician for a husband."

"Hmm."

"Your wife is obviously not one of those who are in the habit of whining. The couple of times I've had the pleasure of meeting her, at any rate, she seemed to be in the best of spirits."

He answered seriously and almost deferentially, "She's an exceptionally good person."

Pause.

"Curious," I then said, "how husbands praise their wives but very often snipe at marriage."

"Of course," he replied. "People are as a rule all right, but the institutions——." A shrug.

"Are you sure that you don't attach too much importance to institutions? Isn't it nature itself that——?"

"Nature is brutal enough," he snarled, "but what's the use of complaining about nature? The fact is that we smart animals always change nature's iniquity for the worse, rather than what we should be doing, changing it for something relatively good."

"Hmm. Love *can* be beautiful, you know."

"Love is beautiful when it's forbidden, old chap," he yelped. "When it's not regulated, I mean. As far as society is concerned, love is simply——tolerated, just so; neither more nor less. Licensed love is boredom.

"Matriarchy," he went on——"we must get matriarchy back again, obviously in a different form. Society has nothing to do with those things. They will fall into place by themselves, hidden away as a poetic mystery in the inner sanctum of private life. Then woman too will come into her own again and become what she has to be for us if we are to be men: the Great Mother, the high sovereign not to be approached with unwashed hands or with a sleepy, routine love in the warmth of a bed. Men do not become men except when they fight over——or for——the woman they themselves have made a queen. Well, you must have read about that. In the age of gynecocracy men were heroes, they fought and died like regular braves for this mystical-sacred mother-mistress; but what is man today, when he has pulled woman down along with himself, and turned her into Mrs. Persen in Skipper Street? They have turned into oxen, yes sirree; heavy, dull oafs laboriously schlepping the burden of life behind them along the beaten track, thoroughly trapped under the yoke."

He had gotten red in the face and nervous. I suddenly felt I knew this man. And it was somehow a disappointment to me: the question of "woman and marriage" was evidently the very substance of this individual. I had really thought there was greater depth to him.

And the question itself came to seem more hopeless than ever. When such an intelligent man, after reflecting on it for an entire lifetime, finds no way out other than in these ravings, then the question must be unanswerable. Whether the established order is "rotten" or not, whether it is sinister or not, we shall quite simply have to let it remain in place. And love will be the same as ever: our greatest torment.

I have been curiously blind: I went in pursuit of woman to find rest!

I'm recovering out here; my head is clearer, the apathy is wearing off. Thanks to the country air and plenty of sleep—and probably also lack of money, which compels the gang to go easy on the cognac.

Besides, I'm so fed up with this endless swilling that I would stay dry anyway. Kvaale is also staying out here "on a diet," and we fortify each other in virtue and good morals.

And, God knows, it's really too shoddy: to have to console oneself with the bottle. Boozing is plebeian. It's only for coarse nerves. I've practiced it in my despair, because I *willed* my destruction; but good heavens, in that case one should behave like a well-bred individual and swallow cyanide.

"It's not only the degrees of latitude that count," Kvaale says, "it's lack of culture. A well-developed human being appreciates the finer pleasures; he wants to see clearly and perceive sensitively. But then, hang it, he can't afford to reek of cognac or have his head befogged with beer."

"No, that's disgusting," I said. "It's that Siberian town in there that demoralizes us: what can anybody cook up there, among all those tubs of lard. You would be bored to death if you didn't stoke up with spirits—since the *esprit* is lacking."

"One has to choose one's company, old chap. One has to find somebody or other who doesn't have too much lard, who has risen above this Germanic heaviness. On the whole, alcoholism is a Germanic disease. We must try to become a bit Mediterranean and hand over the *Bier* to the Germans and the *brandy* to Scandinavians and Englishmen. It will suit them with their bearish bulk and their solid smell of heating stoves and tobacco."

"In my veins flows Spanish blood, I've heard say, and I know for a fact that the only thing I can truly enjoy is a glass of genuine burgundy."

## XXX

Kr—ia. September

We were at Jonathan's today; argued the whole time.

I spoke about the most recent literature in France and defended it. Jonathan still knew about the movement only through some English journal articles; nevertheless he was perfectly ready to give his verdict, and he didn't pull any punches. "Those tepidly sweet, weepily soft feminized men who produce literature in Paris at the moment," etc.; "they have given themselves a name that is worthy of them: decadents—poets of decline, decay, putrefaction. This is the bourgeoisie starting to disintegrate. They no longer believe in anything, are interested in nothing whatsoever, and lack the strength to uphold anything at all; so they have nothing better to do than to fiddle-faddle with their own insipid feelings, until they can squeeze a bit of literature out of them. By comparison, the naturalist is the epitome of wholesomeness; he notes down, coldly, elegantly and without flippancy—and without coquettishness—the world picture that has presented itself to him. That's how he has seen it, black or red; though it too may be insipid enough, impersonal and what you will, he is nevertheless an aristocrat compared to these spiritual self-abusers of most recent date."

Dr. Kvaale shrugged his shoulders and said that this new lunacy was just as crazy as the previous one. "It's a ridiculous idea to wish to reproduce reality; it is so impossible that every honest naturalist must have told himself so. But to 'reproduce one's feelings'—that is self-contradiction pure and simple. As soon as a feeling has passed through consciousness and been translated into language, it is no longer a feeling, it has become thought; feelings, after all, cannot be expressed—except through music. For a feeling is a stirring of the soul that has not yet found its form; if you want to express it in words, you will at best end up with witty pronouncements *about* it, but certainly not with the thing itself. That's impossible, once and for all."

"The naturalists never wanted to reproduce reality," Jonathan asserted. "They wanted, like all the world's poets, to reproduce the world picture they bore within their consciousness, and that could be done. But when people go soft inside so they can no longer hold a picture of the world in their heads, they begin to rummage in their guts for moods and sensations, which they then represent in the most artificial and unlanguage-like language you can think of. And that is what's called decadence—freely translated, putrefaction. Anyway, the whole affair will die away of itself; in the end the poets will sit around vomiting on their own manuscripts from sheer disgust."

I said that they were both mistaken about the main thing. "The fact of the matter is that we're here confronted with a complete revolution in worldview. Naturalists and materialists take 'nature' as a given and the soul as derivative: 'personality is a product of the environment.' We are now going back to the more aristocratic conception that the self is a given and that the so-called objectivity is only the content of the self; and so literature becomes psychological, subjectivist, and depicts states of mind per se instead of representing them as products of such and such external circumstances," and so on. To all of this Jonathan responded merely by the shallow remark that "Frenchmen are nowadays translating Hegel and Schopenhauer, just as they translated Hume and Locke in the previous century—what an untalented race those Gauls are!

"This business of the soul," he added, "means simply that those French milksops have grown too weak and too sluggish to follow the thorny path of investigation and therefore have chosen the distaff road by way of priest and oracle. Why should anyone perform chemical and biological experiments if he can drive up to Madam Andersen's at the Ekeberg bend and have his life explained in coffee grounds?"

Dr. Kvaale explained the situation in his own way.

"It's the old story," he said: "from woman to God. Every religious impulse is sexual desire. Unsatisfied, overdeveloped, or degenerate sexual desire. This racial drive, as the Germans call it, is the so-called mystical element in us, 'the idea of eternity.' An isolated individual would certainly never think of dreaming about immortality and such; but our core, you see, is race, and somehow or other *that* is the foundation of the separate individual. And the race, of course, does have a 'longing for eternity,' or this idea of enduring for an unlimited time, and it's this idea that becomes 'religion.' And that is also why woman is most religious; she represents the race more than anyone else. But there are plenty of women among the men too; in Paris in particular there are lots of that sort. All in all, I bet we'll never get rid of the parson; the best we can do is to isolate him, render him as harmless as possible."

"In reality, the parson is a useful member of society," Jonathan said, blowing cigarette smoke through his nose. "The cheaters in class must also be included; and these periods of reaction simply mean that the upper classes will now have a holiday till Monday, so that the parson can put the detention class through the mill after school hours. When they have more or less caught up, it'll be our turn again."

Kvaale shrugged his shoulders.

"By the way, you're right, Doctor," Jonathan continued. "The question is: race or individual, woman or man. Right now I can think of nothing more repulsive than those fucked-out Parisian half-men who lie sniveling at every crossroads: '*Hélas*, let's get drunk'!" He rang the bell, a maid stuck her head through the door. "Bring me a drink!" he ordered demonstratively.

I didn't bother answering. I suddenly felt such a distance between these men and myself that discussion was out of the question.

It was a feeling at once sad and agreeable. All of a sudden they appeared to me as incarnations of the period we are beginning to put behind us, while I myself felt, in a peculiarly reassuring way, a kinship with the future.

## XXXI

15 Oct.

It won't work. Here in town you willy-nilly relapse into your old habits again. And become nasty and sick and apathetic.

I'll make a radical break.

There is going to be a brief struggle, but this struggle will be of a certain interest. And I won't really sacrifice very much. What I've sought to achieve by the help of alcohol—oblivion, equanimity—I don't achieve anymore; on the contrary. Just more restlessness, more anxiety. Not long ago those slender bottles with the reddish-gold label started becoming an object of horror: peering out of them was death, a mysterious, cunning maggot that wanted to catch and fascinate me. So the only thing I'll have to sacrifice is just a stupid habit, which in reality merely bores me.

In about a month it will be all set: I shall have arranged my life in the new manner and regained my freedom. So until then: a strict diet.

31 Oct.

It's working capitally. My self-esteem is increasing. Appetite: growing; sleep: normal.

Essentially I'm seeing only Dr. Kvaale, who "observes a diet" on his own account. Find myself liking that man more and more. But I haven't quite figured him out yet.

I'm sitting this moment at the Grand with my coffee, without a snifter, watching the "Teutons" with a certain pity. What miserable cowards, not to be able to keep afloat without paralyzing themselves. Spongy and puffy and in a semistupor, they sit there feeling disgusted, and will become "human" only after alcoholizing themselves to the point of being stoned. Ugh.

I can sense their *Stumpfsinn,* that drowsy-lethargic heaviness that weighs on their brains, until they've gotten up steam and their nervous systems start working, spasmodically. It makes me sick. I don't belong in that crowd anymore.

But I haven't quite pulled through yet. I notice it particularly when I sit at home; the absence of a glass with my cigarette or pipe disturbs me, and I cannot work. Every moment I instinctively walk up to that familiar cabinet. I need something, lack something; my whole being needs, lacks—I feel so dry inside, a certain burning, something that wants to be extinguished, it's almost like feeling thirsty in one's sleep. Then I suddenly remember; I stand there miserable and shamefaced.

But in a couple of months the cure will be over. Then I'll be a free man and able once again—if I wish—to have a liqueur with my coffee.


Was at Jonathan's for coffee today. When the liqueur was brought, Kvaale said, "You'll have it all to yourself from now on. Gram and I have gone in for being good."

Jonathan had the liqueur taken away. "I have been drinking just to keep you company, you know," he said.

Then he expatiated on optimism. "Existential angst? That's nothing but hysteria. What sort of abyss are you talking about? You've read too many decadents, Gram. There is no abyss. Certified: George Jonathan.

"The great mystery is not 'dreadful,' it's beautiful. You see, it's life itself—its sun-drenched glory makes it too hard for us to figure it out.

"The only thing that's ugly is death. Long, barbaric torments, finally convulsions; frothing at the mouth, vomiting, cold sweat, bad smells—after which you stretch out, gape idiotically and plunge the back of your head into the pillow. And so you lie there staring. Such a thing is not for human beings.

"Can you think of anything more helpless and stupid than to go your whole life waiting for this abominable so-called natural death? Instead of taking death into your own hand and arranging it humanely and comfortably. You see, death doesn't have to be ugly, not at all. We need only come to grips with the thing and make sensible arrangements, then we'll soon be able to say, more justly than the apostle, 'Death, where is thy sting?'"

And the two men of the present set about discussing the question of how death should "be arranged." Not a bad idea, incidentally. But I wasn't all there. I'm sometimes plagued by hallucinations. George Jonathan's elegant liqueur service, for example, haunts me as the naked beauty did Saint Augustine. And my soul is nothing but a dry, cracked sensation of thirst. . . .

Jonathan wants to become a newspaper editor. "My position is now so secure," he said, "that I can start the preliminary work of subversion."

I gave a shrug.

"One has to do something," he responded. "I can't go around like a Frenchman winning women's hearts forever!" He leaned back in his rocking chair and looked very serious.

"Women's hearts or voters' hearts," I mumbled.

"Very well, tastes differ. Anyway, my particular lunacy is that I must have an army behind me. And besides, there is my megalomania: I can't sleep soundly until I have saved the world."

"If your newspaper is to preach your personal ideas, you will certainly have no army behind you."

"My personal ideas? You don't think I want to be a martyr, do you?"

"All due respect for the martyrs, for that matter!"

"Sure, insofar as one lunacy can per se be just as crazy as another; but the martyrs are inferior in my eyes. That sort of thing is acting like a little boy—being unable to hold your tongue, feeling absolutely compelled to blurt out the truth on every occasion. What for? We know, after all, that it takes a hundred years for a truth to be grasped, so we can take it easy and shut up—leave truth behind in a brilliant posthumous work and thus avoid this fiasco and bad taste called martyrdom. I won't claim that I am myself secretly engaged in such a work; I only say that I'm going to enjoy the good things in my lifetime and still render just as many services to truth and progress as a few average martyred simpletons."

"*C'est possible.*"

"My paper will be conservative, naturally—or perhaps liberal—or something of the sort; whatever catches on most easily. I'll make the empty vessels of the day rumble, so that people will fall over backward with astonishment. But at the same time one can very well subvert faith and virtuousness."

"Very politic."

"If we want to go by rail across the Alps, we have to dig tunnels. If we want to gather the people around us, we must fly the banner of 1789—its ideas are now roughly old enough. Simultaneously we'll quietly dig that tunnel to the future. You understand?"

"Yes."

"Will you join me?"

"I? What can I do?"

"Dr. Kvaale will be science editor, we'll hand over the arts to you."

"Really? But I'm a heretic."

"With a certain weakness for the decadents? Doesn't matter. The main thing is that you can handle those things with a certain degree of intelligence."

"You'll give me complete freedom?"

"Sure."

"And space enough?"

"Sure. We'll cultivate those areas. We're going to have a model paper, you see, a first-class paper that will make the natives sit up. Anyhow, it's high time to work up a little culture in this town, which in fifty years will be the capital of the North."

I stared at him. He nodded.

"So?" he asked.

"I—almost think I'll give it a thought, by Jove!"

*"Well, sir."*

Not such a bad idea, not at all. If one has nothing else in this world to live for, then it's necessary to find some work.

To be a force for education, culture; to civilize all these half-shaven bears, provide possibilities for a richer intellectual life in this city, where intelligent men have so far been obliged to sit at the Grand drinking whiskey and soda. . . .

The young are doubtless beginning to long for something deeper, finer; they want to get away from noisy politics, Bohemian chatter and morals debate, and all the rest of the corny stuff, to a more European culture. If these young people got some help, we might have a fairly cultivated public in a few years. Then it would be possible to live here too.

"The young are the future!" What business of mine is the future? Even so, one somehow feels a desire to influence that future, God knows why.

A last illusion. If only I were allowed to hold on to it!

## XXXII

"Time is old."—"The world is old"; "Time is old."—"The world is old," comes the chime from Paris. It sounds like the tolling of funeral bells from the tower of Notre-Dame.

Oh well. To have no illusions, no faith anymore, is after all the very definition of old age.

What sort of faith exactly did we have the last time around? Ah, "evolution," of course. Then some philosophical oaf or other comes along and blurts out with what every initiate has known privately: that evolution can only bring about more suffering. Evolution is differentiation, refinement; the more refined we become, the less ability we have to put up with the disharmonies of life. That bubble has burst. Paradise is not behind us, said the positivists; it is not in front of us either, adds the decadent.

And our generation sits by the wayside, its arms drooping. And its eyes are staring and empty, like those of a madman. Darkness ahead and darkness behind. Meaningless and irrelevant, the will-o'-the-wisp of science flutters about on endless bogs.

But in the air worsening winter storms are howling, and existence is filled with falling leaves.


*(Seven beatitudes.)* Blessed are the poor: for if only they had a million . . .

Blessed are the oppressed: for if only the revolution came . . .

Blessed are the misunderstood: for if only there arose a real critic . . .

Blessed are the disappointed in love: for if only they could embrace that one and only . . .

Blessed are the drunken: for if only they could restrain themselves for just one year . . .

Blessed are the sick: for if only they became well again . . .

Blessed, blessed are all who suffer loss and pain: for they still possess the illusion of happiness.

But woe to you, ye wealthy, ye mighty, ye healthy, ye famous, ye who are lucky in love and in war: for your heads are no longer shaded by any curtain of illusion from the consuming sun called truth.


Asia, Asia . . .

Have I really been able to go around believing that Asia has been left behind by Europe? The truth is that Europe has several thousands of years to go before it catches up with Asia.

Over there they knew long ago what we can see only now: that no "evolution" exists, only a constant going in circles. Everything returns, and we ourselves return; the only wisdom is quietism. And the only hope for the individual is to work himself out of the limitations of individual existence through self-denial and renunciation and blissfully merge into the boundless all, Nirvana.

Buddhism is the deepest and the highest of all religions. Just as Christianity is too deep for the Negro, so Buddhism has to this day been too high for the Europeans. But finally those most advanced are beginning to catch on: Buddhism is making its way into Paris.

Dr. Kvaale won't lend me his books on hypnotism, spiritism, etc., "not yet," and so I've got hold of a few on my own.

They're weird things. But one needs only to read about the Indian fakirs and such to know that there's certainly more between heaven and earth than $H_2O$, $HO_2$. . . .

The Asiatic philosophy is brilliant, the only real philosophy in existence.

Several thousands of years ago something was discovered that we still won't quite believe: that there exists no real contentment. All that we call contentment is a fraud, a fraud that brings about fresh agony; the only reality is the sense of loss. To achieve contentment, therefore, we have to suppress the sense of loss, the Asiatic concluded with chilling logic. And behold, fakirs and dervishes and all who had reached the heights of wisdom mounted rocks and pillars and died to the world. They hypnotized themselves by constantly becoming absorbed in meditations on Nirvana; and they had no sense of loss anymore, and their soul found peace.

Christianity with its doctrine of self-abnegation is nothing but an imperfect imitation of Buddhism.

## XXXIII

*(Delirium.)* Why are murderers punished? An absurd idea. A state is about to burst from overpopulation—but if a good-natured fellow comes along and helps that state get rid of a few individuals, the above-mentioned state grabs the fellow and chops off his head. Not very intelligent.

"For the sake of the consequences!" Fiddle-faddle. The aptitude for murder is a special talent; one is a born murderer, just as one is a born genius. No fear!

So the state wants to have a monopoly of the craft? It is itself the best judge of the matter? The private killers are cheats. Finish the job too quickly, too painlessly; the children of men shall be murdered methodically, according to a plan; be put on the rack and slowly tortured to death, starved and worked to death on departmental stools and by means of other instruments of torture—and in this business the state is an expert. Well, now you're talking!

But if there were any humanity on earth, the murderous souls would be rewarded, honored, and encouraged, so that there would be many of them, and many able ones. As soon as a man had carried out a fairly acceptable murder, he should be sent to Paris, London, Italy on a government stipend in order to further develop his art; and if thereafter he carried out five deaths in a satisfactory manner, he should receive a permanent appointment, with salary and uniform, in addition to a handsome title: Royal Norwegian Death Helper, Royal Norwegian Chief Sorrow-Extinguisher, Royal Norwegian High Steward for Court Preferment Relations. . . .

That's what the military is for, isn't it? Well, fine. But they are appointed solely to kill Swedes! The national killers, on the other hand, those who devote their abilities to the service of the fatherland, who seek to deliver their fellow countrymen and compatriots and fellow Christians—they, damn it, receive no encouragement but have to place their shaven heads on a low, rough-hewn block.

And yet they work well, as a rule. Make a fairly correct selection: throttle old misers, usurers, wealthy single women and the like, people who actually get what is coming to them. But such matters are not considered; these individuals have their lives cut short without further ado—instead of being appointed lieutenants, captains, generals of the true Salvation Army.

Strange, this prudishness concerning murder. As if those usurers weren't bound to die in any case! Today, tomorrow. . . . And even a mediocre murderer dispatches them more nicely and quickly than clumsy, filthy nature.

Hey, Jakob Shoemaker, another stiver's worth of brandy. . . .

Yes, I've fallen.

That particular virtue is just *too* boring. After all, you can't wander about by yourself all the time, and if you are with people it gets to be in poor taste to just sit there like a Pharisee and as the others' bad conscience. You take a glass for the sake of propriety, just one; when that's been emptied, the principle has been broken, and you might as well take another half glass. And so it ends by your having to let yourself be taken home by a cabby.

On the whole, to go around being bound by your will—this and that you don't dare, etc.—is really impossible for an intelligent human being. And why torment yourself? It's all so indifferent anyway. That is to say, if one could really believe in the transmigration of souls.

I'm a cultivated man. I've proven to myself that I can go back on my habits and frailties; hereafter I shall prove to myself that I can be free.

It's a base, merely semihuman standpoint to bind one's will.

## XXXIV

*Scene:* Karl Johan Street. *Characters:* A whippersnapper; George
Jonathan; G. Gram.

WHIPPERSNAPPER. Oh, but N. N. no longer has the young on his
side.

G. J. Is that so important?

WHIPPERSNAPPER. Important? The young are the future, aren't
they?

G. J. When they get old, sure.

WHIPPERSNAPPER *(somewhat taken aback).* Yes, but . . . yes, but, you
must understand that—

G. J. Anybody who knows how to make noise can get the young on
his side. I'll tell you something: one becomes a human being
only around forty, when the worst womanizing is over and one
starts having a smut-free view of the world.

WHIPPERSNAPPER *(angry).* One is a human at twenty: that's the
time for love, for hate, for enthusiasm. Then one wants to do
something!

G. J. Oh dear, our twenty-year-olds! Why, they have still to be fully
cured of their self-abuse. Nor do I hear a lot about enthusiasm
in that quarter, but that much more about listlessness, weariness, lack of energy, ennui. They go around whining that they
don't fit in anywhere, that they don't take an interest in anything. Since the time I became an adult I've heard nothing but
these blues from the camp of "the young." No, we cannot use
the young. Their métier and task is to lie around billing and
cooing with the little girls and write sniveling verses and sex
books.

WHIPPERSNAPPER *(flushed).* And I who thought you were a modern

man! Excuse me. Goodbye. *(Does a complete about-face—
disappears.)*

G. J. *(whistles, smiles).* All right.

GRAM. Irritating fellow. But what you said about the young
should've been left unsaid.

G. J. Oh?

GRAM. You have taken my public away from me. What can I do for
your paper now?

G. J. You must create your own public. Have a good dinner!

---

"The aristocracy of the future." Every once in a while I hear those
words. It's what I was supposed to help create, isn't it?

But where do I find material to create it from?

An aristocracy cannot be made, as one makes a democracy; it
must be born. But where's the mother?

The old aristocracy is dying out. Or has given up hope and mixes
its blood with that of the stock exchange crowd. On the whole,
effete. A plant whose root has withered.

"Aristocracy of wealth?" Good Lord, yes, such a thing does
exist; wealth through several generations does refine. But all things
considered, the dollar is a plebeian: it feels as comfortable in the
pocket of the usurious Jew as in the purse of the fine gentleman,
and has no validity as a patent of nobility. Every moment some
chap from the riffraff moves up into the ranks of the nobility of
wealth, and consequently this nobility will always retain its
mixed—unaristocratic—character.

The military? Alas. War is no longer heroic deeds and dreams,
but applied mathematics, an impersonal affair that's led by engi-
neers. Moltke is the Napoleon of our time; he will die as a dutiful
department head and member of the national assembly. There is
now just one martial virtue, namely discipline: to stand where you

were stationed, to go where you were sent. Good followers are produced that way, but no commanders. A lieutenant is extremely different from a hero; and the captain, the major, the colonel, and the general—they're all government officials.

And the government officials? They are servants. Clerks. Non-personalities, "offices." "The County has the honor to transmit . . .";
"The Department is of the most humble opinion. . . ." But servants are slaves and will always remain slaves.

The scientists? With their inky fingers and head colds and tiny little inventor's ambitions? A scientist gets, at best, to be a professor, and his son becomes a ne'er-do-well and obtains a government position with the help of connections. No good.

Writers and artists and such—they are simply the proletariat. A poet, for example, was at all times the male *prostitué*. Previously he compromised his feelings in the interest of any well-paying lord of the castle; now he prostitutes himself to the public. Makes capital out of his intimate life, concocts tender feelings to achieve three editions, erases the best and most sincere things he wanted to say to obtain a publisher. Such a caste of slaves will not generate an aristocracy.

The farmers? They might be the only ones. It's princely to own land, to be sole ruler of a piece of the planet, however small; and the old well-to-do farm families are alone in this country in having a noble aura about them. But—the land is already a commodity. And the men of the future dream about turning the earth into "communal property," whereby the basis of this only thinkable aristocracy will be completely removed.

But "the young?" They are the not yet fully developed lieutenants, government officials, artists, and proletarian peasants. . . .

"The future" is a horrible idea. Factories and well-to-do workers. A world full of informed, well-fed petit-bourgeois souls who eat, drink, and reproduce scientifically.

I will *not* be part of it. I simply will not.

## XXXV

*Fin de siècle, fin de siècle. Fin de la culture européenne.*

Black-fisted proletarians pull down the Vendôme column, burn Notre-Dame, break into the Louvre, and reduce the Venus de Milo to crushed stone with good hammers. The Madeleine is converted to a hall for workers' balls, the Tuileries to a public soup kitchen. The Arch of Triumph is torn down and replaced with a magnificent up-to-date universal *cabinet d'aisance,* parading, in large letters, the inscription *Liberté, Egalité, Fraternité; entrée 5 centimes.*

But on every corner the guillotines operate like stamping mills. For all must die whose hands are white and whose noses are too delicate for the unadulterated odor of petroleum and rotgut and people's sweat.

I'll have myself guillotined.


Astronomers tell us that our sun, with its entire retinue of planets and satellites, is falling through outer space at a speed of millions of miles a second—toward some star or other in the constellation of Hercules.

One fine day our earth will hurtle down on this star and evaporate like a drop on a hot stove.

For *what* did it exist? When the good Lord someday in the next eternity counts his flock of stars, he won't even notice that the planet Tellus has disappeared.


O God, how long?

When will I get the better of this perpetual uneasiness, this gnawing discontent and dissatisfaction, this dryness and thirst through my whole being? I'm like an animal in a desert where there's no water, like a captured lion loping back and forth behind the bars of its cage in search of freedom. All that is uneasy and aspiring and watchful and yearning and restless has gathered its torment in me, it lies in my breast like a lacerating anguish.

When I go out I hope to meet peace in the shape of a young, full-bosomed woman, who puts her white arm around my neck and whispers in my ear the infinite understanding of love. When I get home, I hope she sits there waiting for me, still and beautiful, with an intriguing melancholy in her dark eyes.

I sit down in my most comfortable chair but cannot rest; I lie down on my softest couch, but there is no peace. I'm constantly on the watch, on the watch, every nerve taut, my senses strained to the point of hallucination: don't I hear those familiar footsteps? Won't it come, that blissful revelation?

But the only one who comes is the bill collector.

### XXXVI

Is it beginning now?

I don't see flies precisely. But these odd, feeble, addle-brained fancies that pester me present themselves with a certain idiotic, guffawing importunity as strokes of wit, and the worst of it is that I sometimes feel they're good:

"Olsen has no fate, one must at least be called Ohlzén, and even so it will only be a fate at ten øre. . . ." Can something like this possibly arise in a brain that functions normally?

I have to take care. Not too much absinthe either—.

Buddhism is not for me. I'm stuck head over ears in barbarism. I find this business of self-denial to be too negative: my being thirsts for satisfaction, happiness, love. The barbarian cannot resign himself; he always believes that life *cannot* be that cold, there *must* sit a fatherly God or a tender goddess someplace.

\*

*Scene:* My room. *Characters:* Dr. Kvaale; G. Gram. Twilight.

GRAM *(comes in with Dr. Kvaale).* That was nice of you. Now we'll have a cigar and chat sensibly together. It's been long since the last time. *(Lights the lamp.)*

DR. KVAALE *(flops into the rocking chair; listless).* I never have time, you know. Now too I have *(looks at his watch)* . . . only forty minutes. Then I must go down to my suicide again.

G. *(brings cigars).* Suicide? Really? That sounds interesting. *(Lights his cigar.)* Didn't make it, eh?

DR. K. *(shrugs).* Of course not. Confounded bungler; can't ever do it right. *(Lights his cigar.)*

G. *(sits down).* And you really have the heart to "save" a guy like that?

DR. K. *(shrugs).* Duty, damn it.

G. A very immoral duty.

DR. K. Hmm.

G. Is he young?

DR. K. A young whippersnapper, of course. Felt bound to do this thing when some business came up; but he didn't know anatomy. Put the bullet in where it couldn't do any effective damage.

G. So, a revolver. Choice of weapon in poor taste. A bang and fuss. Don't you agree? You prefer opium too, right?

DR. K. Yes.

G. By the way, to drown while swimming isn't bad either. But one risks getting saved.

DR. K. Yes. People are so compassionate—when it isn't necessary. *(Pause.)*

G. *(with forced superiority)*. What would you do, for example, if a good friend called on you someday and asked for—a sufficient quantum of morphine?

DR. K. Well, he could complain of pain someplace or other, you know.

G. Nervous pain . . . that kept him from sleeping, for example?

DR. K. Sure. For common insomnia, of course, we use other means.

G. *(artificial laughter)*. But you even boggle at giving me chloral.

DR. K. Chloral is a damn nuisance, sure. Are you still bothered by insomnia?

G. Occasionally—when I get those nervous pains. In my arms and legs, you see—and my head. I lie tossing and turning as though I were feverish; rest is out of the question.

DR. K. *(with a quick, searching glance)*. Hmm.

G. *(affectedly cheerful)*. Don't worry, doctor. I'm an old-fashioned guy. I intend to die in the prescribed way, from pneumonia.

DR. K. To tell the truth, it is also—probably—the mildest way.

G. At any rate the correct way. And with death and marriage and that sort of thing, one ought to be correct.

DR. K. Yeah. Also from a scientific viewpoint. It's safe to assume that nature performs that work best, despite everything.

G. Oh, really?

DR. K. It . . . carries out certain preliminaries, you see. It undermines one's resistance to a certain degree, makes the body somehow—more disposed to die, more in the vein, so that *mors* in the end has a relatively easy job of it. On the contrary, violent means, introduced from the outside without preparation, will have to deal with an unprepared, resistant body and must therefore proceed ruthlessly, resort to force, choke and break with tetanus and devilment, so that in all likelihood *mors* becomes a rather unpleasant affair.

G. *(with forced indifference).* Oh, as long as the dose is large enough—

DR. K. Well, yes.

G. Anyway, it's good to be finished with that sort of thing. I too have had my periods, of course. But partly I don't have sufficient energy, and partly I have such an aversion to scandal. So I intend to die in an unequivocally Christian manner, and I'm glad to hear that presumably it's also the most comfortable.

*(Pause. Dr. Kvaale looks at his watch.)*

G. *(quickly).* But as I've said, if insomnia should get too bad—. All in all, an intelligent human being should always have a vial of morphine in his medicine cabinet; it confers a certain sense of security and self-respect to know one is prepared for everything. Let's say I lie here racked with pain one night—you don't feel up to seeing the doctor exactly, not at that hour, but the pain may be such that it makes it quite unpleasant to lie there and wait till morning. It may simply be a tooth that starts aching, and there you lie—

DR. K. Yes, I'm familiar with that. However, one doesn't kill oneself so easily even when the means is at hand. Then, you see, one knows one can always do *that,* so why not wait awhile yet? And so one waits. And in the meantime the attack wears off.

G. Yes. So, maybe I'll come one of these days—

DR. K. Sure. You're an educated person, after all; you know how to handle a morphine vial. *(Gets up as if to go—sits down again.)* Come to think, you may have it right now. *(Takes out his notebook and writes a prescription.)*

G. Thank you, doctor.

DR. K. You're welcome. *(Gets up, puts on his gloves.)* And *should* the
devil ever tempt you, just remember what I've said. Well, now
I have to get down to my clumsy fool.

G. *(has put away the prescription).* Is there . . . enough?

DR. K. *(takes his hat and stick).* For a horse. Have a good evening.

*(g. grasps his hand and squeezes it in silence.)*

## XXXVII

Holy Communion. What is there about this expression that fascinates
me? God's blood in the golden chalice sparkles before my eyes like
a shower of rubies in a wave of sunlight.

The deep, hot purple blood; this bubbling fountain from the
eternal wellspring of life. I would bathe my soul in that darksome
depth and rise therefrom pure and fresh and young, like the goddess
from the shining foam of the sea.

I'll go to Løchen. I'll make confession to him and receive the
great pardon. And I'll enjoy—Holy Communion.

Sunday evening

A frightful winter. Every moment I slip back into these breakers,
which want to suck me in and devour me.

"Will." What is man's will? Pastor Løchen said in his student
sermon today that if it lacks a "living" center it dissolves into mutually conflicting drives and desires, and man drifts on the choppy
sea of life like a ship without rudder. That explanation may be the
correct one.

An idea, too, can be the center of a soul's will, but not of the whole will, he claimed, only for a larger or smaller part of it. Such an "ideal" person can, therefore, be great and admirable as regards a particular aspect, while in regard to others he is adrift like a wreck, a defenseless prey to wind and waves. Only something personal can be the "central center" of a human soul.

Ah yes, something personal, a woman or a God! All abstractions are dead. Even the profound philosophy of Buddhism is not sufficient when the will is broken. A paralyzed or decrepit person gets nowhere from having explained to him the theory of walking; what he needs is someone who can tell him with authority and force, "Rise, take up thy bed, and walk!"

I lie here adrift in my breakers, like a disgusting mollusk without a center. The awful thing is that I wouldn't be able to accept help even if offered. If God revealed himself to me in all his glory, I would fall down in a faint, but afterward I would say to myself: a hallucination, go see the doctor! And if Christ appeared and commanded me to be healthy, and I was healthy, I would say, Verily, he's no prophet; he's one of the more capable hypnotists.

My waking is a semisleep, my sleep is a semiconvulsion.

I wake up in the morning as if stupefied, sore and aching in limbs and joints, my brain collapsed and limp in my head, painfully tired, incapable of being properly awake. This must be how an epileptic feels after an attack, I imagine. And I stagger shakily up to the cabinet.

I'll have a nervous shock one of these days, I know that. I don't dare walk alone anymore; after all, it can come at any time. Frightened and shy, I wander about imagining I can hear voices; when, once in a while, I take a buggy ride I turn around again: that person over there could be a murderer. And if the road is lonely, I become afraid of the driver—he could suddenly go crazy, you know.

My corner at the Grand is the safest place.

*

"You study yourself too much," Kvaale says, "one should take care not to do that. One becomes much too interesting and disgusting to oneself that way; and the will dwindles and egomania swells up, so that in the end one falls an all too easy prey to the madhouse. Try to think of something else to be interested in, something external; there is certainly no lack of things to be annoyed at."

"Yes, but seeing that the only thing I'm concerned about is this lone, unhappy disgusting me—"

He gave a shrug. "We'll send you to the mountains again, when an opportunity offers."

"Come with me," I said. "You look as though you might need an excursion yourself."

He shook his head with a weary smile. Then he grew serious and said, "For me a longer trip will probably be necessary."

He gives the impression of being so broken, so ruined, now. Maybe he, too, is fallen.

Every once in a while I steal into the Catholic church, for vespers, when the lights are turned on. I hide in a dark corner and sit there bathed in organ sounds and choral singing till I cry.

The Nativity celebration the night before Christmas was, to me, an hour of salvation. I became a child again; I believed.

Cursed be the criticism that has eaten away the backbone of faith in us, and science, which sullies and defiles all that should remain sacred and untouchable with its impudent experimentalist fingers. For a long time Mephisto could do nothing with God's people. Then he disguised himself as science and was admitted to the Holy of Holies. And behold—suddenly that tiny peaceful, holy gleam of light from Bethlehem was extinguished.

Why am I so unhappily made? Why must I have this leak in my

brain, this crack in the wall which offers an open view? Why can I not "believe"?

True or not true—how abysmally indifferent! A wall has been knocked out in my soul; the full winter cold of existence blows directly in, and I can see the wolves prowling about out there in the night, with yelps and howls and foaming at the mouth. I sit here, my teeth chattering with cold and dread, and pray gods, devils, and the blue inane for a warm hand to shake, a warm eye to look into, to lose myself in, until the terrors of the night wear off.

Oh eternal wisdom from the lips of a child! Adam was in paradise, but paradise itself came to be horrid to him because he was alone. And behold: there was woman, white and warm, with deep, dark eyes that forgave. . . .

I rarely see Jonathan now. He's cold and self-righteous and shallow, with no inkling of life's depths.

If we meet there's argument. He has an all but half-educated contempt for what he doesn't understand. And despite his "pride" he's by no means above having recourse to tricks—disingenuousness, distortions, empty derision, extravagant postulates.

"Spiritism is not merely something to be laughed at," I said. "It's still groping its way in ignorance and childishness and is enveloped in humbug, but at any rate it seeks to put us in contact with eternity. And when all is said and done, that is really the one thing needful."

He shrugged his shoulders and looked at me. "Can't one get off with less?" he said.

"What do you mean?"

"I too have lately thought of assuming a *fin-de-siècle* mask," he scoffed, "but I must confess that if it requires reverence for the English-speaking Cicero, then—."

Such absolute lack of understanding!

## XXXVIII

20 March

The mailman brought me a black-edged letter; I thought I knew the handwriting. Stabbed by a sudden fear, I tore it open; it was signed Dr. Kvaale.

I'm still trembling. This terror is insurmountable—.

Dear Gram,

I can't any longer. When this letter has been mailed, I shall empty my last glass. I write to send you my farewell greeting.

I recognized in you a brother in suffering. Maybe you'll soon follow me. In that case, congratulations!

It's the decision that's difficult. Once it has been made, one feels confident and free. This may have been my one and only happy moment in life.

My account is settled, everything is in order. In half an hour all the world's sorrows and afflictions will knock on my door in vain; Johannes Kvaale will have escaped.

I presume there is no immortality. But if I live on, and if I should have something to report to you, I'll get in touch with you. Don't be afraid, I won't scare you. I'll watch out for a time when you're not nervous or weak, a time when you'll be able to endure it. Perhaps someday you will meet a man whose name you can't remember but whom you think you must have known once; if that man engages you in conversation and tells you things that no eye has ever seen and no ear has heard, and that have not arisen in any man's heart—that's me. And then you must give me a glance of recognition, and a friendly word I can take with me to my supposedly rather lonely beyond.

Goodbye, Gram. Skoal. Welcome after.

Very sincerely yours,<br>*Joh. Kvaale*

P.S. Only you and a physician, whose discretion is assured, know the truth.

I'm sleeping in a hotel during this time; there are people and traffic from evening till morning, and in a pinch I can call the valet. Curiously enough, insanely scared; soft in the head—.

If I knew a hypnotist, I would look him up and have my fancies hypnotized away.

Impossible?

Why?

Suppose the old wisdom is correct, the one that has reigned throughout the world until now and which the spiritists are trying to retrieve—and why shouldn't this be just as correct as the opinion of a few pedestrian materialists from the last century, people who stopped at nothing to banish spirit from existence, since they couldn't place it under the microscope? Suppose that the soul is the original element, eternal, so that the body is nothing but an outfit that the soul puts on and throws off as it pleases. . . . Why, exactly, should the body be the essential thing, this sick, wretched body which we know has no self-subsistence, this conglomerate of cells that is held together by some shaping principle or other and falls apart in putrefaction as soon as that principle ceases to function? A ridiculous idea, a typical idea of the professors and the laboratory: since we can see the product, the product exists; but since we cannot see the productive principle, there is no productive principle, notwithstanding the fact that the product could definitely not exist without the productive principle!

I have at bottom never believed in any of that. At bottom I've always imagined "death" as a transition; imagined that I would go on living, float about with the drifting clouds and the soughing winds, move from planet to planet and see new sights and new truths. The soul possesses the immediate certainty that it will not die.

Should energies and consciousnesses, these highest and most finished forms of existence, the peaks of creation, its explanation and *raison d'être*—should they cease to be, disappear, fade away into nothing and everything, when even the most paltry atom of dust cannot be annihilated? That's just utter drivel.

Or how about my poor doctor, that strong man in a miserable body, a rich, deep, fine soul which, hidden behind an unimpressive exterior, had barely managed to begin living?

What did Fanny say? And she had intuition: "There *must* be a second part to the novel." I put more faith in this childish outburst of spontaneous emotion than in five hundred professors who deny what they cannot smell.

Dear unhappy friend, keep your word. You know I'm still nervous and weak; do not follow me. . . .

I was drawn by an irresistible fear; I had to see him. He was frightful.

Absolutely unrecognizable. The face dismally black, haggard, with open, staring, gelatinous eyes; the mouth gaping, the nose broken, an idiotic fearful smile frozen on the razor-thin, blue-black lips. Large yellow teeth grinned brutishly from the middle of the twisted picture of horror. The sight paralyzed me. I was going to feel sick; the body began floating and swaying before my eyes, nodding. . . . I tore myself away and staggered out, pursued by a strange, intimate terror that held me in its embrace, breathed on the nape of my neck, whispered in my ears, enveloping me in the stench of decay and oppression of spirit, suffocating me. . . .

Some time later I found myself, God knows how, in Pastor Løchen's drawing room. Had a nervous attack and turned the house topsy-turvy. The family doctor was fetched, a serious, energetic young man; he sat down at my bedside and talked to me. I calmed down and fell asleep.

He persecutes me. Whenever I'm alone, he is nearby, behind me, like a nerve center in the air; I can feel him, as one can perceive a pair of eyes staring fixedly at the nape of one's neck.

Pastor Løchen said that I should pray. It does help sometimes, especially in the evening, when I've gone to bed; but in the daytime, when it's light, I can't. It's just playacting.

## XXXIX

I have followed him to the grave.

Officially he died of a heart attack. The funeral was very nice. Amazingly large funeral procession; the shy, lonely man had more friends on the quiet than he knew. An older physician and George Jonathan acted as pallbearers.

Løchen spoke. He had as his text these words from Ecclesiastes, "All is vanity, vanity and vexation of spirit." He said many apt things about life's sorrow.

The book of Ecclesiastes was accepted into the Bible because it shows, in an inspired way, the necessity of salvation by representing to us the world as it appears from the viewpoint of the godless. A world without hope, without a deeper explanation, is nothing, nothing—except vanity and vexation of spirit. Everything that human beings attempt to fill their existence with, pleasure, work, great ideas, common humanity—without a deeper explanation it's all meaningless and empty: vanity and vexation of spirit. This book of the Old Testament looks as though it was written for the present time; it is the true introduction to Christianity for the highly educated present generation, since it gives expression to the despair, the pessimism, at which a more highly developed human being is bound to arrive when trying to live without God. "This man whom we today follow to the grave was an honest quester, and he didn't hide from those who knew him the fact that his quest and his thought had led him away from faith and the God of faith. He was an able and energetic laborer in his vocation, and his heart was full of love for mankind; his thought was constantly occupied with problems and projects for the improvement of the human condition, and we can safely say that the nobility of his character matched his high development. And yet the sum total of his realization was this: all is vanity—vanity and vexation of spirit. Confirmed in this realization, he was suddenly snatched away.

"But when he had reached this realization, he found himself on the threshold of Christianity, of salvation. And we hope that at the last moment he did find favor with God, the merciful one, and was permitted to enter. For all who knew him believe that his quest was sincere. And he in whose mouth was found no guile has promised and said that whoever seeks—he *shall* find."

A certain peace came over me. The terrible uneasiness that had plagued me since I received the message of death wore off.

Who knows the last sigh of the dying? Who knows what may have opened up for him when the shadows of death were already beginning to settle on his heart? And who knows precisely what awaits us behind that dark gate?

Dr. Thisted, Løchen's new family doctor, is an interesting man. Very different from the common run of our physicians.

He has traveled a lot and has some ideas he must "keep quiet about here at home"; for example, he believes in hypnotism.

"There is nothing mystical in this teaching," he says, "but it will create a revolution all the same, and not just in medicine and the administration of justice. You see, it tacitly contains the truth—one that is dangerous to all so-called modern science—that the soul is the main thing, and that poking around in cadavers is no longer the only scientific way.

"Spiritism? I'll take a wait-and-see attitude. If it can prove its thesis, then it's true. Nothing is more idiotic than repudiation in advance of everything unfamiliar, an attitude so characteristic of present-day science. By and large, if you want to know what dogmatism and dogmatic narrow-mindedness are, then you should go not to theology, but to medicine."

Sunday forenoon

Yes, he's here. He is in the room, in the corner, five or six feet behind my chair. He looks at me with those strange, faraway eyes.

Does he have something to tell me? The suspense is simply awful. . . .

Dear unhappy friend, if it's possible, if no spiritual or natural laws stand in your way, then reveal yourself to me, now, in this moment, when I'm expecting you and am prepared; or reveal to me the truth without which I can no longer live. Answer me with signs. If there are two knocks, it's yes; if there are three knocks, it's no.

*Is there life after death?*

Ten trembling, suspenseful minutes. Dead silence.

Maybe he can write. I'll pick up my pencil—.

Half an hour of experiments. Useless. To be sure, my hand moves, quite automatically; at times it's made to move with a certain force. But all it amounts to is meaningless lines and squiggles.

Is there too much light?

I darkened the room by hanging blankets before the windows. Afterward I experimented for over an hour. No result.

I'm not a medium; even if he's here, he cannot communicate through me. My skeptical, stubborn nature offers unconscious resistance.

Another medium then.

But—as soon as this other medium comes in between, we have at the same time the possibility of deception—conscious deception or self-deception. Hopeless.

How strangely weak I have become. Out. Take a short walk.

During dinner at Løchen's today they talked about Mrs. Ryen. Dr. Thisted is the family doctor out there too and knows her well.

Pastor Løchen knows her too, from religious associations. She has turned Christian.

"A striking proof of the psychiatric method's correctness," said the doctor. "You see, she was in a rather bad way, suffered from hysterical headaches, insomnia, and constant anxiety; she had already started with morphine shots. Her nervous system was altogether in a rather sorry state. Now she's just fine."

"How exactly did it happen?" I asked.

"I simply persuaded her to go to church."

"Oh, I see."

"The real reason why there are so many nervous illnesses in our time is that our view of life is out of order. An individual loses— let's say God; with that his spiritual life has lost its center, it's without a regulator, so to speak, and takes to dashing off in an abnormal, wild flight, without any control. And all at once the spring breaks. Besides, Mrs. Ryen was . . . not very happy in her marriage, which made the situation even worse. She occupied herself with a thousand things just to fill time, to take the edge off her thoughts—it's the usual way, of course; and by now, you see, she had gotten to the point of taking morphine. But it quietly sorted itself out again when she gradually regained a more harmonious conception of life; that brought peace to her soul and, along with it, peace to her nervous system."

"Are you—a Christian, doctor?" I asked diffidently.

"In a dogmatic sense—no. But I'm definitely religious and uphold Christianity on essential points. Our honored host, the pastor, doesn't think I'll be damned," he added with a smile.

"Well, yes, those dogmas," the pastor sighed, "which by an unfortunate misunderstanding hinder so many religious souls from finding the way. But now we shall see," he added more cheerfully, "how the Christianity that we clergymen have dogmatized out of existence will be medicated in again by our esteemed physicians!"

"Pardon me," the doctor said politely, "it's our esteemed clergymen who will help medicine on its feet again."

The conversation drifted to other areas; I sat in silence thinking about Fanny.

Perhaps she's now just as beautiful again.


"But what can be the use of believing in a God whose existence cannot be proven?"

Dr. Thisted replied, "It's the other way around. It's impossible to have doubts about a God whose *non*existence cannot be proven. Anyway, what do you mean by this antiquated-sounding expression 'prove'? Do you want to put him under the microscope?"

"That, obviously, wouldn't really prove anything either."

"No, that's an old mistake. The microscope is useful in examining bacteria, but if one wants to examine the sun, for example, other instruments are used."

"To tell the truth, doctor, the more I consider, the more I find that nothing really stands in the way of my adopting your . . . more modern view of life. Nothing objective. But it avails me nothing. Positivistic skepticism has corroded my soul like an acid, until the very *ability* to believe has been lost. As a matter of fact, I do believe only in what I have under the microscope—and when all is said and done, not even in that. The organ has become paralyzed."

"Can't there possibly be some other explanation?"

"For example?"

"I remember those days when I started taking an interest in hypnotism. I studied it in secret but scoffed at it openly. In the end I really believed, but I continued to scoff. Why?"

"Yes, why?"

"Finally it dawned on me; but for three months I tried to deny it. My entire disbelief was due to the fact that I had a very clever and gifted friend whom I feared; I was afraid of his ridicule—and the ridicule of my other friends. Oh, it does sound wretched, but the considerations that keep us away from what we have ourselves realized are often that cowardly."

"Well, I never!"

"Yes. And so I made a clean break and said to myself: I don't give a hoot about those fellows! I'll no longer permit others to prescribe what I shall assume or not assume! And I possessed sufficient independence to really make myself free."

I didn't hear what he said anymore. I was thinking about George Jonathan. Could it really be that?

## XL

April '90

I go to church and listen to Løchen every Sunday. And I always go home with my mind at rest.

This quiet depth, this holy simplicity, this beneficent clarity as regards those questions that, in the end, are the only ones that concern us—why haven't I had the courage to seek these pavilions before?

Here is none of the flashiness of "science," the hullabaloo with which they try to consign the hopeless "we don't know" to oblivion. The river of faith, which is so shallow that a lamb can wade and so deep that an elephant can swim in it, flows tranquil and clear, and refreshingly pure.

She, too, is there. Pale, thin, with the traces of much suffering and with an ethereal glow in those deep eyes. I again have a sense of security and contentment such as I haven't felt since we two, she and I, wandered together on darksome paths.

I'll have to get over this notion of "him who follows me"; it sometimes becomes too strong. Once in a while it overwhelms me with a fear that makes me helpless.

Today, as I was walking up Ullevold Road, a pale man dressed in black went past me; there was a somber, dark air about the man's whole manner, a sepulchral mood. His irregular face with those small, rather shy eyes attracted my attention. He himself stared at me with a curious look in his eyes—it suddenly occurred to me that I must have known him, but I couldn't recall his name. The next moment it flashed through me, It's him! *him!* And overcome by a fear that spread chills through my whole body and nearly paralyzed me, I saved myself through flight.

Who is unhappy? He who has become the carrier of a dark secret.

Such a secret is like a devil in a cage: it wants out, it wants out! I catch myself saying aloud to myself as I walk, "Dr. Kvaale took poison, Dr. Kvaale took poison." Then I give a start, terrified, and look about me; there could be someone nearby who had heard it.

No more whiskey and soda—and no absinthe. What if, in an unguarded moment, I should blurt out this insinuation, which is on the tip of my tongue!

"Madness or Christ!"

I'm weary. My anxieties overwhelm me. I cannot sleep at night for fear that he will manifest himself; I lie with the lamp burning, reading the Bible.

Jesus is the good shepherd. In his arms one does not need fear Satan anymore, nor his envoys.

Oh, that old godless existence, which turned the world into a snow-covered chasm, gray as twilight and full of ghosts! It's high time, high time, that I save myself. New, brighter times shall come. Once more the Easter bells will ring out through the world; once more the morning song will sound:

> Christ ist erstanden!
> Freude dem Sterblichen,
> den die verderblichen,
> schleichenden, erblichen
> Mängel umwanden . . .

To pat a dog, to make a child's face all smiles, to enable an old woman to breathe easier by giving her a krone, to help a young man feel a zest for life, however briefly, by making him enthusiastic about something—all in all, to contribute something, much or little, so as to increase life's pitiful legacy of joy: won't that weigh more on the Day of Judgment than twenty volumes of ennui?— says Dr. Thisted.

I began to glimpse a calling. We shall meet, she and I, in a better way than we once imagined.

Dr. Thisted has a remarkably beneficial effect on me.

It's not what he says, even less the household remedies he gives me to strengthen my nervous system—it's he himself who affects me. His own clear, strong personality.

Ultimately that's the only true medical science: not the physic, but the physician. One soul affects another, and then again the soul affects the body.

He manages to make me believe in him. That way he gives me the staff with whose help I, taken with palsy, can suddenly stand up and walk. Now I understand that Jesus of Nazareth could perform miracles.

Every physician who cannot perform miracles is a quack. Every physician who isn't also a spiritual adviser is a quack.

He tidies up in my innermost self, removes difficulties, breaks down obstacles, sweeps away fancies, exorcises fear. He takes hold of all the healthy fibers of my soul and nurtures and strengthens them. He restores my self-confidence, my faith in my will, my *spirit;* he gives me the courage to have courage, God knows how.

He sets up values for me; what lay scattered and trashed and meaningless before my eyes, becomes coherent, full of soul.

He reconstructs existence for me by giving it a center.

I cannot believe like Løchen or like her. But my heart is filled with a strange tranquillity and peace at the notion of "the good shepherd."

The good shepherd who sacrifices his life for the flock—it sounds so marvelously good and simple, and so positively reassuring.

Never in my anxious dreams did I have any idea of the quiet grandeur of the figure of Christ. Never did I find in the world, under the most vociferous glamour, anything that in purity, loftiness, and noblesse compared even tentatively with that which was hidden behind his humble poverty.

He has promised to give me rest, and he gives it me. I don't know exactly what the situation is with regard to his divinity, but from now on he is my hero. My old doubts, etc., are schoolboy wisdom from my senior high-school class; schoolboys, naturally, are too wise for God. From now on I'm a truly "proud man," who couldn't care less about the world's opinion, that is, the opinion of "science," and who seeks peace where peace can be found.

Løchen was right. The world is a discord. And a discord has its truth, not within but outside itself, in its resolution. But the resolution is called eternity.

"Have you noticed," Løchen said today, "that nearly all great apostles and leaders of freethinking are Jews?"

And he set forth how the so-called freethinking, this cold, flat negativism, was nothing but a continuation of the great crime on Good Friday. "It's the Wandering Jew who walks about to the end of time, persecuting the victorious Galilean with his undying hate. He has nothing to give, nothing to offer; he can only tear down, steal, and rob. He has nothing but his hate, and hate is barren, just as love is life-enhancing."

And he said one more thing that is true, "All truly great spirits are religious."

Such a painful struggle for "peace" and "light"—and then the light is right here among us.

As Pastor Løchen said today: I have gone about believing in Christ a long time. The only thing necessary was to acknowledge it to myself. From now on I belong to the new century, the century of the imagination, faith, the heart. I go to church and listen to the song of bygone days of greatness in a different spirit than before, because I can join in the singing, it's my song—as it is that of my ancestors.

But I feel happiest in the Catholic church, where the authentic old church singing can be heard, and where the eternal flame burns at the flower-trimmed foot of the Madonna's altar.

You pure, holy one who still understands, you blessed among

women, you Virgin Mother—you I shall worship beside your glorious son; for only that religion is a true religion which also has an altar for woman, for the Holy Virgin and the Holy Mother—for the threefold holy Virgin-Mother.

"He" doesn't pursue me anymore. As if my new doctor had hypnotized him away, he's gone.

That "man in black" I saw again today—at Pastor Løchen's. He's a very real and a very intelligent man; his name is Pastor Holck, and I want to talk more with him. He was going to a meeting of the Association for Provision of Free Meals to Poor Schoolchildren with Mrs. Ryen and some other women. I took out membership in the association right away.

A difficult path lies ahead of me. Only then will I feel a true child of the new age when I have definitively broken with all the old things.

I'll go once more to George Jonathan.

## XLI

Not without a certain emotion did I sit down today in my old chair in George Jonathan's private office on University Street.

He was the same as always. And as I sat there listening to him, it became almost unbelievable to me that I had been able to maintain this friendship for so long.

That conceited, smug, self-righteous manner! Great God, what exactly do we mortals have to give ourselves airs about?

And then that curious dandyism of his, self-ironic only by half. He even wants to pass for an (illegitimate) son of an English lord. Accordingly, everything must be English. Long reddish whiskers, strongly pomaded hair with parting front and back; white, fat, strikingly well-groomed hands; that perpetual gray angler's garb with the bankruptcy hat; that stiff nape of the neck and that monocle-crowned expression of feigned indifference! In reality, his whole being repels me, from outermost to inmost.

He devoted a few friendly words of feigned indifference to Dr. Kvaale; then the missus brought the coffee. I exchanged the customary sentences with her. Then he asked what was the "state of my teetotalism at the moment." I thanked him and said, "I have, as a matter of fact, lost the taste for pleasures of that kind; but I can always take a glass of liqueur."

All of a sudden he sat in the midst of "the society of the future." He probably hadn't had a chance "to hear George Jonathan speak" for some time.

"For instance," he said, "you don't have any idea what an evening party will be like in the future." And he related how the guests, after partaking of a royal supper—"at 50 øre per cover, wine included"—when the coffee was served would be handed a "program for the evening's enjoyments" which, translated into the language of the present, would look roughly like this:

THÉÂTRE FRANÇAIS: *The Miser.*

GRAND OPÉRA: *Don Juan.*

OPÉRA COMIQUE: *The Barber of Seville.*

THÉÂTRE D'EDEN: Grand Ballet.

CIRCUS RENZ: Gala performance.

SAINT PETER'S BASILICA: High evening mass with
    processions.

HOUSE OF COMMONS: Evening session; great speech by
    Gladstone.

PHILHARMONIC: Bülow concert.

    And so on, and so forth.

"Then the gracious host asks each one individually: 'Have you made your selection? Which play do you want to see, which opera do you want to hear?' Whereupon everybody makes himself comfortable at his telephone and his screen—you understand: the screen which picks up the photographic snapshots of the play in question, so that not only can one hear what is said but also see what happens, every movement, every facial expression. During the intermissions they walk and exchange impressions. One is jubilant about the Spanish ballerinas at the Eden Theater, while another is dying with enthusiasm over Gladstone's speech. That will be some entertainment!"

I smiled. "You still believe that happiness is to be achieved by external means, don't you?" I asked.

"Happiness? What do we need happiness for?" he said. "Happiness, well, that's boredom; happiness is to sleep or to be dead. I can't imagine anything more hopeless than to be happy. I assume that people will always be so dissatisfied that they will continually find a reason to aspire to better things. No, life is just going to be humane, fit for human beings. Those little prosaic, pernicious quotidian troubles must be put out of the way, to make room for the great troubles, the grief of Juliet and Romeo, Hamlet's and Faust's despair."

"And those who are in despair—what will you do for them?"

"For them I have my death festival."

I got up; the moment had arrived.

"All this masked despair is quite indifferent to me," I said.

He too got up. Stood face to face with me, staring at me with eyes in which I glimpsed something satanic.

"I've suspected as much," he said. "So you don't want to join my paper?"

"No."

"You're going to the clergyman."

"I have liberated myself," I said. "I'm giving up all the old clichés. I'm seeking satisfaction for my soul—where it can be found."

"To him, all right!" he mumbled.

"Goodbye!" I said, wanting to go. He stood in my way.

"I took you for a man," he continued, determined to vent his spleen, "one of those who bend but do not break. So you were too weak, after all; there was that fatal crack in your spine. *Fin de siècle— agonie de la bourgeoisie.* I'm very sorry, Gram. But it cannot be helped. The weary ones go to the clergyman. Goodbye."

"I did bend," I said, "because I didn't want to break. You go and do likewise. Farewell."

I left. Behind me I could hear George Jonathan's laughter.

It sounded as though it came from hell.

## »)»» AFTERWORD «)«(«
## GARBORG AND DECADENCE

> *Fin de siècle.* Strange times. The world is on the eve
> of another turning point. The more we know, the
> more we see that we can know nothing; all we can do
> is to recognize this and seek remedies elsewhere.
>
> (*Weary Men,* part 2, chapter 28)

*I*

Immediately after the publication of *Weary Men* in 1891, Arne
Garborg (1851-1924) wrote to Jonas Lie that the book was "somewhat 'thrown together'—gotten up in a hurry."[1] Even if we do not
take this literally, it should at any rate indicate that Garborg was
surprised by the lively debate triggered by *Weary Men.* The book
found more readers than any of his previous books, and the amount
of discussion it elicited was unprecedented in his experience. Garborg's place on Parnassus was decisively strengthened. A well-
known German critic, Johannes Schlaf, who read the novel when it
appeared in translation shortly afterward, felt justified in calling it
"the most perfect psychological novel" in recent literature.[2] It is
still the one among Garborg's books that is of greatest interest to
foreign critics.

However, the reason why so many contemporary Norwegians
were moved by the novel was not literary. They were chiefly interested in the author's value system. What was most important in

their eyes were Garborg's opinions on moral issues and his attitude toward Christianity. In order to understand this, we have to remember that the 1890s were a period of acute crisis and conflict in every domain of cultural life, and that the intellectual support of Garborg and other prominent thinkers was considered extremely important. Christians in particular detected in *Weary Men* new and positive signals from a writer hitherto known as a freethinker and anarchist. What they emphasized above all in their reading of the novel was Gabriel Gram's eventual conversion, interpreting it as the story of Garborg's own. The book was simply understood as a personal testimony and, generally, as a religious work. Indeed, there were instances where people would go to the bookstore and ask for that new collection of sermons there had been so much talk about!

On the other hand, many readers had great difficulty discovering what Garborg's intention had been in writing *Weary Men* and how he perceived his own relationship to the hero he had created. The critic Christopher Bruun (1839–1920) was one of those in doubt. An 1892 meeting of the Student Association in Kristiania (now Oslo), called in order to discuss the book, came to no conclusion; since the debaters were unable to formulate their views on the morality that the novel embodied, the meeting was also rather boring.

A third group dismissed out of hand the allegation that *Weary Men* was about Garborg finding his way to God. This group was firmly backed both by the author himself and by his wife, Hulda. Incidentally, Hulda Garborg was assigned to interview her husband on this very issue by the daily *Verdens Gang*. She used the interview, among other things, to vent her sarcasm at the Christians' reading of the book and ridiculed the very idea of a conversion. Anyway, if her husband were to have converted, she intimated, he would have espoused an optimistic Christianity, in sharp contrast to that of Gabriel Gram. Garborg himself engaged in a polemic with Bjørnstjerne Bjørnson (1832–1910): he had noticed, he said, that some people obviously *needed* to convert freethinkers. All the same, he had not turned Christian. On the other hand, he now thought that dogmatic freethinking was just as bad as dogmatic belief. Therefore, he wanted to *include* Christianity in his view of life, and he admits that he might need to liberate himself "on various points."[3]

The Swedish writer Hjalmar Söderberg (1869–1941) probably echoes Garborg's own view when he considers Gabriel Gram to be "the author's underground self, so to speak—that self which rears its head again and again in moments of loneliness and weakness, in hours of idleness, in unguarded nocturnal dreams." Gram is to Söderberg "the personality that an author avoids becoming in reality through making him live on paper."[4]

In sum, *Weary Men* is a work of such complexity that no one has been able to come up with a univocal norm or an unambiguous message. The same problem has confronted all those who have wanted to see this novel as a typical work of decadence. It both is and is not such a work.

In order to understand how this is possible, we must first briefly examine the notion of "decadence."

*II*

In its definite form the word "decadence" as used in literary discussion denotes, first, a diverse group of artists in the latter half of the nineteenth century, and, second, the artistic movement this group represented; in its indefinite form it stands for a general attitude toward life that we also today associate with the adjective "decadent." Etymologically, decadence means "decline." But no matter which of these phenomena one is interested in, the road takes us to France. It was there the concept was created, where the most central artists were found, and where the "decadent" milieus were most extreme.

The credit for having made the expression *décadence* current in intellectual debate goes to a classical philologist. His name was Désiré Nisard, who in 1834 published a book of criticism on "les poètes latins de la décadence," that is, the Latin poets from the period when the Roman Empire was on the decline. But he also wanted to demonstrate that, from about 1775 on, French literature itself had been "decadent." In this way he intervened directly in the contemporary debate.

While Nisard was trying to counteract this state of affairs, there were many poets who identified themselves, warts and all, with the picture of the decadent artist and accepted his representation of decline and decay in intellectual culture, and in society as a whole. This was true whether they used the word "decadence" or not. Charles Baudelaire is usually seen as the chief source of inspiration for the decadent writers who appeared several decades later. He called his principal work of 1857—*Les Fleurs du mal (The Flowers of Evil)*—a "product of the muses of the end-time,"[5] and wrote that he had more memories than if he had lived to be a thousand years old. Like Gabriel Gram he was in many ways "born old." Baudelaire's literary universe is replete with the nightside of the human psyche—passions, phantasms, nightmarish visions, incurable wounds, jarring disharmonies—but also with a deep longing to overcome loneliness and self-division. The key words in Baudelaire are "spleen" and "ennui."

But it goes without saying that the decadents did not content themselves with worshiping a dead poet; to create a milieu they needed, beside a collective name, a living leader and a journal. They got both.

The writer and critic Paul Bourget did a great deal to give the concept of decadence a positive content. Thus, in 1876 he wrote that without "being humble and without being proud, we accept this terrible word *decadence*. . . . The great centuries could not last for ever."[6] To us, it is interesting that Bourget is one of the Frenchmen Gabriel Gram admires: "I also like Bourget; he presents in his essays a very straightforward *philosophie du pessimisme.*" Gram must have in mind his *Essais de psychologie contemporaine* of 1883 and 1885. In his essay on Baudelaire, Bourget included a "Theory of Decadence."

Beside Baudelaire and Bourget, poets like Paul Verlaine and Stephane Mallarmé, along with others, influenced the decadent movement. But its principal figure turned out to be a modest government official, much against his will and on account of a single book. That author was Joris-Karl Huysmans, and the book was the remarkable work *A Rebours* (*Against the Grain,* 1922) from 1884. It has been said that *A Rebours* became "la Bible de l'esprit décadent."[7] With its refined, hyperintellectual, deeply divided and neurotic hero, the novel acquired a greater influence in European literary milieus than we can easily imagine today. Interestingly, the title character in Oscar Wilde's *The Picture of Dorian Gray* (1891) receives no less than nine copies of the first edition of *A Rebours.*

Nobody has been able to establish with certainty whether Garborg had read *A Rebours* or not. According to the Norwegian scholar Rolf Thesen, Hulda Garborg thought that her husband "had hardly read anything by Huysmans."[8] In that case it is strange how many parallels there are between the literary world of Huysmans and that of Garborg; I shall come back to this later. Here it may just be mentioned that Huysmans is another Frenchman whom Gabriel Gram appreciates: "he's excellent. And queer"—he notes. And why should not Garborg, just as well as Gram, have read something by him? He knew French, after all, judging by the fact—pointed out by Johs. A. Dale, another Garborg expert—that he had read the Goncourt brothers' novel *Germinie Lacerteux.* And in a letter to Amalie Skram, Garborg is looking forward to "hearing a civilized language, namely, French." [9]

However this may be, there can be no doubt that Garborg knew a lot *about* Huysmans and the other decadent writers, and that he was well acquainted with the thinking behind the decadence and with the milieus where the movement prevailed. During sojourns in Paris in the mid-1880s and from 1889 for a couple of years in Germany, he had had the opportunity to make firsthand observations of the European literary scene.

### III

A reader of *Weary Men* familiar with Garborg's production will soon discover clear thematic links to his previous works. One such theme is that of marriage, along with its contraries of bachelorhood and loneliness. In *Bondestudentar* (1883; *Peasant Students*), *Mannfolk* (1886; *Men*), *Hjaa ho mor* (1890; *With Mother*), as well as in several of his stories and essays, questions like these are central: Why do people get married? On what basis do women marry? On what basis do men marry? What is the real state of affairs within marriage? And what happens to those who, for different reasons, remain beyond the pale of established family life: old maids and old bachelors, domestic servants, prostitutes, and those individuals—women and men alike—who consciously *choose* to stay single? Similarly, it seems significant that such questions are to some extent thematized through the same characters from one book to another, at any rate through the same names. Daniel Braut appears in *Peasant Students* as well as in *Men,* and both Gabriel Gram and George Jonathan turn up in *Men* and *Weary Men.* Gabriel Gram is also found in *With Mother,* where the main character is Fanny Holmsen, the woman that Gram is so obsessed with in *Weary Men.* When we know, besides, that Garborg discussed the topic of marriage in articles and letters, we come to see that *Weary Men* is anything but a book apart in his oeuvre. Just like *Peasant Students* and *Men* it may be called a bachelor novel, though to a greater degree than the two others. Anyway, a "weary man" full of "ennui" would seem quite unthinkable as the father of a family.

Gabriel Gram's main problem seems to be that he is neurotically divided, both in regard to women and to marriage, with its many obligations. He is even divided with regard to his own divided emotions. In the view of the decadents, and as many of Baudelaire's poems had shown, to be morbidly self-conscious is one of the marks of the modern intellectual. In one moment devoured by love for a woman, in the next cursing everything having to do with women, thereafter occupying himself by analyzing his changing attitudes—such is Gabriel Gram. About his attraction to Fanny he says that it was "a painful, sick, divided love, a dissolution of my being." But just as often he attacks her and blames her for everything. At other times he defends his own life style as a positive alternative to marriage: "longing, loss, pain, and worry—that's just what life *is* . . . , while being satiated and content—well, that is simply the end of everything." At such moments he is glad not to belong to the number of "all those distressed married men." But Gram's internal conflict never ends, and he has to admit that he is lonely and misses the experience of sharing. Also, his acquaintances are getting married. "Soon I'll be alone," he says at the beginning of Part Two.

This is the main reason why he begins to think of the shared values represented by religion and the church. For a long time seeking salvation is merely something he debates with himself intellectually. Gradually it becomes a real way out: "I will fold my hands in humility during the confession of our forefathers' faith—and *wish* I could believe as they did." His resumed friendship with a drinking companion from his student days, now become "Pastor Løchen," plays a certain role in this connection. Gabriel Gram is deeply impressed when Løchen relates that, for him, the choice had been between "madness and Christ." Moreover, the suicide of his friend Dr. Kvaale, the representative of science and freethinking, is a shocking experience to Gram. At last he feels that he is moving further and further away from George Jonathan, with whom he has associated more than with anybody else. Their final meeting is very eloquent in this respect: the attorney appears as a cold cynic who makes fun of Gram's conversion, which—rather than being an occasion for hallelujahs—is accompanied by profound despair and an agonizing inner struggle.

It is not surprising that Gabriel Gram calls the world a "bin" and a "sewer" and that he perpetrates a merciless analysis of practically every single social group, an analysis concluding with the statement that he refuses to go along anymore: *"Fin de siècle, fin de siècle. Fin de la culture européenne."* The most odious group, in his eyes, is the moneyed aristocracy, but he spares no one. Of particular interest is his showing-up of both art and artists, since this implicates himself and his plan to turn his "notes" into a book: "someday, maybe, *this* could become a novel," he muses, and after Dr. Kvaale's suicide he thinks that *he* shall "represent contemporary pessimism" in the novel, by contrast to George Jonathan. But Gram's attitude to the vocation of the writer is ambivalent.

## IV

There can be no doubt that literature is important to Gabriel Gram, as it is in the novel as a whole. Thus, numerous novelists and poets are alluded to and discussed in his "notes." But Gram's attitude to *other* writers is no more unequivocal than his attitude to *himself* as a writer. Partly he is satirical, saying how it amused him to "tease" George Jonathan with the "religious reaction" in French literature, partly he is serious about the same writers, as when he mentions Huysmans and Bourget (and Hennique). Gabriel Gram is a very slippery character, not easily grasped. Nor is it easy to determine when and in what respect he speaks for the author, whether the subject is literature or something else.

I have already mentioned that nobody has been able to discern a clear authorial norm in *Weary Men*, with its many-layered irony. Though the author himself feared that his irony would not be sufficiently manifest on account of his use of first-person narration, it does become apparent in several ways. For one, Garborg's very use of "Dano-Norwegian," as he called it, implies distance. The literary historian A. H. Winsnes correctly describes the language of *Weary Men* as "a flexible and elegant *riksmål*"[10]—traditional Norwegian, similar to Danish. But one cannot help asking why this was the only one of Garborg's novels which did not appear in *landsmål* (New Norwegian, a written language based on rural dialects). Was it not in order to underscore how urban and European the problems of Gram were? And yet, Garborg's use of *riksmål* did not imply distance alone; it was also, after all, the language he used in most of his articles.

The same double vision informs Garborg's treatment of his central character in *Weary Men*. The author's compassion with his despairing hero is authentic enough, as shown by the presence of the superficial George Jonathan as the hero's foil. On the other hand, Gram is viewed with unmistakable irony. The irony may apply to his view of women, as in the following: "Up here one becomes so poor in spirit that one even finds time to concern oneself with women's liberation"; or it is directed at his religious yearning, as in this passage: "A desperately sick yearning to throw oneself at the feet of someone or other, a woman, a priest, a god, and howl, weep, confess, be whipped, cursed, condemned, finally to be lifted up by a pair of trusty, loving arms like a sick child.—I have to be a bit careful, I might get the horrors." In these lines we detect a hint of something that will be further developed later on, namely, a conflation of religious and sexual longing. In an apostrophe to the Virgin Mary, Gram calls her "you blessed among women"; she is at once "the Holy Virgin and the Holy Mother . . .[,] the threefold holy Virgin Mother." Viewed in light of the novel as a whole, there is no doubt that this must be read ironically, as is Gram's equation of eros and love of mother, "the holy woman in whose arms . . . [the male] experienced absolute security."

It appears, therefore, that *Weary Men* is constructed around a dialogical play between seriousness and mockery, irony and non-irony. And the irony is partly Gabriel Gram's self-directed irony, partly Garborg's irony at the expense of Gram, partly Garborg's own self-directed irony, partly his irony aimed at other literature. Already the introduction casts an ironic light on the novel. Thus, Gram speaks about "pretend[ing] to be a writer," thereby trivializing his "notes and impressions" as the product of a mere dilettante; yet, going by the fiction, it is none other than he himself who has written what we read, while the title page carries the name of Arne Garborg. The relationship between author and central character is in the highest degree a *literary* relationship. On the whole *Weary Men* has a literary character that is quite striking, and in more than one way: first, through its peculiar impressionistic style and the dialogical play within the text, second, through its numerous references and allusions to other literature.

*V*

*Weary Men* is a happy hunting ground for the intertextual critic. In addition to the French authors already mentioned, many others make their appearance in the text. Choosing at random, I may mention Strindberg, Schopenhauer, Wergeland, and Goethe.

Heinrich Heine is quoted, as is the Bible, and one can find traces of Shakespeare, Wessel, Kierkegaard, and Ibsen, as well as of Nietzsche. Rolv Thesen stresses the fact that Garborg went through a "Nietzsche-craze" just before he wrote *Weary Men*.[11] Garborg saw Nietzsche as someone who had opposed the decadence. Yet I find it most fruitful to read *Weary Men* against the background of contemporary French literature, while fully aware that the book is not simply a transposition to Norwegian soil of a foreign literary impulse but instead represents a creative adaptation of considerable originality.

Neither Baudelaire nor Verlaine is decadent in the usual sense of the word, but they were both important to the decadent movement. For this reason it is interesting that the second stanza of Gram's poem in part 1, chapter 6 shares some features with Verlaine's famous "Chanson d'automne." Other passages are reminiscent of Baudelaire. Johs. A. Dale says that a description of smell in chapter 10 of part 2 might give one the idea "that Gram [Garborg] wanted to compete with Baudelaire, that great depictor of smell."[12] And I feel quite certain that Garborg alludes to the prose poem "Enivrez-vous": "Alas, what is life? Alas, let us intoxicate ourselves!" Still, the parallels with Huysmans are the clearest. Interestingly, on closer scrutiny, one discovers that they do not apply only to *A Rebours*.

Like Garborg, Huysmans started off as a committed naturalist; he was a member of the so-called Médan group that met regularly in Zola's home. He too, like Garborg, wrote about women's position in society (in *Marthe* of 1876 [English translation 1927] and *Les Soeurs Vatard* [*The Vatard Sisters,* 1983] of 1879). Similarly, he dealt with the conflict between bachelorhood and family life (in *En Ménage* of 1881), and few have given a more acid representation of an outsider than he (in *A Vau-l'eau* [literally, "with the stream"; figuratively, "down the drain"; translated as *Down Stream,* 1927] of 1882). However, this is not the right place to examine Huysmans's naturalistic writings, though *A Vau-l'eau* in particular is in many ways reminiscent of *Weary Men*. In this connection, a comparison with *A Rebours* seems more likely to throw light on Garborg's novel.

Both des Esseintes in *A Rebours* and Gabriel Gram are unmarried and alone. They both find themselves in a worsening crisis related to a neurotic attitude toward women. At the same time they experience a retrospective longing for harmony: the safety they dream about is that of childhood. In both of their lives art plays a great role, for Gram mainly literature, for des Esseintes all the arts. But art effects liberation for neither; rather, it reinforces their alienation from their surroundings. Loneliness and an aestheticizing attitude toward life are closely interconnected. While the heroes of romanticism tended to find strength in external nature, the latter means very little to the decadent heroes. In Huysmans, the cult of all things non-natural, artificial, aesthetic is part of a conscious philosophy. Indeed, this cult is the very core of the philosophy of decadence.

The situation in *Weary Men* is somewhat less drastic. But his experience of nature gives little joy to Gabriel Gram. True enough, he occasionally comes across something fresh and unexpected, but on the whole nature serves only as a point of departure for intellectual reflections or the writing of poems. "The peacefulness of the church and the quiet of the forest weary me; I must have the chatter of the tavern and the hubbub of the street," Gabriel Gram states, and he hurries home to Kristiania after a vacation in the West Country. However, the life which the main characters of both Huysmans and Garborg lead is so unwholesome that it simply *cannot* be sustained without a breakdown: first physical, then spiritual breakdown. When neither love, art, or nature can give value to life, and when there is an apparent absence of a shared work experience and social commitment, there remain only two possibilities: insanity or conversion. "Lord, have mercy on the Christian who doubts, with the disbeliever who wants to believe," prays the desperate des Esseintes on the last page of Huysmans's novel. "A difficult path lies ahead of me. Only then will I feel a true child of the new age when I have definitively broken with all the old things," says Gram in the next to last chapter of Garborg's.

Despite these parallels, the difference between *A Rebours* and *Weary Men* is enormous. The life of Huysmans's wealthy, learned duke is worlds apart from that of Garborg's civil servant: des Esseintes has no contact with people at all, having withdrawn into complete isolation. But this fact does not minimize the features that the two works have in common.

Typically, these common features no more escape Garborg's irony than anything else. For des Esseintes, for Huysmans himself, and for the decadent writers in general, the "religious reaction" was the solution to the existential crisis they had ended up in. It is also the solution for Gabriel Gram. But we have already seen that Garborg treats Gram's approach to the church ironically: he presents it in part as regressive, in part as aesthetic, in part as sexually tinged. And since Gram's pattern is so close to the usual pattern in the literature of decadence, it is safe to say that the irony applies to the whole pattern and implicates all writings in which it is most distinctly present. In the case of des Esseintes (and Huysmans), the religious longing is partly concretized as a longing for the cloister, specifically directed toward Gregorian chant. We find this very same aesthetic longing for the cloister in *Weary Men*, but by and large Garborg treats it ironically.

And with this we are again confronting the play between irony and nonirony. As I see it, this is what holds the novel together. Still, I can well understand why so many find it difficult to accept ambiguity in a literary work.

Traditionally, a work of literature is supposed to have a positive unity, not only in a literary but also in a moral sense. When this unity cannot be found, one tends to feel that the key to the work has not yet been discovered, or one chooses to see the work as a necessary link in the author's development. In Garborg's case, the latter immediately suggests itself, considering the books before and after *Weary Men* as well as the author's comments about the novel. Nevertheless, from the perspective I have chosen, it is its multivalent, disparate, playful, and creative aspects that are the most important. In saying so, I am also thinking about its dialogue with other literature, both with Garborg's earlier books and with the works of others. The novel seems to present itself explicitly as what it is, namely, a piece of literature. At the same time two myths about literary creation are exposed: literature is neither a natural or necessary expression of private emotions or thoughts, nor simply experience committed to paper. Rather, it is an extremely intricate process, and the point of departure for all literature is other literature. Other literature is also one of the most important elements in a literary work.

By way of this "literarization," *Weary Men* is seen to be an early example of a modernist novel in Norway. I use the term "modernist," as do many other critics, to describe a novel that is partly about itself and does not try to disguise—or *cannot* disguise—the fact that it is a novel. Obviously, such a novel cannot be an ode to joy. No modernist novel is.

If, then, one wants to call *Weary Men* a novel of crisis, the crisis is more literary than religious. Garborg himself hinted that he had put too much faith in naturalism; with *Weary Men* he was trying to find a new direction. But as he himself was fully aware, the book also had many naturalistic features, and anybody looking for *one* new direction—*one* single message—will look in vain. Thus, the novel also problematizes a common method of reading novels.

Per Buvik
University of Bergen
Translated by Sverre Lyngstad

# Notes

1. As quoted by Rolv Thesen, *Arne Garborg*, III: *Europear og jærbu* (Oslo: Aschehoug, 1939), p. 64.

2. As quoted by Johs. A. Dale, "Garborg i Tyskland," *Garborg-studiar* (Oslo: Det Norske Samlaget, 1969), p. 113.

3. As quoted by Thesen, pp. 64–65.

4. As quoted by Thesen, p. 67, from "Arne Garborg," *Ord och Bild*, II (1893), p. 136.

5. As quoted by Hugo Friedrich, *Die Struktur der modernen Lyrik* (Hamburg: Rowohlt, 1956), p. 31. See also the English translation by Joachim Neugroschel, *The Structure of Modern Poetry* (Evanston, Ill.: Northwestern University Press, 1974), p. 25. Friedrich's term *Endzeit*, which Neugroschel renders as "terminal era," is here translated as "end-time."—TRANS.

6. As quoted by François Livi in *J.-K. Huysmans: "A Rebours" et l'esprit décadent*, 3d ed. (Paris: Nizet, 1991), p. 29, from Bourget's article in *Le Siècle littéraire*, April 1, 1876.

7. See, e.g., the blurb of *A Rebours*, ed. Marc Fumaroli (Paris: Gallimard, 1977), and Livi, pp. 7, 12.

8. Thesen, p. 58.

9. Letter of December 5, 1885, in Arne Garborg, *Verk*, ed. Sveinung Time (Oslo: Aschehoug, 1980), XII: 70.

10. Francis Bull, Fredrik Paasche, and A. H. Winsnes, *Norsk litteraturhistorie*, V: *Norges litteratur fra februarrevolusjonen til verdenskrigen* (Oslo: Aschehoug, 1937), pt. 2, p. 322.

11. Thesen, p. 51.

12. Dale, "Impresjonisten Gabriel Gram," *Garborg-studiar*, p. 60.

# European Classics